D0610635

# In Search of Adam

## Caroline Smailes

First published in hardback in 2007 by Friday Fiction. This
paperback edition first published in 2008 by Friday Fiction
An imprint of The Friday Project Limited
33 The Cut, London SE1 8LF

www.thefridayproject.co.uk
www.fridaybooks.co.uk

ISBN    978-1-906321-02-4

British Library Cataloguing in Publication Data

A catalogue record for this book is available from the British
Library

Cover design by Snowbooks Design
Internal design and typesetting by Wordsense Ltd, Edinburgh

The Publisher's policy is to use paper manufactured from
sustainable sources

**For my Gary**

*Unto the woman he said, I will greatly multiply thy sorrow and thy conception; in sorrow thou shalt bring forth children; and thy desire shall be to thy husband, and he shall rule over thee.*

**Genesis 01 : 003 : 016**

*The Owl and the Pussy-Cat went to sea*
*In a beautiful pea green boat.*

**Edward Lear, 1871**

# 1980

On March 26 1980, I was six years, four months and two days old. I was dressed and ready for school. It was 8:06am on my digital watch. My mother was still in bed. I went into her room to wake her. I found her lying on top of her duvet cover. She wasn't wearing any clothes. Her ocean eyes were open. She wasn't sleeping. And from the corner of her mouth, a line

of

**lumpy**

**sick**

joined her to the pool that was stuck to her cheek. Next to her, on her duvet I saw an empty bottle. Vodka. And there were eleven tablets. Small round and white. And I saw a scrap of ripped paper. There were words on it.

*jude, i have gone in search of adam.*
*i love you baby.*

I didn't understand. But I took the note. It was mine. I shoved it into the pocket of my grey school skirt. I crumpled it in. Then. Then I climbed next to her. I spooned into her. Molded into a question mark. Her stale sick mingled and lumped into my shiny hair. I stayed with my mother, until the warmth from her body transferred into me. We were not disturbed until my father returned from work. At 6:12pm.

* * * * *

* * * * *

In the days between my mother's death and her funeral, I noted that someone from every one of the thirty-one other houses in my street came to visit. Some just stood in silence in the hallway. Some drank coffee at the wooden kitchen table. Others sat with my father in the lounge. Smoked cigarettes and drank from tin beer cans. My father liked these visitors the best. There were some neighbours who came each day. Just to check on my father. And between them they decided on how best I should be cared for.

I was six years old. I was more than capable of taking myself to school at 8:30am. My father left for work twenty minutes before I left for school. 8:10am. That was fine. I loved those twenty minutes. I was alone in the house. I was king of the castle. I spent the twenty minutes sitting. Sitting on the bottom red stair. Staring at my watch. Glaring. Terrified that I would be late for school. I loved those twenty minutes. School was a ten-minute walk away. Over only one main road. But a lollipop lady watched out for me. *They'd had a word*. Then coming home from school. I could manage the walk. But. But they thought it best that I wasn't at home alone. My father came home from work between 6:10pm and 6:17pm. So together. Those smoking drinking neighbours and my father. They decided where I should go each night.

| Monday. | (Number 30) | Aunty Maggie. |
| Tuesday. | (Number 19) | Mr Johnson. |
| Wednesday. | (Number 14) | Mrs Clark. |
| Thursday. | (Number 21) | Mrs Roberts. |
| Friday. | (Number 2) | Mrs Hodgson. |

I had my key. Tied to a piece of string and fastened with a safety pin inside my brown parka. That key was to lock the door each morning and only for emergencies at night. That key would allow me to escape from my neighbours.

During those days. Between my mother's death and her funeral. I used to watch my neighbours slowing down as they passed by my mother's house. I could sit on my bed and watch them from the window. I could open the window. Just slightly. Just enough to let their words fly in. They didn't look up to me. I was already invisible. They never saw me. They never looked for me. Some neighbours would stand talking. Curlers in their hair. Slippered feet. Dressing gowns pulled across their chests. They would point at my mother's house and they would chitter and chatter and yackety yacker. Gossip. Gossip. Gossip. Always about my mother. My precious, my beautiful mother. She was in the tittle-tattle. She was in the chitchat. Her demise. My demise. My mother's house, Number 9 Disraeli Avenue was the centre of the universe. Front page gossip. The neighbours talked of *a pure evil* that was within my mother. They spoke of her *lack of motherly instincts*. They talked about a *murderous past*. I didn't understand their words. But. But they were tinged and tanged with mean-sounding twangs. They talked. I listened. I heard them. Through the open bedroom window.

On the day of my mother's funeral. Five days after her death. My father told me to put on my school uniform. A grey skirt. A blue blouse. A blue and yellow stripy tie. My blouse was creased. Crumply and worn. My tie was stained with baked bean juice.

My mother's coffin was in the box room. The lid had been removed. She looked so beautiful. Her long blonde hair had been styled. She looked like a glamorous film star. She was covered in a white sheet and her bare feet were poking from beneath it. I crept into my mother and father's bedroom. I took my mother's favourite shoes from her wardrobe. I also took a blouse and hid it under my pillow. Her scent still clung to it. Combining Chanel, musk and Mary Quant. Then. I returned to the box room. I took her purple stilettos. I lifted the white sheet to see her ankles. I placed her purple shoes onto her blue feet. Touching her skin sent a throbbing ache into my stomach.

*I feel sick. I feel sick.*

I fought my weakness. I stopped myself from being sick. I needed her to be wearing shoes. I didn't want her feet to become raw. She was off to hike through foreign lands. My mother was not smiling. Her face was blank. As I looked at her I realised that all expression came from her eyes. I longed for those ocean eyes. *Open your eyes, please open your eyes.* Just to connect with her one last time. My hair was tangled, still matted with her sick. So I sat on her hairdressing stool. Next to her coffin. In the box room. And I counted each stroke as I brushed my hair. *One ... two ... three ... four ... five ... six ... seven ... eight ...* I needed my mother. I needed her to get rid of the tatty tatty clumps. I reached into the coffin. Her coffin. I held her cold hand. I heard people laughing and chatting downstairs. *Ding dong. Ding dong. Chatter chatter. Laugh laugh laugh.* Aunty Maggie from Number 30 had brought rice, Mrs Clark from Number 14 had brought a platter of sandwiches and with each ding dong my father poured drinks and welcomed his guests. I sat. Holding my dead mother's hands. Wishing that she had taken me with her on her journey. Downstairs they talked loudly. And then. Then hushed and whispered. *She hadn't left a note, she was so very selfish, how could she be so cruel to little Jude.* They talked badly of my mother. I wanted to go and scream at them. To stop their evil gossiping. My father said that he wouldn't speak ill of the dead. But. *Sarah was an evil whore and ahm glad that she's deed.* And. *She'd been threatening te dee it for years.* And. She was *an evil lass. A selfish murdering whore. She divvnae care aboot anyone but horsell.* I hated my father. I hated that he fed the neighbours lies. I didn't understand. Liar liar. Pants on fire.

My mother loved me. She did care about me. I didn't understand why my father was telling lies. My mother was magical. She was beautiful and she loved me. Right up to the sky and back. She was thirty-two. She was clever. She was just going to explore the world a little. She would come back when she was done. She had gone in search of Adam. Her explanation was simple. I had no idea who or what an Adam was. She would tell me all about it when she found it. She'd come back then. She'd come back and carry on being mine. I'd wait. I'd always wait. I stroked her long slender fingers. She was cold. Too cold. Back into my bedroom. A hot water bottle. I took it into the bathroom. Turned the hot tap till it was burning. Burning. I filled my plastic hot water bottle. Then I returned to my mother. I placed it under her sheet. I gave her the shiny fifty pence that Aunty Maggie, Number 30, had given me the day before. Just in case. She may have time to buy herself a treat. An ice cream and a ten-pence mix up.

My father shouted for me. I stood. Over my mother's coffin. I looked at my mother. The last time. She did not look back at me. Her eyes were closed. Sleeping. Sleeping Beauty. I would not cry. I could not cry. I had to be brave. They would think badly of my mother. My father had told me. He had warned me. *Big girls don't cry. Do you hear me? Big girls don't cry.* I bent down and kissed my mother. She did not wake. I was not magic.

I sat next to my father in the large black car. I lowered my head and tried to name all the foreign places that I could think of. My fists were clenched. I recited names. I could think of only five.

Spain ...
France ...
Scotland ...

**America** ...
**London** ...
Spain ... **France** ... **Scotland** ... **America** ... **London** …
Spain ...
**France** ...
**Scotland** ...
**America** ...
**London** ...

I tried to picture my mother in these countries. The Tower of London. Loch Ness. Disneyland. The Eiffel Tower. On the beach. Sunbathing. And in my head I could see her smiling. Her eyes twinkling with excitement. As she grasped her sketch book, charcoal and lead.

The funeral ended. Mr Johnson, from Number 19, took me to school in time for lunch.

Mashed potato.
Peas.
And carrots.
Mixed together.
Fish fingers.
One, two, three.

Jam sponge.
Custard.

The afternoon of the funeral passed quickly at school. Children avoided me. My teacher cried at the front of the class. I sat at my small wooden desk and held my tightly clenched fists in front of me.

Spain ...

    France ...

        Scotland ...

            America ...

                London ...

                    Spain ...

                      France ...

                        Scotland ...

                        America ...

                        London...

                        Spain ...

                        France ...

                        Scotland ...

                        America ...

                        London ...

I would not cry. I did not move during afternoon playtime. Teachers walked past the classroom window and peered in at me. My nails dug into my palms, but my knuckles were fixed and I concentrated through the pain.

          Spain ... France ... Scotland ...

          America ... London ... Spain ...

**France ... Scotland ... America ...**
**London ... Spain ... France ...**
**Scotland ... America ...**
London ... Spain ...
France ...
Scotland ...
America ...
**London.**

I didn't draw an Easter card. I didn't practise my writing. I didn't listen. I didn't speak. Nothing. Nothing. Nothing.

The final bell rang.

I left my desk. Children moved out of the way. Terrified that a touch from me would make them catch the evil eye. I had the evil eye. Mothers at the school gate turned their backs. Talked in packs. Always in hushed tones. No one wanted to look at me. No one could find the words. My mother was fresh in the ground. I was at school. The neighbours were drinking. Eating. Celebrating. I had to walk home alone. Alone. Alone. Alone.

It was a Wednesday. But Mrs Clark was at my mother's wake. In a pub called The Traveller's Rest. A wake. The neighbours were trying to wake my mother. I had tried that too. Given her a kiss. It hadn't worked. She needed a handsome prince. The neighbours would wake her. They were old and clever. Aunty Maggie was nearly one hundred and ninety-five years old. She was the oldest person in the world. She had to be the wisest person in the world.

I used my key and let myself into my mother's house. It was cold. It was silent. I rushed to the box room. Ran up the red stairs. *Quick quick quick.* Just in case she was still there. But. But the room was empty. She was gone. I went into my mother and father's bedroom. I opened my mother's wardrobe. It was empty. She had taken her clothes with her on her travels. She had packed. She had gone. I went downstairs. Into the kitchen. I found her things. Next to the door. Waiting to go into the garage. They were in black plastic bags. Waiting to be thrown into the garage. Ready for the bin man. One bag for her clothes, one bag for her secrets. For her stuff. I took her secrets. A bag full of letters and beads and books and her sketch book and a box. I took that bag. I hid it in my room. Buried within a basket of teddies and dolls. I would keep it for my mother. I wouldn't look. She could show me when she came back. We could take it with us. When she took me away. When she had found herself an Adam.

When it was time.

I took my mother's blouse from under my pillow and held it to my nose. I tried to sniff in her smell. But. But already it was fading. I was forgetting. I curled onto my bed. Onto my blue duvet. I curled into a question mark. I held my mother's blouse tightly to me and I stared out of the window. I stared up to the sky. I watched the day fall into night. My father and some of the neighbours returned home. I heard them chatting and laughing and cheering and singing. I felt their happiness. It kind of stuck into me like a fork. They sat downstairs, smoking and drinking beer out of warm tin cans. They didn't come into my room.

* * * * *

Life entered into a robotic routine. I existed. I grew. I was quiet. A thoughtful child. I had no friends. I carried the world inside my head. I carried the world on my shoulders. In my hands. There was no room for play. There was no way of playing. I sat. I thought. Always about my mother.

Aunty Maggie gave me a shiny fifty-pence piece. Every Monday evening when my father came to collect me. I saved all of them. And eventually. I was able to buy an Atlas. I held the world in my hand. It was a large hardback book. Glossy. The pages stuck together. New. Crisp. I learned of new places. Unsure if my pronunciation was correct.

Spain ...

France ...

Scotland ...

America ...

London ...

Libya ... Malta ... Tibet ... Victoria ... Boston ... Greenland ...

Spain ...

    France ...

        Scotland ...

           **America** ...

               **London ...**

Libya ... Malta ... Tibet ... Victoria ... Boston ... Greenland ...

        Spain ...

        France ...

        Scotland ...

        **America ...**

        **London ...**

        Libya ...

        Malta ...

        Tibet ...

        Victoria ...

        Boston ...

        Greenland ...

Spain ... France ... **Scotland ... America ... London** ... Libya ... Malta ... Tibet ... Victoria ... Boston ... Greenland.

I placed a small heart-shaped sticker onto a country. Onto a place. Then. I moved it around each day. I plotted my mother's travels. I watched her move through my book. I watched her move around the Atlas. I held the world. I held her world. I carried the world with me. Always. Always with me. My room was tidy. Always. I asked for and received so very little. Yet with the uncluttered space came calmness.

I started to write poetry. I started to draw. I spent hours scribbling words. Or sketching my mother. In different countries. Outlines of her, with signs pointing to her next destination. My drawings weren't very good. They weren't good enough. I had no photographs of her. My father had taken them all. I tried to sketch her. In case I began to forget. But. I couldn't capture her ocean eyes. I wasn't good enough. My drawings were rubbish.

But.

*Her eyes.*
*They penetrated to my soul.*
*At night.*
*As I closed my eyes in the cold darkness of my room.*
*My mother appeared and her eyes warmed me.*
*I longed for my mother. My precious mother.*
*As I closed my eyes.*
*In my darkness.*
*My mother.*
*Behind her a signpost.*
*Pointing.*
*Four different directions.*
*All leading to Adam.*

*All searching for Adam.*

Her bag of secrets.

Her bag of her. Still buried. Untouched. Waiting. Waiting for her return.

\* \* \* \* \*

In the year that followed my mother's death, my father entertained many women. I would be sent to my room, as he played his records, smoked his cigarettes and drank from cold tin cans. Lionel Ritchie would float through my floorboards. He would dance around my room. I hated his voice. I hated my father's music. I hated those women who giggled and groaned in my mother's front room.

The women came and went. *Good riddance.*

But. But then one woman started coming around more and more and more. It was in December 1980. Just over eight months after my mother went away. I didn't take much notice at first. Thought she'd be replaced. Like the others. My father liked to have a different woman to visit. A different woman every night. Then. Then she started coming back. More and more. She was in my mother's house every day. Every night. Her voice was squeakier and her groans were louder than the rest. She called my father *babe* and she slept in my mother's bed. She slept under my mother's purple duvet. She slept on my mother's sheets.

She was introduced to me.

She was called Rita. *Jude pet, come and say hello te Miss North East 1981. Jude meet Reta.* I didn't understand my father's words. He was smiling. He was excited. Rita's hair was bleached white and she wore short skirts. Her thighs were really fat and dimply. She wore blue mascara. It clogged on her lashes. Her lips were ruby red and her skin was orange.

## She was a monster.

She talked of sunbeds, fake tan and keep-fit videos. She was fat and ugly. She wasn't like my mother.

My father liked Rita. She kept her toothbrush in our bathroom and within the year after my mother's death, Rita would walk around my mother's house without any clothes on. Her breasts were saggy and her nipples were huge. She was hairy. Black hairy. She was scary. She wibble wobbled about. Her fat wibble wobbled about. She smoked cigarettes. Between twenty and twenty-four a day. She drank out of tin beer cans. One two three four five. Sometimes she would wake me in the night. She'd be giggling. Cackling. Squealing. Falling downstairs. Or. Coming into my room. I didn't like her coming into my room. She banged the door. She cackled. She breathed her nasty smell into my room. Onto my things. I didn't like Rita. She didn't smell very nice and her eyes didn't sparkle.

I missed my mother. As I curled up in bed. I covered my ears so that I couldn't hear them. I thought of my mother's ocean eyes. I longed to be with her. Maybe. Maybe one morning I wouldn't wake up. I'd just go away. I'd go off looking for an Adam too. If I was really lucky. If I wished and wished and wished. Then just maybe I'd wake up in my mother's arms. She'd have come back for me. If my mother wrapped her thin arms around me. If she pulled me tightly to her. Then. Then I'd be safe and nothing else would matter.

I could sleep. I looked forward to bed. It was the waking that destroyed me.

# 1981

Two years, six months and twenty-one days before I was born, my parents moved to New Lymouth. From a block of flats that were as high as a giant. My mother's house was brand new. It was shiny. Spick and span. There were two new estates being built in New Lymouth. The housing estate that I was to live on and another one. They each had four parallel streets and formed a perfect square on either side of the main road.

On this Coast Road, there were *The Shops*. Dewstep Butchers was also New Lymouth Post Office and displayed a smiling pig's head in the window. New Lymouth Primary School. My primary school. Was a perfect E-shaped grey building with a flat roof. Mrs Hodgson (Number 2) told Rita that *many cuckoos were put in nests on that roof*. I didn't understand. New Lymouth Library was on the Coast Road too. It was a rectangle. Like a shoe box. Inside the library there were eighty-seven Mills and Boon novels and three Roald Dahl books. There were signs everywhere. 'Absolute silence at all times'. The grumpy librarian liked to read her *Introducing Machine Knitting* magazine. I read the first chapter of *Danny Champion of the World* twenty-seven times. I read all of *Matilda* and *The Twits*. Thirteen times each.

Brian's Newsagents stretched across 127–135 Coast Road. Inside the shop I heard gossip being tittled and tattled, as I stood looking at the jars of delicious sweets.

Rhubarb and Custard. Chocolate Raisins. White Gems. Aniseed balls. Coconut Mushrooms. Brown Gems. Cola Cubes. Pear drops. Cherry Lips. Licorice Comfits. Toffee Bonbons. Jelly Beans. Edinburgh Rock. Pontefract Cakes. Pineapple Chunks. Sweet Peanuts. Scented Satins. Sherbet Pips. Midget Gems. Sweet Tobacco. Chocolate Peanuts. Toasted Teacakes. Rainbow Crystals. Sour Apples. Lemon Bonbons.

Unable to decide. I wished that I had the courage to ask for one from every one of the twenty-five jars.

On the other side of the Coast Road there were five really big houses. My class teacher Mrs Ellis and Mrs Hughes the local librarian lived in two of them. I didn't know who else lived there. The children in those houses didn't go to New Lymouth Primary School with me. The children in those houses didn't play foxes and hounds around the estate with us *local bairns*. I walked down that road on my way to school. I peered into those large houses. I stopped walking to stare in. I tried to look past the fresh flowers in the window and I thought about all the nice smelling things that would live inside.

The Coast Road ran a slope from New Lymouth down to the Lymouth seaside. The estate that I lived on was at the top of the hill. As the road continued up, it travelled through a number of similar estates and villages. Signs warned drivers when they were leaving one village and arriving in another. My father said that the *nearer yee lived to the coast, then the richer yee were*. We lived about a ten-minute walk from the coast. I'm not quite sure what that made us. All I know is that when my mother was alive, my father talked about one day living on the sea front. The houses there were enormous. Five stories tall. They went up and up and up to the sky. You could stand on the roof and your head would be in the clouds. I thought that really important people lived in *those* kinds of houses. People like the Queen could live there. A *hacky lad* in my class at school lived in one, with about twenty other children. His mother and father hadn't wanted him. They, the twenty other children *and the hacky lad*, lived in their mansion that looked out over the beautiful Lymouth cove. They were very very lucky. They must have been very very rich. They must have been the richest people in England.

Lymouth Bay was shaped like a banana. There was a pier at each end and three caves lived in the cliff. Just over the left pier. Sat tall on a throne of rocks. There was a lighthouse. The most beautiful. The most elegant. A white lighthouse. Legend had it, that hundreds and thousands of small green men with orange hair lived in it. I never saw them. But. Paul Hodgson (Number 2) had seen one buying a quarter of toasted teacakes in Brian's Newsagents.

There were one hundred and twenty steps to climb down. One hundred and twenty steps before touching the grey sand. The sand was unhappy. It looked poorly sick all the time. A green handrail wove next to the steps. I never had the courage to touch it. The paint was covered in carved initials, decorated with lumps of hardened chewing gum and topped with seagull droppings. Yackety yack. Hundreds and thousands of lumps. Hacky yack yack. Paul Hodgson (Number 2) told me that his uncle caught an *incurable disease* from touching that handrail. He said that his *uncle's hand had dropped clean off*. I wasn't going to risk it.

To me, the Coast Road seemed to go on for ever and ever and ever. I was told that it was a perfectly straight road, which travelled from the seafront and through four villages. You could catch a bus on the Coast Road. The road passed by my school, up the slope, close to my house and then on through village after village into lands that were unknown. Into lands that sounded magical and exciting. North Lymouth. Marsden. Hingleworth. Coastend. Mrs Hodgson (Number 2) told me that Coastend was *famous for its cheapness of tricks*. A magical place.

I lived in Disraeli Avenue, in between Gladstone Street and Campbell-Bannerman Road. The neighbours all said it dizz- rah- el -lee (four chunks) Avenue. My mother's house was a semi-detached on a street with 31 similar-looking houses. They looked identical but I knew that they weren't. There were differences.

Thirteen had red front doors. Seven had green front doors. Five had blue front doors. Seven had yellow front doors. The garages matched the front doors. Except for Number 17. Mr Lewis had a yellow front door and a green garage. I didn't know why.

**green,**

**red,**

**red,**

**yellow, green, red, red, yellow, yellow, green, red, red, red,**

**green, blue, blue,**

**red,**

**blue,**

**green,**

**yellow, red, blue, blue, yellow, green, green, red, red, red,**

**yellow, red, yellow.**

I wanted the numbers to fit better. I wanted the colours to fit better.

It should have been sixteen red front doors. One half. Eight green doors. One quarter. Four blue doors. One eighth. Four yellow doors. One eighth. It was simple. The colours could look really nice. I had worked it all out.

**red,**

    **red,**

        **green,**

            **red,**

                **green,**

                    **red,**

                        **blue,**

                            **blue**

**green, red,
yellow, red, green,
red, yellow, red,
red, green, red,
green, red, blue, blue,
green, red, yellow,
red, green, red,
yellow, red, red.**

I wasn't happy with Mr Lewis (Number 17). His colours didn't match. Maybe he didn't realise. I wished that I had the courage to talk to him about it.

There was a little wall in front of the garden. A dwarf wall. A dwarf wall for Snow White's friends to play on. There was also a drive for my father's Mini. There was a garden to the front and a slightly larger one to the back. The front lawn was just big enough to squeeze onto it a folded tartan picnic blanket. The soil surrounding the perfect square of grass was always packed with flowers. I watched the flowers. I noted them all in a little lined book. It was green and lived on my windowsill. Thorny rose bushes, coordinating colours and then down to a mixture of blossoms. Depending on the month.

*Gaillardia 'Burgunder'.*
*Shiny red flower, with light yellow centre.*
*June–October. 30cm.*

*Dahlia.*
*Really orange and red.*
*June–November. 60cm.*
*Narcissum 'Amergate.'*
*Orange outside with a darker orange*
*in the middle.*
*March–April. 45cm.*

I liked to write things down. In the green notebook that I kept on my windowsill. Flowers. Colours. Number plates. Full names. Times. Routines. All of the first chapter of *Danny Champion of the World*. So I wouldn't forget.

\* \* \* \* \*

Hold your palms out. Let me read your fortune.
I see that you are destined for great things.
Love … yes. A great love.
Children … bend your little finger …
　Ah. I see a boy and a girl.
It's all here. Written within your palm.

\* \* \* \* \*

Aunty Maggie lived at Number 30 Disraeli Avenue and every Monday she looked after me. Her hallway walls were jam packed with black and white photographs of her *darling husband Samuel*. Who *passed away in his prime*. They were all the same photograph, but in different-sized frames. Aunty Maggie had *never been blessed with children*. I didn't understand. Before my mother died, she liked

Aunty Maggie. Aunty Maggie used to make boiled rice for my mother. She'd cook it to a fluffy perfection in one of my mother's pans. Then. She'd walk along Disraeli Avenue. Number 30 to Number 9. Both hands clutching the black handle of the steaming pan. My mother used to pretend to my father that she had cooked it. My father used to like Aunty Maggie's feathery white rice.

When Aunty Maggie looked after me. I would sit in her pink room and she would open a cupboard brimming with untouched toys. They were shiny and perfect. Treasures. Aunty Maggie was always old. Always one hundred and ninety-five years old and her face was a web of wrinkles. I wanted to run my finger along the tracks. Round and round and round and round. I never did. Her breath was smelly. Mint. Toothpaste mint. And about her lingered a flowery scent. Sweet and lasting.

In the pink room, where everything was pink, I was surrounded by smiling faces on photographs of school children who sometimes visited. I would play with her Bible Fuzzy Felts and sip at milky tea. I was on my best behaviour. As I left she would always give me a shiny fifty-pence piece. A whole shiny fifty pence. I was rich. Aunty Maggie spoke with a swish accent and her house was always tidy. Always. She used to watch me from her window and I knew that she longed to be my mother. I was glad that she was not my mother.

On February 1 1981 I was seven years, two months and eight days old and it was within the first year after my mother's death. Although

Rita was nearly always in my mother's house, I still visited the neighbours after school. Aunty Maggie was expecting me. As I entered her house, cigar smoke was swirling from her pink room.

### She had a guest.

Eddie was her brother. He was fat. He wore brown and his big belly was forcing the buttons on his shirt to cling to the holes. His trousers stretched over his solid fat belly. Up and over. Up and over. He looked like a brown egg. With little chicken drumsticks coming out the bottom. He was perched on the edge of Aunty Maggie's special chair. Not daring to touch her plump cushions. He wore a brown cardigan with a thin mint green tissue sticking out of the pocket. His hair was flat and looked like it had been drawn on with black felt tips. He was shiny. Very shiny. But he had a laugh like I imagined Father Christmas would. *Ho Ho Ho.* He boomed and he chuckled. I thought that I liked him. When I left he gave me a fifty-pence coin too. I was rich. Two fifty-pence coins. One hundred pennies. One whole pound. They asked if I would like to visit them again the next day. I knew that I would be given more coins and I had had a nice time. So Aunty Maggie said that *she would have a word with Mr Johnson.*

On February 2 1981 I went to Aunty Maggie's straight from school. Eddie was perched on the edge of the special flowery chair. Ready to swoop. I saw him watching me through the dirt-free windows. Edged with coordinated flowery drapes. He was ready. He opened the door. A fat cigar balanced in between his fingers. His shirt was a dirty cream. A hot wash of whites and browns. Tight shirt. Old shirt. His forehead glistened with tiny beads of sweat. A tiara of sweat. His nose was a purple plum and as he spoke stale smoke escaped between his narrow lips. He smelled. Sweat. Sour smoke. Chip fat. Smelly smelly man.

Eddie was happy to see me. I liked that he was happy to see me. He'd been looking forward to it all day. He smiled. He smiled and showed me his painted brown teeth. Aunty Maggie had had to nip out. She wouldn't be long. He led me into the pink room. Where everything was still pink. He told me to take off my shoes. He liked my white socks. Aunty Maggie didn't like shoes to be worn in her house. I didn't know that. Eddie had shoes on. Brown shoes.

He sat down on the pink chair. Daring to sink into the freshly plumped cushions. He patted his lap. He wanted me to sit on him. I stayed still.

### Again.

He slapped his thighs with the palms of his fat hands. He was telling me where I must sit. I didn't want to. I didn't feel happy. I didn't want to sit on Eddie's lap. I wanted to sit on my own chair. He told me not to be a naughty girl. His face went all screwy. Angry lines sprouted on his forehead and around his eyes. Not happy anymore. Not smiling anymore.

I sat on his lap.

He rubbed his fat fingers over my cold thighs. Pushing the tips into my skin. He was strong. He kissed my neck. Kiss nibble kiss kiss. A nibbling eagle. His breath was getting faster and faster. His fat fingers were playing harder and harder. His hands moved up to the top of my thighs. Up up up. Gripping. Gripping. Gripping my thighs. Pulling me into him. He asked me if it felt nice. I didn't say anything. Silence. Fear. Silence. He told me that it felt good. His angry voice asked me to like it. I said yes. I said that it was nice. It wasn't. Really it wasn't. I didn't like it. I didn't want to be on his lap. I didn't want him to touch me. I didn't know what to do. I was drowning. Drowning. Drowning.

A key in the door.

A humming accompaniment. Aunty Maggie was home. Eddie jumped onto his heavy feet. I was pushed forward. My legs were shaking. Shaking quaking shaking shaking. My knees buckled to the floor. I stayed on the floor. He scuttled to help his sister with her heavy bags. I stayed still. Rooted. Rooted. I didn't understand. I didn't understand what was happening. I wanted to cry. *Big girls don't cry. Do you hear me? Big girls don't cry.*

Eddie and Aunty Maggie came into the room. Aunty Maggie was looking at me. She wasn't smiling. She was looking at me. Over me. Up and down. Up and down. Eddie told Aunty Maggie that we were just about to play Bible Fuzzy Felts. He winked at me, as he carried the box from the cupboard that brimmed with toys that failed to excite. Eddie was excited. He was all happy and jolly and all *ho ho ho*. I didn't understand. He was happy again. He was funny again. He liked me again. As Aunty Maggie prepared her feast, she bustled in and out of the pink room. I placed Noah beside his arc, but baby Jesus could not be rescued. Two by two. Two by two. There had to be two. I knew that baby Jesus would die. Two. There had to be two. Eddie sat close to me. Too close. Knees touching. His smell was next to me. His smell was on me. Waiting. Waiting. *It's oor little secret. You're me special girlfriend. Here's an extra fifty pence.*

As I left, I clutched my shiny coins. Three shiny coins. One hundred and fifty pennies. Two days of coins. Totalling two hundred and fifty pennies. I was rich. Really rich. Eddie said that he liked having me around. It made him feel young. It was nice to have a youngster around the house. Aunty Maggie thought I might like to come again the next day. *She would have a word with Mrs Clark.* She liked to see her only brother happy. He was very dear to her. He was such a lovely man.

On February 3 1981 Eddie was lingering with a camera. He wanted a nice shot of me to take home with him. Aunty Maggie had a spare frame. I was to have pride of place on his mantel. Over the electric fire. In between his Madonna and a clock that had stopped working at ten minutes past three. But he wasn't sure if it had happened in the morning or in the afternoon. *Ho ho ho.* Aunty Maggie thought that it was a wonderful idea. Her brother was such a lovely man. He was so very dear to her. Aunty Maggie was cooking in the kitchen. She was humming. She was buzz buzz buzzing. I could hear her. Eddie could hear her.

He told me to lift up my skirt. He told me to do it. An angry voice. I knew that I had to. No choice. No choice. I had to keep Eddie happy. Aunty Maggie liked her brother to be happy. Pink knickers with tiny butterflies fluttering over them. They were too tight. A little bit too tight for me. Click. Click. Flash. Quick. *No one need know.* I was a funny-looking thing. He thought that I was a funny-looking thing. He asked if I had a boyfriend. He asked if I would like a boyfriend. I didn't understand. I was seven years old. I didn't understand. He told me to sit on the chair. On the edge of the chair. He told me to pull up my skirt. *Higher higher.* He told me to open my legs. *Wide wide wide.* Click. Click. Flash. Aunty Maggie droned a happy song. *It's oor little secret. You're me special girlfriend.*

My father came for me. He told Eddie that there was no need to give me money. Eddie insisted. He was such a nice man. *A real gent.* I clutched my shiny coins. Two coins. One hundred pennies. Totalling three hundred and fifty pennies. Three pounds and fifty pence. I was rich. Very very rich. Eddie told my father that we were having such good fun together. *Ho ho ho.* He winked at me. He smiled his special smile for my father. A brown painted smile. Eddie asked me if I had had a good time. I said yes thank you very much. I hadn't had a nice time. I was being polite. I was being a good girl. Good manners were very important. I had to be polite. Please and thank you. Please and thank you. My father suggested that I visit again on Thursday. He was sure that Mrs Roberts wouldn't mind. Eddie was pleased. I didn't feel very happy.

On February 4 1981 Eddie put his hand up my school skirt.

We were sitting at the table. In the pink room. Cups of milky tea and still hot scones were placed on white lace doilies. Aunty Maggie went to fetch a jar of strawberry jam. Eddie pushed his fingers up my skirt and inside my knickers. He rubbed and rubbed. It hurt. He was being hard. Big, heavy, fat fingers. He was trying to push his fingers into my skin. Aunty Maggie was coming. He swiped them out. He lifted them to his mouth and sucked.

Suck suck suck.

He turned to me, just as Aunty Maggie bustled nearer. *It's oor little secret. You're me special girlfriend. Here's an extra fifty pence.* Eyes down, cheeks red. I didn't understand. Aunty Maggie spooned the jam into a delicate bone china dish. She didn't speak. She didn't speak to me. Eddie heaped the jam onto his scone. Dribbling in delight. Eyes glistening. He guzzled scone after scone. One two three four. Forgetting to swallow. Scoffing. Wolfing. Devouring. Moaning with pleasure. Staring at me and smiling. Not a nice smile.

His eyes were not smiling. A dollop of strawberry jam escaped. It tumbled down his brown shirt. Tumble tumble tumble. It stopped. Next to button number five which was desperately clinging to its nearest hole. When I left he gave me an extra fifty pence. One hundred and fifty pennies. Totalling five hundred pennies. Five pounds. I was richer than I had ever been.

On February 5 1981 I went to Aunty Maggie's house. I thought about the two or even maybe three fifty-pence pieces that I was sure to get. Eddie asked me to go for a walk with him. It was getting dark. We would have to hurry. He wanted to see the Lymouth coast. The street that I lived on was a ten-minute walk from the beach. Surfers enjoyed the North Sea. Pirates explored the Lymouth caves. Eddie told me all about pirates. Eddie told me that there was buried treasure in the caves. He had a map in his pocket. But it was a secret. It was our secret. I held his hand and he took me into the cave. It was dark in the cave. It was salty. I could see him. Just about.

He took off his brown cardigan and laid it on the grey floor. I kneeled onto it. Waiting for the treasure map. I wanted him to hurry up. Before the pirates came. Eddie told me to lie down. I did. He unfastened his belt and pulled his trousers down to his knees. He put his hand up my skirt and pulled off my knickers. He threw them into the cave. I didn't speak. I watched as he climbed onto me. I was winded by his weight. He hurt me. He burned into me. He ripped me. He filled me with damp sand. I opened my mouth to scream. No sound came. He placed his hand over my mouth and he ripped

31

into me further. Rip rip rip. The pain. Such pain. It took away the sound. I tried to scream. No sound. No sound.

## He stopped.

He told me to move off his cardigan. I could not move. The pain ran from my belly and down my legs. He pulled his cardigan from below me. It rolled me onto the damp sand. My knees were shaking. My body was shaking. Cold cold cold. He shouted at me. His cardigan was ruined with my blood. He threw it deeper into the cave. His cardigan. My knickers. Buried treasure. *It's oor little secret. No one would believe a strange bairn like yee. Tell anyone and I'll get yee.* He left me. I lay on the wet sand. Shaking shivering shaking. I could not move. I tried to think of my mother. She did not come to me.

Spain ...
France ...
Scotland ...
America ...
London ...

Spain ...
France ...
Scotland ...
America ...
London ...

I knew more countries. I used to know more countries. But. But they were gone. I wanted the sea to visit me. To sweep me away. I was riddled with sand. My teeth chattered. My knees were shaking. I needed help. I didn't understand. Pirates. Treasure. Pain. Such pain. I was dying. This had to be the end. My mother had not saved me. Eddie had taken her memory from me. I had nothing left. Nothing nothing nothing.

I stood. Blood and wee slid down to my white ankle socks. He had lit a fire inside me. My hair was matted with sand. My blue school blouse was ripped. I was seven years two months and twelve days old.

I walked out onto the beach. It was quiet. It was dark. Too dark. The lighthouse was still. No eye. No yellow eye. No green and orange little men. No one was watching. I climbed the one hundred and twenty steps. I did not touch the green handrail that wove next to the steps. I had to keep stopping. Doubled in pain. Difficult to breathe. Difficult to carry on. I walked myself over and along the main Coast Road. The lollipop lady had gone home. I walked past the Dewstep Butchers that doubled as the New Lymouth Post Office and displayed a garnished pig's head in the window. Past New Lymouth Primary School. Past New Lymouth Library. Past Brian's Newsagents. Stretched across 127–135 Coast Road. Past the detached homes which housed the professional types. I walked to my mother's house. Eyes never looking left or right. I hoped that a car would hit me. I walked slowly. I had ripped clothes but my brown parka covered them. I had a single line of blood trickling down my inside thigh. Inside my brown parka. I was covered in sand. Nobody stopped me. Nobody asked me what had happened. People looked away. Neighbours called their children in from play. Nobody. Nothing.

\* \* \* \* \*

*A greedy decision. A need for shiny fifty-pence pieces. A greedy need. I was saving to buy a globe. One that lit up with the flick of a switch. Paul Hodgson (Number 2) had gotten one last Christmas. I needed fifteen pounds. That was a lot of money. A greedy need. Misguided trust. My whole life stepped onto a path. I stepped onto a path. I sometimes imagine that my palms were smooth and blank. Right up until that week. That precise week. That my palms had promise. I still had a future. That I still had exciting challenges and a glossy journey ahead of me. With my decision. With my greedy need. The lines appeared. Abracadabra. Hey presto. The lines were engraved. Tattooed. Forever. Scraped in a web of complications. My palms told of the self-destruction that lay ahead.*

*I never bought the globe.*

* * * * *

*Sand*
*In my pants.*
*Itchy itchy sand monster.*
*Sand*
*In my tummy.*
*Sand*
*In my head.*
*Nasty nasty sand monster.*
*Sand*
*Make me vomit.*
*Sand*
*Make me die.*
*Naughty naughty sand monster.*
*Never to be gone.*
*Dirty dirty sand monster.*

I used my key. It was tied to a piece of string and fastened with a safety pin inside my brown parka. I fumbled with the pin. My hands were shaking. Sand and blood poked from the tips of my nails. I was dirty. Sand clung in between my fingers. Dirty dirty dirty. I needed to wash my hands. I needed to scrub and scrub and make my hands clean again.

I let myself in. Wiped my feet on the welcome mat and slowly climbed the ruby carpeted stairs. Each tiny footstep sent a flame

35

up my inner thigh. Rita and my father were in the kitchen. My movements were slow. I wanted them to come out. I wanted them to see my pain. I had no voice. Eddie had stolen my voice. I could not speak. No energy. No power. Slowly. Slowly. Slowly. A tiny skulking mouse. Pain flicked with each step. My father shouted a hello and then turned his attention back to Rita. They did not come out to me. She was giggling again.

Alone in the bathroom. I took off my school uniform. Blood damp socks and ripped school shirt. I neatly folded my soiled clothes and placed them beneath the radiator. A perfect pile.

Undressed. Exposed. Naked in the centre of the small square room. Too late to cry. I did not cry. I had not cried. *Big girls don't cry. Do you hear me? Big girls don't cry.* My father and Rita had moved into the lounge. I could hear their laughter. The cackles and giggles and boom boom booming. They were drinking from their tin beer cans. Their laughter glided up the red stairs and squeezed under the locked bathroom door. Their joy rebounded between the ceiling and linoleum floor.

Bounce

    bounce

        bounce

           bounce.

As I stood stark naked. In the centre of the bathroom.

I faced the bathroom cabinet. Focused on a perfect thumb print smeared on the bottom right hand corner of the mirror. I forced my eyes to fix on the girl who was hidden beneath that smudge. Through the smears. I stared into myself. I saw my blue eyes. My mother's blue eyes. I stared at my matted brown hair. *Dirty dirty hair.* I needed the sand off me. Get off me. Get off me. Nasty nasty sand. It was everywhere. It was swallowing me up. I opened the bathroom cabinet. I took out a pair of scissors. They were sticky and blunt. I tugged at my hair.

Chop.

Chop.

Chop.

Clumps fell into the sink. A nest of hair. Grooming and nurturing collected and then plunged. Congealed feathers over onto the linoleum floor. I didn't have my mother's skill. Long strands clung to my gluey fingers, mingled with the knotted blood and sand. I needed to be rid of the sand. I wanted it off my skin. I wanted it out of my hair. It clung. Sticky sticky sand. I yanked. I tugged. It had climbed my hair and grafted onto my scalp. I wanted to scream. I wanted rid. Get off me. Off off off.

I turned the chrome taps. Hot and cold. I waited in the centre of the room. I climbed into the pea green bath. The water was cold. Rita had used all of the hot water. Rita liked a hot bath. The bath had not been cleaned. An orange ring clung to the slippery sides. I climbed in. I gasped. I was numbed. *Pain pain go away. Pain pain go away.* I lay stiff. I was rigid. Straight. Head bobbed. Ears submerged into the rising cold. Muffled reality. Frozen sounds. Arms stiff. Blue feet. I dared not move. Sand began to sink onto the bottom of the pea green bath. Floating in my sea. Sailing in my dirt. Away away for a year and a day. I drifted. I danced by the light of the moon.

The water needed to enter me. To wash away his dirt. I stung. The fire roared. I dared not move. I could not let the water in. The fire roared. And roared. And roared. Tiny white body. Flat and smooth. A swarm of bruises erupted from my veins. Gobbled up my skin. Decorated my secret places. *Pain pain go away.*

I heard my father calling. I sat to attention and listened. He was going to the pub with Rita. A swift half. Then they would be back. A swift half and then I would tell him all about Eddie. I had to tell him. I didn't understand why, but I knew that it didn't feel right. I needed my father to make everything better. He would know what to do. Too many secrets. Hush hush. My head was pounding. Whirling. Swirling. Round and round. Twirling secrets round and round. Hush hush.

Again. My father called. I wasn't to open the door to any strangers and I could have some chocolate from the fridge. It was Rita's chocolate, but I could have some. Just that once. Four squares. They were in a hurry to get to the pub. Meeting Mr Johnson from Number 19. *Just a swift half. Don't open the door to any strangers. Did you hear me Jude?* I didn't know what a stranger was. Surrounded by neighbours. No strangers in Disraeli Avenue. No need to fear strangers. I was alone. All alone. I was naked in the bath. I was seven years, two months and twelve days old.

My father and Rita went out. I heard the door. Slam.

He left me all alone. I needed him and he had left me. I needed someone to make me better. I needed someone to explain the pain. I needed someone to make that pain go away. *Pain pain go away.* This wasn't how it was supposed to be. Slam and alone. Fear attacked the veins in my toes. I stayed upright. Bolted within the bath. Shivering. Blue. Trembling. Shuddering. I was alone. The house suddenly seemed so big. So empty. So still. Cold. So cold. I was terrified that Eddie would come back. He would be watching them leave. He would know that I was alone. He would enter my mother's house. I was naked in the bath. I would be trapped. He would kick down the door. He would hurt me. Aunty Maggie had a spare key. He could let himself in. I wouldn't be able to stop him. *Help me. Help me. Help me.*

I was sick into my bath.

Sand and sick mingled. *Dirty dirty bath.* I dried myself. Delicate touches made me gasp in pain. Numbness faded and my secrets flared. I dressed ready for bed. Purple pyjamas covered with cream teddy bears in purple boots. Father Christmas had left them for me on Christmas Eve. I had been on the good list. I would not go to bed. I wanted to wait for my father. I needed to wait and ask him about Eddie. Slowly, I moved down the stairs. Tiny steps caused cascades of pain to rumble in my tummy and tumble down my inner thighs. I sat on the bottom red stair.

Through the frosted glass panel on the green front door, I watched the darkness stumble down to the ground. I saw the streetlamp flame. I waited for shadows. Then. I hid in those shadows. I watched the twinkling star. In sight of the frosted panel of glass. I was a guard. A quivering sentry. I waited.

I heard my father. He was singing as he walked and Rita's pixie boots click clacked a rhythmic beat. I heard them coming. He had had his swift half. He was happy. I had not turned the light on. I was rooted on the bottom red stair. Alone in the dark. My nails dug into my palms, but my knuckles were fixed. I concentrated through the pain. So much pain.

Spain ... France ... Scotland ...
America ... London ...
Libya ...
Malta ...
Tibet ...
Victoria ...
Boston ...
Greenland ...

Spain ...
   France ...
      Scotland ...
         America ...
           London ...
           Libya ...
         Malta ...
      Tibet ...
   Victoria ...
Boston ... Greenland ... Spain ... France ... Scotland
... America ... London ... Libya ...
Malta ...
      Tibet ...
         Victoria ...
           Boston ...
              Greenland ...
                Spain ...
                  France ...
                  Scotland ...
America ... London ...
   Libya ... Malta ...
      Tibet ...
   Victoria ...
Boston ...
Greenland ...

*What are ye doin in the dark ye silly bairn?*

My father broke my journey. I didn't say that I wanted Eddie to think that I was out. I didn't say what Eddie had done to me in the cave. My voice had not returned. I had been waiting to tell my father about Eddie. I needed my father to explain my throbbing. I was crying. *Big girls don't cry. Only whinnying bairns cry.*


My father saw my hair. He was staring at my hair. I had forgotten. I had forgotten about the nest of hair. On the linoleum floor. Rita laughed at me. Rita said it was sweet. My wanting to be a hairdresser like my dead mother. My father got angry. He said that my mother was *an evil whore*. He said that I was *a whore's brat* and then he slapped my ear. Buzz fuzz. I was sitting on the bottom red stair. I turned and dashed up those stairs. As fast as I could caper. He caught my ankle and pulled me down. My chin counted each step. One two three four five six. He pulled down my pyjama pants and he slapped me five times. Rita was cackling. As she exhaled the room was filled with stale fumes. Invading. I could smell their swift halves. He pulled me up and twisted me over. He slapped my face. An erupting sting peaked and lingered. He yelled. Loud. In my face. In my ear. *No brat o' mine could be s' fuckin strange.* I looked down to the floor. I could still feel his palm on my cheek. Pain. More pain. I focused on a tiny swirl woven into the carpet. I had never noticed it before. Not until that moment. That precise moment. Snot and tears twirled together at the tip of my chin and gently dripped onto the ruby fitted carpet, just missing the peak of that perfect swirl. I counted six drips. Drip

drip

drip

drip

drip

drip.

The carpet absorbed them. My father went into the kitchen and Rita staggered after him.

I stayed. Feet rooted to the hallway carpet. Alone. Rita wobbled back struggling with a glass basin. Rita would fix my hair. She put the empty fruit bowl on my head. She cut around it. Her fingers never touched my hair. The scissors scratched and slashed. When she had finished, she removed the bowl. She chuckled. She said that I looked like a boy. She wasn't my mother. She had a funny smell. She pinched my arm. It hurt. More decoration. She whispered just loud enough for me to hear. *Evil brat just like ye killer of a mam.* I hated Rita. She was fat and ugly. She was not like my mother. She was a nasty nasty beast. I didn't like the way she looked at me. Her eyes were angry. Little piggy stare, with lines and lines exploding from them. Lines buried in her skin. Lines that made her look angry and sad and mean and ugly. She was never happy. She was not my mother.

My hair looked silly. I looked silly. My pain bubbled inside. I ached and I ached. I went to my room. I lay on my blue bed. Reached under my pillow. I took my mother's blouse. I held it to my face. Her scent was gone. I held it to my chest. I slept.

Hoping.

\* \* \* \* \*

Eddie went away. He had been a guest. *How nice of him to visit.* He came for a week. He ripped me. *It's oor little secret. You're me special girlfriend. Here's an extra fifty pence.* Nobody noticed. On Monday. Three days later. I went to Aunty Maggie's house. She was mad. She was all shouty. Eddie said I had run away on the beach. I was a rude little girl. She did not give me a fifty-pence piece. I was angry. I needed that fifty-pence piece. Saving to buy a globe that lit up with the flick of a switch. Eddie was *such a nice man. A real gent and the perfect house guest.* He would visit again soon. I was a naughty girl. *It's oor little secret. No one would believe a bairn like yee. Tell anyone and I'll get yee.* I didn't say anything. Eddie had stolen my voice.

I never bought the globe.

\* \* \* \* \*

Timothy Roberts (Number 21) was in my mother's house. Rita was on the phone. Talking to Mrs Clark (Number 14). Rita was talking about Mrs Roberts (Number 21). Mrs Roberts had to go to the hospital. Had a *woman thing* wrong with her. She asked Rita to babysit Timothy. Just for a couple of hours. Timothy Roberts was two and *a bit of a bugger at times.* Timothy Roberts was emptying the kitchen cupboards. Banging pans onto the floor. I went to see him. Stood at the kitchen door. I listened while I watched him.

Apparently. Mrs Roberts (Number 21) had *had a bit of Mr Johnson* (Number 19). They lived next door to each other. Their garages joined onto each other. During the day, *lazy arse Mr Johnson would nip round for a bit of how's ya father.* I didn't understand. Apparently. Mrs Johnson was *blind as a fuckin bat to what was going on right under her nose.* I didn't understand. Apparently. Mr Johnson and Mrs Roberts *were taking the piss.* Rita said that she'd *been staring at the brat for the last twenty minutes and couldn't figure out who the bugger was like.* She reckoned that he was either Mr Dewstep the butcher's, Mr Johnson's or possibly Mr Scott's (Number 25). I didn't understand. Rita was laughing. Cackling. She thought it funny that Mr Johnson was *pulling a fast one expecting to get away with fiddling on his own doorstep.* She was telling Mrs Clark (Number 14) that Mr Johnson would be *caught with his pants doon.* I didn't understand.

I stood in the kitchen doorway. Watching Timothy Roberts bang bang banging. I was staring and staring at him. Waiting for Mr Dewstep. Waiting for Mr Johnson. Waiting for Mr Scott. Waiting for the three men to step out of Timothy Roberts. I really didn't understand.

Rita had changed her yackety yack yack yarning. She was talking about Karen Johnson now. *A reet pretty bairn.* She was telling Mrs Clark (Number 14) all about Karen's accident. I'd seen it happen. I knew what had happened. I'd watched it from my bedroom window. Karen Johnson had been roller skating. Up and down. Up and down. Up and down the street. She had new skates. They were red and had huge rubber stoppers at the toe. I liked them. I really liked them. Anyway. Karen Johnson had fallen over. Apparently she had slipped on *some crap or other that the lazy arse bin man had dropped.* I didn't know. I had seen her fall. I had watched her land on her hand.

Snappety.
    Snap.
      Snap.

Apparently. You could have heard her screams in Wallsend. I heard them through my bedroom window. I saw them escape from her mouth. All the neighbours came rushing and pushing to help. *Emergency. Emergency. Help. Help. Help.* I saw Mr Johnson. He came flying over the other neighbours. He was faster than a speeding bullet. He was faster than an aeroplane. He was faster than the wibble wobblers. Rita was telling Mrs Clark (Number 14) the story. Apparently. *Mr Johnson flew in the air like fucking Superman.* Mr Johnson was Superman. He had scooped Karen in his arms and ran all the way back to his house. From just outside Number 4 to Number 19. Rita was laughing again. Cackle cackle cackle. *I wouldn't mind suckin on his super power.* Cackle cackle cackle. I didn't understand.

Karen Johnson was taken to hospital. Mrs Roberts (Number 21) had given Mr Johnson and Karen a lift. *Dirty buggers.* Cackle cackle cackle. Apparently. Karen Johnson had been a *reet brave bairn.* Her wrist had snapped in two places. Snappety snap snap. *Poor bairn.* She had a white plaster cast on her arm. I saw her from my bedroom window. I had seen her every day for the last four. She sat on her front wall. Clutching her white plaster. Clutching it as it changed colour. One two three four days. All the neighbours stopped to talk to her. All the neighbours wrote their names. Some drew pictures. I saw the colours. I saw the squiggles. But. But I never wrote my name. Mrs Roberts (Number 21) took her sweets. Mrs Shephard (Number 15) bought her a little teddy bear. Karen Johnson kept them all with her. All her new things. Along her front dwarf wall. *A reet pretty bairn. A reet brave bairn.*

Timothy Roberts started screaming. Piercing. Shrilling to the ceiling. He had hurt his eye. Hit it with a wooden spoon. Rita was angry. Rita had had to end her natter. Her yackety yacking cut short. She stormed past me. Slapped my head. Sharp. Sting sting sting. *Fucking useless ye are. Can't be fucking trusted te look after a little bairn.* Timothy Roberts stopped crying. He stared at me. He was sad. He was angry. I had let him be hurt.

\* \* \* \* \*

> Inside me
> Thousands of your waste
> Swim.
> Penetrating, burrowing,
> Tails wiggling,
> Worming into my essence.

You forced them into me
And now I exist with part of you.
I long to turn my insides out,
To scrub,
Till blood-filled scabs replace the dirt.
I have become you.
We remain one,
Till death us do part,
Till your dirty thousands die with me.

I hurt inside. I felt sick. I had a strange feeling that was with me all the time. It made me breathe faster. It made me feel as if something bad was about to happen. In the days and then weeks following my walk with Eddie, I began to hear noises. I heard voices. I jumped with fear. I shook. I was cold. Everything was inside of me and it needed to come out. It needed to escape from me.

The neighbours weren't always there after school. Eleven months and one day since my mother's death and I was known to be *a reet strange bairn*. They said it was alright for me to be alone. They liked me to be on my own. They found me odd. *She's strange, that Jude.* It was a Tuesday evening and I didn't go to Mr Johnson's (Number 19). I used my key instead.

Rita came to my mother's house before my father got home from work. She cooked his tea and ironed his shirts. She wanted to marry him. She wanted to live in my mother's house. She always came at the same time. Number 28 bus from Wallsend to Marsden. Arrived at 4.45pm or 5.15pm depending on which one she caught. I had sixty minutes. She had a key.

I went into my father's garage. It was attached to the house, through a wooden door from the kitchen. The stone floor was cold. I felt the cold through my white ankle socks. I looked around. The walls of the garage were my father's. Shelves of goodies and racks of tools. Half empty cans of paint. Brushes. Turpentine. Buckets. Jars of screws. Tins of nuts and bolts. Rakes. Brooms. Hammers. Screwdrivers. Saws. Spades. Never just one of a sort. I saw a tin. A pretty tin. A navy blue cylinder. It had a gold trim and $E^{II}R$ in gold lettering. It was dusty. It was neglected. It was too special to be on a shelf. In my father's cold garage. My father liked his garage. His special things were kept there.

The bricks of the garage were damp. It stank of the oil which had leaked from the bottom of my father's yellow Mini. A pool of oil was in the centre of the stone floor. A rusting lawn mower slumped against the wall waiting to be cleaned. I was looking for something to help me. I was standing in the doorway, scanning the room for something. Something to help me.

A paintbrush. Too soft.

A spade. Too heavy.

A hammer. Just right.

I took down a hammer from my father's tool rack. It looked very old. A thick dull metal head, with a wooden handle covered in scratches and dents. It spoke of experience. It was heavy and cold. I went back into the kitchen.

The kitchen. A rectangle that was divided into two separate areas. One where you ate. One where you cooked. When the house was empty I sat in that area where we used to eat. Special occasions. **Christmas Day.** Ripped-open Selection boxes. Chocolate for breakfast. A Curly Wurly poking out, waiting to be sneaked before lunch. Turkey dinner. Snapping crackers. Paper hats and funny jokes. **Toon Moor night.** Fish and Chips from the chippie on the seafront. Eaten straight from the newspaper parcel. Placed onto a plate. A bag of candy floss saved from the fair. Fluffy, pink and promising to be delicious. **Easter Sunday.** A leg of lamb, roast potatoes and lashings of mint sauce. Easter eggs lined up on the kitchen worktop. In sight and waiting.

Timber panels were nailed to two of the three walls giving a Scandinavian woodland feel while we ate. It was a simple setting. A matching stained wooden picnic table, resting against the panelled wall. A themed location. Hardly used anymore.

I sat at the table clutching the hammer. Hovering its cold head over my wrist. Plucking the courage. Finding the courage. Deep within me. Somewhere. Just a little tap at first.

Tap

    **tap**

          tap.

It felt nice. It wriggled and jiggled and tickled. I liked it.
I tapped a little harder.

Tap

      tap

          **tap.**

Pain. Physical pain. Actual pain. Throbbing, pounding, thumping
pain. I could breathe again.

I hit a little harder.

**Hit**     **hit**    **hit.**

Pain. Again. **Again.** Again. The pain released me. The pain
cleaned inside my head.

My wrist was red. The white bone was shining through the stretched
skin. I saw my bone. It shone. Tears gushed from my eyes. My legs
were shaking. Shock. Cold feet. Pain. Again. Again.

Enough. The hammer was too heavy to continue.

My wrist was swelling. I stood. Shaking. Colour jumped from my cheeks and plummeted to my toes. I wobbled. I went back into the garage, clutching the heavy hammer. The stone floor was cold. I wiped the handle of the hammer. I don't know why. I replaced the hammer, back on my father's tool rack. It swayed. I went back into the house. Slowly slowly.

A plan. A simple plan.

Fourteen minutes later. Rita came. I was sitting at the bottom of the stairs. I was crying and clutching my wrist. I could cry. My red swollen wrist made it alright to cry. I told her that I had fallen down the stairs. Fallen onto my wrist. It was a simple plan. She was worried. My father would be in trouble. No one was looking after me. She told me she would buy me sweets. She told me that I was not to tell anyone that I had been left alone in the house. *It's our little secret, bairn.* Whirling. Swirling. Round and round. Hush hush.

She would say that she saw me fall. I didn't have to lie. She would help me. She phoned my father at work. He came home and he hugged me. He hadn't hugged me before. He smelled of cigarettes and his breath puffed out stale beer. I didn't want him to let go of me. I wanted to stay. At the bottom of the stairs. Standing on the red carpet with my father's arms wrapped around me. He said that it would be alright. My father promised to make everything alright. Rita would look after me too.

\* \* \* \* \*

We all went to hospital. They told my story. I had an X-ray. My scaphoid bone was cracked. *A clear crack in the small boat-shaped bone in Jude's right wrist. This type of crack is consistent with a fall downstairs.* The doctor didn't know about my father's hammer. He didn't know about my tap tap tapping. I would have to have a plaster cast on for *up to six weeks*.

A nurse was waiting for me. She had blonde spiralling ringlets, coiling to just above her shoulders. Her silver eyes twinkled and sparkled. They had been speckled with enchanted fairy dust. She wrapped the soft white cotton wool around and around and around. My wrist felt safe. Snug. Warm. Then the bandages wrapped around and around and around the cotton wool. Securing. Cuddling. Then. Water was dripped onto the bandages. Magic. A white plaster oozed between the nurse's fingers. I watched the enchanted nurse manipulate the white lumpy mess into a perfectly smooth shell. She created a faultless capsule. It shrouded my tiny wrist. I admired how she could manipulate the gluey substance between her slender fingers. I watched as the plaster began to dry and white patches decorated her bitten finger nails. I thought she was magical. So magical. When she finished, she gave me a real smile and then offered me a shiny sticker. It was a brown teddy bear with a golden star on his round tummy. I had won a prize.

As we left the hospital Rita and my father promised to look after me. I cried through the pain. I cried out my pain. It was fine to cry.

Crying made the pain real. I rested my heavy arm within a powder-smelling sling. I liked the pain.

I could have some time off school. I could eat sweets and watch the television. A ten-pence mix up. Pink Shrimps. Gum rings. Foam teeth. Black Jack. Fruit Salad. Candy watch. Strawberry lace. Flying Saucers. All neatly placed in a crisp white paper bag. Aunty Maggie brought me a magazine. The *Beano*. Edition 2015, February 28 1981. Sellotaped to the front was a shiny fifty-pence piece. I liked the pain. The pain made them notice me.

I was here again. I was visible.

The pain was lovely. The cold hammer was miraculous. The smell of the damp plaster made me happy. My father tucked me in bed. I was a clever girl for not telling the doctor. Some secrets were good. Hush hush. Pain was nice. My father was proud of me. I was not alone. That night I slept and wanted to wake up.

\* \* \* \* \*

Exhibit number two –
sticker from nice nurse.

\* \* \* \* \*

My plaster cast had magical powers. Really really magical. I was magical when I wore it. My plaster cast made my father notice me more. It even made Rita nicer. Sometimes. The magic lasted for the whole six weeks. Forty-two happy days.

Rita and my father bought me sweets. Every day. They talked to me. Asked me how I was. Sometimes I was allowed to watch television with them. *Coronation Street*. I had to go to bed when it finished and I didn't understand it. But. But I tried to be interested. *Annie. The Rovers. Mike. Deirdre. Ken. Emily.* I liked sitting in my mother's front room. With them. Watching *Coronation Street*. The theme tune started and Rita waddled in with a plastic tray overcrowded with goodies. Always. A bottle of Cola. Three glasses. Four tin cans of beer. A large packet of Cheese and Onion crisps. Salted peanuts. A big bar of Cadbury's Whole Nut chocolate. Rita kept it in the fridge. It was solid and stiff. I would sit on the floor, Rita and my father on the sofa. Rita would give me three chunks. Thick chocolate. Her special chocolate. I sucked. I savoured. I tried to work out what was going on between *Mike, Deirdre* and *Ken*. Rita said that she loved Mike Baldwin. She wanted him to do things to her. I didn't understand. I stared into the screen. Tried to use my magic. Tried to magic Mike into whisking Rita away to Manchester. That was far far away. Practically the other side of the world. I liked watching television with my father and Rita. I liked the tray of goodies. I liked that the tray was not removed until everything was guzz guzz guzzled.

Forty-two happy days. But. But then my plaster was cut off.

A revolving blunt blade split my pod into two. The hairs on my arm were thick and dark. My hand smelled. Dead skin rolled and clung around my thumb. Dead pain clung in between my fingers.

My wrist was stiff and ached. My wrist missed its plaster. My plaster cast came off and my father was happy. Rita was happy too. They were not in trouble. They had tricked the doctors. Nobody knew that I had been home alone. We had a secret. Hush hush. I had more secrets. Whirling. Swirling. Round and round. Twirling secrets round and round. I wanted to tell them my secrets. They had been nice to me. I wanted to tell them about Eddie.

When my plaster cast came off. My magic was taken away. Stolen from me. And. Rita and my father just stopped being nice. They just stopped. They didn't have to prevent my talking with doctors. They didn't have to be nice anymore. No more shared secret. They said *thank fuck for that*. They could breathe again. They stopped buying me sweets. No more ten-pence mix ups. No more chunks of solid chocolate. I was alone again. No more hugs from my father. When I went near to him, he told me to move. I blocked his television. I was a big girl. I never cried. *Big girls don't cry*. I was sent to my bedroom. They preferred me out of the way. *Fuckin' pain in the arse watching is all the time. Do you see sheh looks a' the tray, to see wha sheh can 'ave? Fuckin' greedy brat*. Rita didn't like me. I didn't like her. I wasn't allowed to watch *Coronation Street*. Things had changed again. My plaster cast was taken from me. I had nothing again. I didn't understand. The hammer would understand.

Over the next two years, the hammer was used four times. Every six months. Every six months to the precise date. Always on the

27th of the month. Always. Nobody ever asked the question. I was *such an accident prone bairn.*

\* \* \* \* \*

In the six months following Eddie's visit, my hobbies began to slip away. No ballet. No Brownies. No friends for tea. Nothing excited me. Nothing interested me. I didn't understand why I was different. I didn't understand. My father stopped smiling at me. He stared. He glared. *No brat o' mine could be s' fuckin strange.* Rita told me that I was evil. *Like your killer of a mam.* My father had Rita. They had each other. He wanted to drink from tin cans. Every night he drank and played his records. Lionel Ritchie. Kenny Rogers. Dr Hook. He liked to make Rita squeak. He liked to make Rita moan and groan and screech and yell. He liked her. I didn't. I chose to stop the violin. I didn't want to play the recorder. I didn't want to be in the end of year play. I hated music. I wanted my life to be silent. I was waiting.

## Waiting.

Always waiting.

\* \* \* \* \*

On the last day of term. July 16 1981. I walked home from school. Followed the crocodile of children that moved up the slope of the Coast Road and towards the estate. Head down. Anchored at the tip of the crocodile's tail. Mrs Andrews (Number 18) and Mrs

Hodgson (Number 2) walked in front of me. Big squishy bottoms in flowery skirts. Blocked the path. Wibble wobble. I tried to move past them. Tried to slide in between the round squishy wall. But. Their squishiness squashed me. Bounced me back behind them. I squeaked politely. They didn't hear me. They didn't want to hear me. Their children, Gillian Andrews and Paul Hodgson, were seven like me. They had raced ahead. Chatting. Laughing. Tig tagging. I tried to zig-zag my way through, but the huge flowery bottoms had swallowed my pathway. Mrs Andrews was talking about Mr Johnson (Number 19). Loud chatter. Tittle-tattle. Chitter-chatter. Snail trail. Wibble wobble. They blocked the pavement. I couldn't get past. Instead I walked near to them. Almost brushing their backs. I listened. I liked to listen.

Apparently. Mr Johnson had been *sacked from his job*. I didn't understand. *Over a year ago*. It must have been before my mother went away. He'd been *full of booze once too often*. I didn't understand. Apparently. He'd gone to the library every day for two weeks. Apparently. He'd sat all day. Reading a newspaper or staring at the books. Never spoke a word. Apparently. He hadn't had *the balls to tell his wife that he'd been sacked* and then one day Mrs Johnson bumped into Mrs Hughes the librarian in the Dewstep Butchers. Apparently. *Holy hell had broken out that night.* I didn't understand.

I liked Mr Johnson. He was a nice man. He always picked Karen and Lucy up from school. He waited at the school gate with the mums. He held his girls' hands and he talked to them. All the way home. I watched him. Chitter chatter. He smiled a lot. Yellowed mouth with a little gap in between his front two teeth. He often came around to my mother's house, smoked cigarettes and drank out of tin cans with my father. He laughed a lot. Sounded like a horse hiccupping.

Hic-cc-**cup-up-up-innnnnnng**.

It made me smile. It made me giggle giggle giggle. Mr Johnson was a nice man. He wore jeans and bright white sports shoes. He wore a blue, soft leather jacket which had huge pockets. Squishy. Squashy. He jingled as he walked. He called Mrs Johnson *wor lass* and talked to my father about Challenge Anneka's *canny backside*.

Mr Johnson had two girls. Karen was in my class at school. *A reet pretty bairn.* Her sister Lucy was two years younger than us. *A bonny bairn and reet clever too.* I didn't play with them. I didn't play with anyone. They liked Sindy dolls, make-up and Girl's World. I didn't see the point. I just didn't see the point in piling luminous blue eye shadow onto a plastic blonde head.

The squishy bottoms slowed at the peak of the Coast Road slope. Wibble wobble. Huff puff. Mrs Andrews talked. Yackety yack. Apparently. Mr Johnson had been *given his cards* and it was putting *a canny strain on his marriage*. I didn't understand. Poor Mrs Johnson was working *every hour to put bread on the table*. I didn't understand. Apparently. Mr Johnson *drank like a fish* and thought *money grew on trees*. I didn't understand. Mr Johnson was funny. He had a laugh like a hiccupping horse. He made me smile. Mrs Andrews spoke her words with a nasty twang. I knew that she was being mean to Mr Johnson and I didn't like her doing it. Mrs Andrews told Mrs Hodgson that she shouldn't tell anyone. Hush hush. I wouldn't tell anyone either. Whirling. Swirling. Round and round. Twirling secrets round and round.

As we walked past Brian's Newsagents, Mr Johnson was coming out. Lucy and Karen had ten-pence mix ups. They were exploring their little white paper bags. Mrs Hodgson said a strange hello to Mr Johnson. She giggled and touched his arm. Then she just stopped. In the middle of the pavement. I carried on walking. Too busy watching. Walked into her back. She turned and shouted at me. *Watch where ye gannin.* I put my head down and carried on walking. *Such a rude bairn tha Jude Williams.* Past the window of Brian's Newsagents. Past the library. Through the cut. Past Gladstone Street. Into Disraeli Avenue. Number 9. I used my key.

\* \* \* \* \*

On Wednesday July 29 1981 Prince Charles and Lady Diana Spencer were getting married. Disraeli Avenue was having a street party. My father and all the other men who worked were given the day off. A national holiday. A day to celebrate.

My father was assistant manager of Rumbelows in Newcastle. Mr Johnson's (Number 19) brother was the manager. *Pulled a few strings*. My father didn't have to have an interview. He said that he was *the luckiest bloke in the world*. And. That if he fell from a plane, he *wouldn't land on his arse*. It was an easy job. He just had to turn up and help people spend money. My father liked his job.

My father was the first person in Disraeli Avenue to have a Philips Betamax video recorder 2020. *Could line up five programmes for up to 16 days in advance*. He never did. That was too complicated. My father sold electrical items, but he could never work them. He liked to have the latest things. It cost a *small fortune*. £519·99. My father didn't pay that. It was ex-display. He had an employee discount and it had a big scratch on the bottom. He made the big scratch on it. He was careful to make it on the bottom. Just enough damage. Mr Johnson's brother had shown him how. *Reet clever bloke*. It cost my father three hundred pounds. The neighbours were amazed by it. Everyone must have thought that we were rich. That we were the richest people in Disraeli Avenue. Three hundred pounds. We were the richest people on Disraeli Avenue.

Wednesday July 29 1981. The Royal Wedding. We had been learning all about it at school. We even sent a card to the Prince and Princess. Mine had a drawing of a yellow-haired princess in a Union Jack-coloured wedding dress. It wasn't very good. I only had forty minutes to think of the idea and to draw it. It was rushed. Inside I wrote. *Dear Prince Charles and Lady Diana. Love Jude Williams*. I couldn't think of anything else to write. I was rush rush rushed. My teacher sent it thirty-seven days before the wedding. But. We didn't get a letter back. I asked my teacher every day. I wanted to know if Lady Diana liked my card. My teacher said that the princess would be too busy to write to our school. I didn't believe her. I didn't want to believe her.

The Royal celebration. Red, white and blue bunting joined the opposite houses. Unified. Celebrating together. It swung in the gentle breeze. Ladders rested against houses. Front doors were open. Music blasted out of windows. The sun was shining. A day off work. A day to party. Posters of Prince Charles and Lady Diana were taped inside windows. They were free with the *Daily Mail*. A souvenir. I bought one from Brian's Newsagents. Used one of the fifty-pence pieces that Aunty Maggie had given me. I didn't stick it on my window. I kept it. Neat. Perfect. Flat. In an *Oor Wullie* album. 1978. In between pages 29 and 30. Like the date of the wedding. There were no page numbers though. I had to count from the beginning of the book. I placed the *Oor Wullie* album containing the special poster into my wardrobe. Carefully carefully.

I watched from my mother's front room window. I watched the sea of red, white and blue. Flapping. Waving. Noisy. The party was in full swing. It was nine o'clock in the morning. Tin cans were already lying empty. Cluttering Disraeli Avenue. I stayed in my mother's front room. I peeped through the window every now and then. I didn't want to go outside. I wanted to soak up every moment that the BBC was supplying. I was excited. Really excited. A princess. I was going to see a real princess.

Every one of the neighbours joined in. It had been arranged. Mrs Hodgson (Number 2) had gone around with a list of food. Rita and my father had to bring sausages on sticks. It was all planned. The men had put up bunting. The women were fussing around the still folded tables. Waiting for someone to put them out. Needing someone to put them out. The children. Some children were playing hide and seek. Noisy. Rush rush. Run and hide. I could see Paul Hodgson (Number 2). He was crouched in my mother's garden. It wasn't a good hiding place. The street was noisy. Alive. Screaming. Squealing. Over the radios. Over music. Screeching. Over the blaring television screens. Everything was on full volume. Everyone switched on. Open front doors. In and out of each others' houses. Rita had cleaned my mother's house. It was polished and vacuumed and spick and span. She was happy to leave my mother's front door open. In and out. In and out. I didn't like it. I didn't like the neighbours being in my mother's house. They were too noisy. I needed to listen. I needed to see. I needed silence. I needed to concentrate.

My father helped Mr Johnson (Number 19) and Mr Douglas (Number 8) set out the tables. They were wallpapering tables. Different sizes. They didn't quite join together properly. Paper table cloths were put onto them. Red, white and blue. The tables stretched from Number 5 to Number 19 Disraeli Avenue. No chairs at the table, but there were some deckchairs. Placed along the pavement. The two entrances to the avenue were blocked off. Two chairs and a plank across. Mr Smith (Number 23) was a builder. He made the two blocks. Mrs Scott (Number 25) said that Mr Smith had done a good job. *First time he ever did something on time. Bloody waste of space lazy arse.* Everything was arranged. Tin cans of beer bobbed around in buckets of cold water. Scattered along the street. The food was foiled. Placed out along the centre of the table. Neatly. Aunty Maggie made rice. Mrs Roberts (Number 21), Mrs Johnson (Number 19) and Mrs Andrews (Number 18) brought plates of sandwiches. Spam, jam, ham and egg. There were other foods. They appeared in between my peeping. Cakes. Crisps. Scones. I wanted to know who brought them. I needed to know how they got there. I wanted to know. But. I was distracted. I was waiting. Watching. Waiting to see the princess.

> Sausage rolls.
> Crispy cakes.
> Jelly.
> Fairy cakes.
> Scones.
> Biscuits.
> Crisps.
> Hard-boiled eggs.
> Crackers.
> Spam sandwiches.
> Ham sandwiches.
> Jam sandwiches.
> Egg sandwiches.
> Rice.

*A reet royal spread.*

At the table, outside my mother's house, Rita poked sausages onto cocktail sticks. She wore a commemorative apron over a short red skirt and a white shirt. Her white stilettos finished off the look. She looked quite normal from the front, but not from behind. As she bent over the table her fat dimply thighs squelched under the hem of the skirt. No tights because it was the summer. It was hot. The sun was shining. Rita was orange from her sunbed sessions. Like a wrinkled Satsuma. Mrs Lancaster (Number 7) told Rita that the tan made her legs look thinner. I didn't understand. She had fat thighs. Big fat orange pork sausages. Juicer than the flimsy ones that she was poking onto sticks. I watched them all from my mother's front room window. I heard everything through the open windows. But I would look only when there was a break or a boring discussion on TV.

Mr Johnson (Number 19) wore a blue vest with his tight jeans. He wore a Union Jack bowler hat. He'd bought four extra and had given them to his *chosen ones*.

## Rita. Mrs Roberts (Number 21). Mrs Hodgson (Number 2).

Mrs Hodgson was wearing a white nurse's outfit. She wasn't a nurse. Hadn't worked. Mrs Hodgson was *on the social*. Hush hush. Her boobs were all squashed together and bursting out of the neckline of the outfit. The white dress had a big red cross on it

65

and she told Mr Johnson that she was wearing blue knickers. You could see the blue knickers as the outfit stretched across her huge bottom. She had pulled her yellow hair into a ponytail and tied it with a Union Jack ribbon. She looked funny. She looked like a little girl. But she wasn't a little girl. Nothing about her was little. Mr Johnson liked her dress. He told her that it was *making me rise to the occasion*. I didn't understand.

I was going to see a real Princess. I didn't have a television in my bedroom. Karen Johnson (Number 19) did. I had to sit on the floor in my mother's front room. I tried to block everything out. All of the noises. All of the people. I sat as close to the television as I could. I sat too close to the TV. *Strain your fucking eyes.*

Then.

Then the Royal Wedding coverage began. Angela Rippon and Michael Wood were in the studio and John Craven was in London. Live. I liked him. He did *Newsround*. He told me lots of things. The BBC was excited about the Royal Wedding. I was excited like them. There were reports from all over England. From castles, boats and staff. The Red Devils and the Red Arrows flew over London, leaving trails and patterns. Twirling and swirling. Painting the sky. Red, white and blue. There were crowds of people. Real people. All shown on the television screen. Thousands and thousands of people turned up in London. I saw them all on TV. I wished that I was there. I wished that I was with those people. They wanted to see the

Prince and Princess too. I sat. In my mother's front room, glued to the TV and recording it all with my father's Philips Betamax video recorder 2020.

**9:45am**

Inside St Paul's Cathedral. People started to arrive. Famous and beautiful people. I didn't recognise any of them. I listened to the descriptions of their clothes. Then. A beautiful lady walked into the church. She looked familiar. She was a princess. From Denmark. She was wearing a pale blue silk gown. It trailed along behind her. I didn't catch her name. She looked like Cinderella. She had yellow hair. I couldn't see her shoes. I wanted to see her shoes. They might have been glass slippers. I think that she was Cinderella. She was very very pretty. She was smiling. She was happy. I was hearing name after name. I was trying so hard to catch them all. But. They were names that I had never heard before. Names that wouldn't stick inside my brain. The television screen was brimming with princes and the princesses. The church was full of them. I was so excited. My face was pushed against the television screen. Too close. Far too close.

**10.20am**

The commentators were excited. They talked quickly. Sing songy. Members of the Royal family were leaving Buckingham Palace.

**10.30am**

Then the Prince left.

# Then.

## 10.45am

The Princess left. Magical. Magical. A carriage. A Cinderella glass carriage. Elegant horses. Her white dress was so very beautiful. It ruffled and fluffled at the neck and the elbows. It fluffed and puffed. It stood alone. A princess decorated in a big fluffy dress. A beautiful dress. She looked a bit like the knitted doll that covered the toilet roll in my mother's toilet. It had been a present from Aunty Maggie. It was white and green. It matched the bathroom. I looked at the detail on Lady Diana's dress. I listened to the commentators. Every word.

## 11.00am

The service began. A diamond tiara. The Spencer family tiara to hold her veil. Lace. Sequins. Jewels. Crinoline. Silk taffeta. The train of material went on and on and on and on and on. A twenty-five-foot train. Designed by the Emanuels. Ruffles and tuffles of material. I had a green notebook. I wrote it all down. Every detail. The commentator said that it was white English silk. Snowy silk for the new princess. Pure. Delicate. Her bouquet was beautiful. The descriptions given precise. I liked precise. I could almost smell the flowers. Gardenias. Lilies. White Freesia. White Orchids. Golden Roses. I wrote it all down. She was a princess. A real princess. Her prince was tall. He wore a uniform. It was decorated with medals. He must have been brave. He would look after her. She was safe. The gold trims on his uniform glistened in the sunshine and the medals twinkled to let me know that she was going to be safe. I looked at Lady Diana. Her sad eyes peeked through her eyelashes. She would be safe. *I do.* Husband and wife.

**By 12.20pm**
The Prince and Princess of Wales had left St Paul's Cathedral.

## Every detail.

Lady Diana was beautiful. She had sad eyes and shiny yellow hair. She was lovely. Rita had a 'Lady Di' hair do. Mrs Thomas (Number 13) had cut it for two pounds. She came to my mother's house and cut it over newspaper in the lounge. Rita said that she needed her roots done too. Mrs Thomas didn't know how to do that. She was doing a night course at the community centre in North Shields. Only been doing it for three weeks. Rita wasn't beautiful and her hair looked silly. Black roots and bleached blonde ends. My father said she looked like a *skunky toon supporter. Divvent want to share me bed with a fuckin Magpie.* Rita would never be a princess and my father was not a prince charming.

On the day of the Royal Wedding, my father took his chance to wear red and white all day. He had a wig. Saved it from the 1973 FA Cup Final. Sunderland beat Leeds 1–0. Best moment of my father's life. I was born that year too. My mother became pregnant after the celebrations of the Semi-Final win. My father still talked about the Cup Final. *The best day of me life.* Bob Stokoe ran onto the field at the end of the match. *The moment of the game. The underdog had won.* The only thing Sunderland AFC had ever won. My father liked to talk about that special day. He caught a train from Newcastle to London Victoria. Travelled through the night. A pilgrimage. His only ever time to London. He went with a man from work. Couldn't remember how or when he got home. The proudest moment of my father's life. My father was so happy after the FA Cup win that he got a needle and ink and tattooed SUNDERLAND across the knuckles on his hands. No room for AFC. He paid to have a black cat tattooed on his right forearm and underneath it read Sunderland AFC forever. On his left forearm in fading blue-black scribble was *Adam* He was the only Wearsider living in Disraeli Avenue. He was proud of it. Every other week he went to Roker Park. Drove through the tunnel. Went on his own. Faithful. Loyal. I listened to the results on the radio. My father would drink to *drown his sorrows*. I knew to stay in my room if they had lost. They often lost. To celebrate the union of Charles and Diana, my father wore his red and white wig as well as his red and white striped top and black shorts.

**At 1.20pm**

The Prince and Princess appeared on the balcony with the Royal family. Buckingham Palace balcony. Prince Charles kissed Princess Diana's hands and then her mouth. The crowd cheered. The neighbours cheered. I watched Diana's eyes. Closed. Tight. Her lips did not move. Joined. Princess Diana had a family now. She had smiling people around her. The Queen of England would be her new mother. She would always be safe. No one would ever hurt her and her eyes would get happier and happier.

## An idea.

I would draw the princess. I would draw her in her beautiful wedding dress. I would draw her with her new family. Smiling. I would capture the happy moment. Then. Then I would send it to Princess Diana. I would send it with a letter. To say sorry for drawing the wrong wedding dress. On my card. The one that my teacher had sent. Thirty-seven days before the wedding. She would never wear a Union Jack wedding dress. I had been silly. I needed to make it all alright. That was why she hadn't written back to me. That was why. She hadn't liked the dress that I had drawn. The Philips Betamax video recorder 2020 would help me. Rewind. Pause. I rushed upstairs to find my sketch pad and pencils.

I was in the bathroom. A quick wee. Rushing before I started my drawing.

## I smelled him.

Stale sweat. I didn't connect the smell. I felt a panic. Terror. I didn't know the terror. I was unlocking the door when the smell of cigar smoke hit me. I opened the door before I realised.

## He was there.

He was still fat. He still wore brown and his big belly was shoving me into the bathroom. *How's me special girlfriend?* Fear. Fear. Fear. A fat cigar balanced in between his fingers. His shirt was the same dirty cream and he wore a red tie. His tie was crooked. The knot curved to the right. Off centre. Scruffy. He had a Union Jack bowler hat. One of Mr Johnson's special hats. His nose. Still a purple plum and as he spoke stale smoke and tin can beer smells escaped from his narrow mouth. His lips were wet. A tiny blob of saliva had formed in the corner of his mouth. Excited. Nothing had changed. Panic. Panic. Panic. He pushed me back into the bathroom. I fell against the pea green bath. My legs buckled beneath me. I curled onto the linoleum floor. He locked the door behind him.

Panic. Panic. Panic. Fear.

Zip.
    Zip.

He held his thing in his left hand. Gripped. His stumpy fingers clenched around it. Stubby. Shiny. Glistening under the fluorescent bathroom light. Pointing into my eyes. He balanced his cigar on the edge of the sink. Carefully. He moved towards me. Swift. One hand gripped my hair. Yanked my head back. Fear. Fear. He pushed it onto my lips. I closed my eyes. Tried to make it dark. Tried to make myself invisible. Couldn't. He smelled. It smelled. Like the dead skin in between my fingers when my plaster cast was removed. Dirty. He pushed. Trying to worm into my mouth. Burrowing in.

Dirty. Smelly. The thing dribbled. I felt drops on my lips. I wanted them off. I wanted his smell to go away. My lips did not move. Eyes tight shut. I tried to keep my lips closed, but I needed to make him stop. I went to scream. *Help. Help.* My lips gave way. He rammed it in. I couldn't make a sound. My mouth was full of his thing. He pushed. He moaned. His breathing quickened. He yanked my head back and forward. My mouth stretched. My jaw locked. Ached. The corner of my mouth burned. I wanted the dribbles to be gone. Sticky rolling off my lips. I couldn't scream, but I could move my arms and my legs. I squirmed. I tried to attack. Eyes closed. My arms flip flapped. Panic. Panic. Tried to grasp hold of him. No nails to scratch. I tried to nip. I couldn't grab hold. I couldn't see. My arms waved in the air. I was too weak. He was too strong.

*Suck it. Suck it.*

He moved my head back and forward. Jerking. I continued to flap my arms. He gripped. He controlled. He squirted into my mouth. Within seconds my mouth was full. My mouth was dirty. I gagged. He pulled his thing out. I threw myself over the bath. Eyes open. I was sick. Salty. Lumpy. Dirty. Tumbling down the side of the pea green bath. Zip zip. Eddie boomed with laughter. *Ho ho ho.*

From the corner of my eye, I saw him collect his cigar. Carefully. *It's oor little secret. Nah one'd believe a strange bairn like yee. Tell anyone and I'll kill yee. Clean that fuckin mess up.*

I watched the lumps sinking down the side of the bath. Falling falling. Eyes fixed on the pool of his dirt. I heard him unlock the door. He closed the door behind him and went outside to join the neighbours. The party was in full swing.

I cleaned it up. I cleaned the pea green bath. Away away for a year and a day. I danced by the light of the moon.

I went to my bedroom window. All the neighbours were outside. Celebrating in the sunshine. Celebrating the union. Partying. Commemorating. Drinking from tin cans. Dancing. Shouting. Eating. The wedding was over. The happy ever after had begun. I watched. I watched the happy ever after. My father congaed up and down the grey slabs with a train of drunken neighbours and he blew on a bugle. His red and white frizzy head bobbed up and down. The bugle was Mr Wallace's (Number 22). He had played it in a war. My father liked the noise it made. *Rasped like a wet fart.* My father blew out the conga rhythm. The neighbours danced along their slabs. I watched it all.

Eddie was below my open bedroom window. Dirty cream back to me. Under the lamppost that flamed outside of my mother's house. He was slumped into a bright red deckchair. Cigar in one hand, tin can of beer in the other. A bucket to his right, with four tin cans bobbing. Aunty Maggie was on his left. She was in a deckchair too. Hers was a grass green colour. Not red, white or blue. They were laughing. They were chatting. They were happy. A special day. Eddie's shoulders kept moving up and down. Chuckling. *Ho ho ho*. His hands lifted to his mouth. Cigar. Tin can. Cigar. Tin can. I watched.

One tin can.
Two tin cans.
Three tin cans.
Four tin cans.
Five tin cans.

He was trying to move off the deckchair. The streetlight flickered. Darkness was coming. I was scared of the dark. I was scared of the light. I was scared of Eddie. The light made me see things. The light gave me pictures in my head. He kept turning to my mother's house. Looking at the doorway. Looking at the open doorway. Panic panic. He was talking to Aunty Maggie, but he was looking at my mother's house. Panic panic. He was moving in the deckchair, trying to shuffle himself out of the dip in the fabric. Shuffle shuffle shuffle. He was going to come back into my mother's house. **Panic panic**. He was trying to get up. He was struggling. Shuffle shuffle shuffle. His drumstick legs were straggling. Slumped in the deckchair. He couldn't quite match his feet to the pavement. Humpty dumpty man. I didn't have very long. Panic panic. I had to be quick.

I knew where to hide. *Such a nice man. A real gent and the perfect house guest.* I had rearranged the boxes under the bed. Just enough.

Just enough space. I scrambled in. Balls of dust. A tiny metal top hat. Red and yellow counters. Broken bits of plastic. Old knickers. Crumbled sweet wrappers. I pushed my way over them. Burrowed in. Flat on my tummy. I rearranged the boxes in front of me. Monopoly. Connect Four. Buckaroo. Bought by Aunty Maggie from a church sale. Too many pieces missing to play. I rearranged the boxes. Neat. Straight. Just enough of a gap for my eyes to peep through. I sneezed. Nose twitched. Dusty dusty. I squeezed the tip of my nose. I waited. My breaths were loud. Too loud. Booming. I tried to make me quiet. I couldn't stop the panic. I couldn't think nice thoughts. **Panic panic**.

I could hear his drumstick legs stomping up the stairs. Panting. Stopping to breathe. The smell of cigar wafted into the room. He was in the doorway. He was leaning against the door frame. Waiting. Waiting. I could see his shoes. Brown. I could see the different coloured laces and the looped bows. They had stopped. Pointed into the room. Waiting. I heard my father. He shouted. *Jude. Where the fuck are you?* Eddie jumped. Quick. He dropped the butt of his cigar into my room. I saw it smoldering onto my carpet. I watched it. *Awreet Bill. Jus usin' the netty. Yee lost that bairn o yeez?* His shoes turned away from my bedroom. I heard him talking to my father as he clumped back down the stairs. *Nowt but trouble that bairn o' yeez. Hope ye divvent mind is usin the netty. Wor Maggie said yez wouldn't mind.* His voice was funny. He spoke too quickly and it all rolled into one big word. No gaps for breath. He sounded like he was going to laugh. *Ho ho ho.* I didn't know what to do. I couldn't move. I mustn't move. Eddie mustn't find me. I had a safe place. Nobody knew where I was. I could stay under my bed. The tiny metal top hat pushed into my stomach.

I dared not move.

\* \* \* \* \*

I could hear the laughter from outside. Even from under my bed. I could hear it all. Getting louder and louder. The music. The cheering. The jeering. The bugle. The neighbours were happy. The noise was too loud. Boom boom boom. The floor was jingling about. My whole body was shivering. The noise. The boom boom booming. I couldn't hear if anyone was coming up the stairs. Too loud. Too loud. I needed to hear. I needed to be ready. Aware. Watching. Watching. Eyes locked on the doorway. I was frightened to blink. In case Eddie returned. In that flicker. In that closing of my eyes. I had to watch. Panic panic. He could appear. Without me knowing. Too loud. Too loud.

My eyes hurt. They felt dry. As if they were going to fall out. Onto the carpet. Then roll away. I wouldn't be able to see them. I wouldn't be able to see. I was scared to blink. My eyes needed me to blink. My head throbbed. Concentrate. Concentrate. My room was getting darker. The cigar remained. Lying on my blue carpet. Nestled in its hole. A piece of Eddie still in my room. I had to watch for shadows. Concentrate. Concentrate.

I tried to stay focused on the doorway. Waiting for shadows. Fearing those shadows. But. But as the time began to tick tock by. My eyes kept dropping. Dropping and locking on the butt of his cigar. In my room. On my carpet. It lay on my carpet. I watched it. It was mine. It was going to be mine forever. I needed it. I needed to keep it. I could smell it. I could remember. I must remember. I must never forget. I wanted to crawl out. I needed to grasp the cigar butt. Then I could crawl back under. But. But I couldn't. I couldn't move. I had to watch the shadows.

I needed to wee. I needed to wee. Quick quick. I didn't know what to do. I didn't know what to do. I couldn't move. I couldn't go into the bathroom. It wasn't safe. Eddie would know. Eddie would be watching. Waiting. It wouldn't be safe. I clenched the tops of my thighs together. I could not leave my safe place.

Concentrate.
Concentrate.

I could not wee.

Concentrate. **Concentrate**.

I could not wee. **Concentrate**. Concentrate.

I could not wee.

I felt the warmth.

I felt the warmth of my wee.

       Covering my stomach.

              Covering my red t-shirt.

                     Seeping through my grey school skirt.

I stayed under my bed until my father and Rita came in. I waited until the music stopped and the neighbours screamed their goodnights and locked their doors. I waited. Still. Under my bed. Waiting.

Safe.

I waited till it was safe. I waited until the lock lock locking of my mother's front door. Then. I moved the boxes and I crawled out from under the bed. Stiff. Aching. I went to the cigar. I picked it up. Evidence. I sat on my bed. Gripping Eddie. Waiting for them. Waiting for my father to ask where I had been. Waiting to tell my father about Eddie. I could show him. I could show him the cigar.

               They didn't come into my bedroom.

Rita giggled. My father giggled too. Rita tripped up the stairs. It was funny. My father thought that it was funny. Rita was squeaky. They had had a good day. *Best day ever.* Rita and my father did not come into my room. I sat on my bed. Rooted to my bed. Waiting. Stiff. Wet red t-shirt. Wet grey school skirt. Smelly. Shaking. Back to the wooden headrest. Knees tight to my chest. Arms wrapped around my shins. Head resting on my knees. My knickers were wet. I could smell my wee. It made me feel sick. Dirty dirty sick. The tops of my thighs were wet. Red. Sticky. I had wet my knickers. I had had to wee. Over and over. I couldn't help it. Too scared to climb from under my bed. Too scared to go into the bathroom. Eddie liked my bathroom. Too scared that he would be waiting for me. My father and Rita didn't come into my room. They went into my mother's room. They groaned and moaned and giggled and banged. I sat. Rooted to my bed. Shaking. Scared. Wet knickers. Under my bed. Not far from that metal top hat. My wee seeped into the carpet.

I stayed awake. All night. I had to. I didn't know what to do. There was nothing that I could do. No one to help. No one to make things better. Cold. Cold. Cold. Dirty. Smelly. No one. My eyes fixed on my basket. Teddies. Dolls. My mother's secrets buried. Buried. I needed her to come back. I needed her to come back for me. For her special things. I had rescued them. I was waiting. Always waiting. I stayed awake. Concentrating. Wishing. Hoping. Willing her to return.

The happy ever after.

\* \* \* \* \*

He is within my mouth.
My tongue touches him.
Caresses him.
Welcomes him into his new home.
My tongue communicates with him.

Teaches him my language.

Gives him my words.

I can taste him.

He shares my food.

He eats off my tongue.

I cannot speak.

 I cannot eat.

He is invading.

He is capturing.

He is controlling.

His flag pole sticks into my tongue.

\* \* \* \* \*

**Exhibit number three –**
**Eddie's cigar.**

\* \* \* \* \*

Friday July 31 1981. The smell of his cigar covered my hair and face. It lived in my skin. It filled my pillow. Two days after the Royal Wedding. The happy ever after had begun. I sat up in bed. Swung my legs over the edge.

Dangled.

Bare.

My pink nightie clung.

Creased.

Twisted.

81

All wrong. Tucked into my knickers. Scratchy. Tight. I hurt. My jaw ached. My hair touched my face. My hair whipped my face. Pain. Constant pain. A dull pain. A dead pain. On my tummy. Just to the right of my tummy button. I touched a small round bruise. The top hat bruise. I sat. Legs dangled. Not yet reaching the floor. Cold. Exposed. I thought about Eddie. I thought about Eddie under my pillow.

I had a tin. It was my father's. I found it on a shelf. In my father's garage. It had had shoe polish in it. I took it. I liked it. It was too special to be in my father's garage. It used to be shoved on a shelf. Shelves of half empty cans of paint. Brushes. Turpentine. Buckets. Jars of screws. Tins of nuts and bolts. Rakes. Brooms. Hammers. Screwdrivers. Saws. Spades. It was too special for that. I rescued it. I had taken it five months and four days before. The day that the hammer helped me. My father hadn't noticed. Rita hadn't noticed. I kept it under my bed. Right at the top. Just below the wooden headrest. Just below my head. Safe. Hidden.

I lay onto the floor.

Stomach flat to the blue carpet.

I stretched out my arms.

I dived under the bed.

My fingers brushed against my cold tin.

Too far away.

I dug my toes into the carpet.

     Edged myself forward.

          Ducked my face to the floor.

               Breathed in the cloud of dust.

It tickled the inside of my nose.

Scrambled a little further under.

     Half a head under.

          My hand grabbed the dusty tin and brought it out.


A navy blue cylinder tin. It used to have tea in it. Before the polishes, before the dirty rag and before the bristly brush. Now it enclosed my secrets. Safe. It kept two secrets already. My tin was rough to touch. Dented and scratched. It had a gold trim and E$^{II}$R in gold lettering. Queen Elizabeth II. Silver Jubilee tin. Three crowns and two images of the Queen and her husband. I didn't know his name. I thought that he was a king, but he didn't wear a crown. It didn't matter. The tin was old. Four years old. An antique. It was mine now.


The lid came off. It had a handle to grip. Had to pull hard. It was tight. It was perfect. Around the lid. In gold capital letters. Queen Elizabeth II. 1952–1977. I pulled and pulled the lid. I pulled and pulled and pulled. Pop. The lid into my left hand. Bang. The cylinder base flew across the room. Bashed against the wall. Banged off the wall that I shared with my father. Hush shush. I dared not move. I held my breath. Waiting. Waiting for my father to shout. Silence. Nothing. I crept to pick it up. Mustn't wake my father. Mustn't wake Rita. Hush shush.

Tiptoe. **Tiptoe.** Tiptoe.

I sneaked back to my pillow. I took Eddie's cigar. I held Eddie. I placed it in the tin. Next to the note from my mother. *jude, i have gone in search of adam. i love you baby.* Creased and crumpled. Ragged with folds. It lived next to the shiny sticker. A brown teddy bear with a golden star on his round tummy. Fluffy-backed. Eddie would live in there too. I would never forget his smell. I pushed the lid back onto the tin. I kneeled back onto the floor. I lay flat on my tummy. I pushed my tin. Back under the bed. I pushed my secrets to where they would be safe. Safe in the darkness. Just under the wooden headrest. Near the wall. Back to their place where the Queen of England would look after them for me.

# 1982

He is still outside.
Still wearing your hat and coat.
I saw him.
Just now.
In the darkness he waved with his twig arm.
Told me to tell you to
Sleep tight.
Night night.

Snow. January 9 1982. One year, nine months and fourteen days since the death of my mother. Eleven months four days since my walk with Eddie. One month sixteen days since my eighth birthday.

I woke. There were squeals outside. I sat up in bed. Then onto my folded knees. I pulled open the orange velvet curtains. I peered outside. A halo of white. Sparkling. Dazzling. Snow in New Lymouth. It was a miracle. A perfectly smooth blanket. Thick thick snow. Quick. Quick. The sea air would take the snow away. It would steal the snow. Robbery. Thievery. Would leave a melted trail all the way down to its shore. All the way down the Coast Road. No time to waste. A day in the snow. A Saturday in the snow.

My father had already left for work. The driveway showed the tracks where his Mini had reversed from the garage. Two parallel trails. A bit wibbly wobbly. Out of the path and curving onto the snow-covered road. Away to Rumbelows. He had forgotten to wake me. He hadn't told me about the snow. I looked at the broken snow. My father's footprints. The postman's or maybe the milkman's footprints. Trailing to and from my mother's front door. They had ruined my snow.

I watched from my window. I saw the neighbours. I saw them in my snow. Mr Russell (Number 10) was raising his arms and shouting at the sky. The snow had come as a surprise. An unwelcome guest. A nuisance. He was a grumpy old man. He had two girls. I didn't know their names. They had come to live there only a few weeks before. They were staying forever, but I didn't know where they had come from. I heard Mrs Ward (Number 12) telling Mrs Hodgson (Number 2 ) all about it. It was when I was in Brian's getting a ten-pence mix up. Apparently. *Their ma and pa were pot heads and the poor bairns were bags of bones.* I didn't understand. Mrs Hodgson wasn't to tell anyone about it. Hush hush. Twirling swirling. Round and round.

Snow. Paul Hodgson (Number 2) was chasing Karen Johnson (Number 19). He had a round ball of snow in each of his gloved hands. Chasing. Running from Number 2 to just beneath the lamppost that flamed outside of my mother's house. Skidding to the white floor as he ran. Clenched gloved hands stopping his fall. In his school shoes. Slip sliding along. Laughing. Karen was squealing. Running. Looking over her shoulder. Pink hat pulled over her ears. Pink head turning. Forwards. Backwards. Forwards. Nowhere to go.

Multicoloured fingerless gloves and a matching scarf. Her cheeks were red. Rosy. *A reet pretty bairn.* She was running. Running slowly in the snow like a flippy floppy scarecrow. Outside Number 14. Paul Hodgson took his shot. Landed the snowball on her neck. Thick snow stuck to the hair that straddled from the bottom of her pink hat. Paul Hodgson turned a slippery circle and ran back up the street towards his house. Number 2. I watched from my window. Karen Johnson tried to pick the lumps of snow from her hair. Her lips were moving. She was saying something. I couldn't hear. Crying. I think she was crying. I watched her from my bedroom window. Kneeling on my bed. Peering out. Curtains pulled open. I watched it all. I placed my right palm flat against the pane. I wanted her to look up and see me. She didn't look up. She turned and walked back to her house. Slip slide slip slide. Gloved hand wiping under her nose. Back to Number 19. Back to Mr Johnson. He would make everything better.

Snow. Real snow. Disraeli Avenue was covered in snow. No time to waste.

I had a coat that used to be Rita's. It was silver plastic. Like a spaceman. Padded and with a silver furry hood. I liked it. It was shiny. Rita said it made her look chubby. She gave it to me. My father bought her a new coat. It was red. It was fake fur. She looked like a fat fox. I put on the silver coat. No gloves. No scarf. I didn't have any. It didn't matter. I put on a red and white stripy hat that Aunty Maggie had knitted. Jeans. A jumper. Quick. Quick. It didn't matter. As long as I wore my coat. My silver spaceman coat. I opened the green front door. Fresh. Clean. White. White. White.

## Crunch.

A firm step onto the thick snow. Footprint. Marking. Capturing my first steps. *One small step for man.* The square of grass had gone. Instead a bedspread of snow. Covering. Swallowing up Disraeli Avenue. Making it different. Making it magical. I bent over. Scooped a handful of fluffiness into my hand. Fingertips tingling. Wiggling. Coldness seeped in through the tips. Freezing them. Prickling the tips. Fingers alive. Tickled. Shocked to red. Fresh. I watched the fluffy flakes resting on my fingers. Floating on my palm. Decorating my naked hand. Weightless. Delicate. Perfect. Pure. Untouched until now. I scrunched my fingers into the snow. The feathery flakes folded. Rounded. Hardened. I turned the downy flakes into a hardened ball. Ready. Ready for Paul.

Snow. Jack Frost had been kind to us. A day of snow. *Make the most of the bugger. Be nowt left the morrow. Thank fuck we live next to coast.* Disraeli Avenue looked magical. Disraeli Avenue was magical.

I built him. Crouched on all fours. Knees sodden and cold. Water seeped into the knees of my jeans. I pushed snow. Packed snow on snow. The fluffy flakes blended. Transformed into his body. I pulled the snow. Used my forearms like a shovel. Trawled the snow. His body grew. It became fatter and fatter and fatter. Burning hands. Not a smooth round. Not a perfect circle. I packed snow on snow. Up and up and up. My hands stopped tingling. My hands stopped burning. Stained red. Ruby red. They no longer felt the snow. Numbness. Nothing. Up and up. Shoulders. Flat. Smooth. He had a body.

I took a handful of flakes. Packed them into my fingers. Hardened. Rolled in my palm. A circle. Rolled in the snow. Round and round. The snow clung. Frightened snow. Round and round the garden. It got bigger and bigger and bigger. Round and round. Stealing the snow. Touching the snow. Leaving a trail. A snowman trail. Changing the snow. Round and round the garden. He had a head.

I went into my father's garage. Walked across the snow. Over the driveway. Through the green garage doors. I stood in the open doorway, scanned the room for something. Something to help me. The walls of the garage were my father's. Shelves of goodies and racks of tools. Half empty cans of paint. Brushes. Turpentine. Buckets. Jars of screws. Tins of nuts and bolts. Rakes. Brooms. Hammers. Screwdrivers. Saws. Spades. Never just one of a sort. My father liked his garage. His special things were kept there. I was looking for something to help me. I was standing in the doorway, scanning the room for something. Then I saw it. In the far right corner. A red bucket. A bucket of coal. I had never noticed it before. I took it. I closed the doors behind me.

He was evil.

He was made evil. Black coal for eyes. The dust off the coal spread around the lump. The dirt from the coal stained my fingers. Made the snow dirty. Big black circles around his dead eyes. Coal for nose. Mucky. Dirty. Four lumps for the mouth. Perfectly straight line. A black line. A dirty black mouth. Two twigs for arms. He would not touch. No hands. No fingers. No legs. He would not move. He could not move. Five lumps of coal down his front. Five buttons. A straight line. Five buttons that would not open. The insides were locked away behind the five lumps of grubby coal. I dug into the body with my frozen index finger. Worked around the body. Into him. I wrote. **Sunderland AFC forever.**

I took off my red and white stripy hat. I gave it to him. He would support Sunderland AFC. I didn't like Sunderland AFC. Sunderland made my father angry. Sunderland made my father hit me. When Sunderland lost, I knew to stay away from my father. Sunderland made my father cross. He would shout if I looked at him in the wrong way. I didn't know the right way. He would hit me. Fists clenched. He would punch punch punch. I knew to stay away from him. I always knew the match results. Always. I didn't want the red and white stripy hat. He could have it. The evil snowman would support Sunderland.

**6:10pm**

My father was due in from work. I sat on my bed. Waiting. Kneeling at my bedroom window. The sky was black. A single star. *I wish I may, I wish I might.* Darkness had arrived without me realising.

The lamppost flamed outside my mother's house. The lamppost flamed into my bedroom. I waited. Peering. Scared. Really scared. I watched for my father's yellow Mini. He was late. He was never ever late. I thought that he had gone. That he had left me too. That I would have to go to another funeral. That I would have to live with the *hacky lad*. In the huge house. On the sea front. I stayed at the window. Watching. Watching. Watching.

I heard it. **6:36pm.** My father's Mini. Home from a day at Rumbelows. My father slowed down to turn onto the small driveway. I watched my father. He looked at the snowman. A smile. A real smile. My father liked the snowman. My father liked the Sunderland-supporting snowman. My father looked up to the window. Smiling eyes. Through the windscreen. Under the flame. Through my bedroom window. Connecting to my eyes. Joined. A real smile. I placed my right palm. Flat onto the window. No smile from me. I reached to my father. He drove onto the drive.

My father came in. Rita was hustling and bustling. Whispered tones. Hush hush. I couldn't hear. I strained to hear. *Nice fucking snowman Jude. Best one on the street.* He shouted to me. He liked the snowman. The snowman made my father smile. I had been mean to the snowman. I didn't like the snowman. I was silly. The snowman was my best friend. The snowman had special powers. I had made my father happy. The snowman had made my father happy.

The snow was magical.

* * * * *

Just before midnight. I should have been asleep. The house was quiet. I had been watching him from my window. On my folded knees. Peering out between the orange velvet curtains. His twiggy arms moved. He was trying to wave. The flaming light was keeping him awake. I crept down the red stairs. Squeak squeak. I unlocked the door. Shush. Hush. A gust of cold air. I shivered. I grabbed hold of my silver spaceman coat. Grabbed it from the coat stand that Rita had brought to my mother's house. My tiny pink nightie stretched across my skin. Polyester. Scratchy. Clingy. The gust of ice wind swirled and twirled around me and into my mother's house. I left the front door open. So I could come straight back in. I had to be quick. The flaming street light would help me. I could not be scared. *Scaredy cat scaredy cat. Hopping off the door mat.* Bare feet. Gasping as I stepped onto the hard snow. My toes tingled. I hopped from foot to foot. A cold cold blanket. Hop hop hop. Outside. He was still there. His perfectly straight mouth had curled slightly. His eyes had brightened. He looked at me. He looked into my eyes. I placed my silver spaceman coat over his shoulders. He must have been cold. I knew that he was cold. I had been watching him from the window. He was shivering under the flaming light. He nodded. Just slightly. Too cold to talk. I hop skip jumped back inside. *Night night Mr Snowman.*

Two days later. My silver jacket and my red and white stripy hat lay crumpled over a stump of melting snow. On the front lawn. Abandoned. *Get ye fuckin coat and hat in from the garden. Yee should take better care of ye stuff. I divvent nah why wi bother getting ye anythin.*

\* \* \* \* \*

On August 26, 1910 Margaret Jones came into being. She was born within the same hour, the same day and the same year as Mother Teresa. She told me that while Mother Teresa was arriving into Yugoslavia, she was being pushed onto an iron bed in a terraced house in North Shields. She said that they were practically twins. I called her Aunty Maggie. She wasn't my mother's sister. She wasn't my father's sister. She was an old woman who lived at Number 30 Disraeli Avenue, New Lymouth.

I sat in front of the garden wall. Street side. Two years and four months and five days from my mother's death. One year and five months and twenty-six days since my walk with Eddie. I was eight. I liked to sit. Back to the wall. As still as a statue. I liked to be invisible. I liked to listen. Mrs Clark (Number 14) and Mrs Hodgson (Number 2) were talking about Aunty Maggie. Mrs Clark knew someone who knew someone who knew someone who knew. Mrs Clark had a *canny jem of tattle*. It turned out that Aunty Maggie had never been married. *Never been blessed with children. My darling husband Samuel passed away in his prime*. Apparently. Darling *husband* Samuel was a man called Samuel Cleggit, who *lived with his real missus of 30 years, in a council house in Wallsend*. That was a bus ride away. She could go and visit. I wanted to go and tell Aunty Maggie. I had found her darling Samuel for her. But.

Mrs Clark (Number 14) hadn't finished her tittle-tattle. Apparently. Samuel Cleggit was *a bit of a lady's man*. I didn't understand. He had *served a bit of time for something minor*. I didn't understand. But now he had come back to life. He must have come back to life. Aunty Maggie liked the Bible. Aunty Maggie was a good lady and maybe she was being given a reward. Maybe her Bible Fuzzy Felts had magical powers. Apparently. Aunty Maggie was a *bit of a tar*t who was stupid enough to *get herself knocked up* before Samuel Cleggit had *done one, refusing to wed her.* I didn't understand. Whirling. Swirling. Round and round. Hush hush. Mrs Clark told Mrs Hodgson that Aunty Maggie had *had the bairn and hoyed it at some nun or other to care for*. Whirling. Swirling. Round and round. Apparently. The black and white photographs of *my darling husband Samuel passed away in his prime*. The ones that jam packed the walls of her hallway, well they were of Samuel Cleggit *back when they were courting*. Apparently. He didn't look like that now. Mrs Clark knew someone who knew someone who knew someone who knew. Said he was a *fat bloke who was on a stick and spent most of his time in the Club playing dominos.*

Mrs Clark and Mrs Hodgson drifted onto another yarn, about the barmaid in The Traveller's Rest. I didn't want to listen. My head was swirling. Twirling. Whirling. Aunty Maggie spoke with a swish accent. I always thought that she was exotic. That she was rich. That she was different from all of the other neighbours. She never called me bairn. She said alright instead of alreet. Never said divvent or canny. Her voice was all sing songy and loopy. It went up and down. It looped and hooped. Aunty Maggie had a nice voice and she smelled sophisticated. On Sundays she wore Youth Dew perfume from a curvy bottle. Strong. Musky. Lingering. Wafted into the room before she did. She wore it for church. Every Sunday morning. 8:45am service.

Aunty Maggie's house was always tidy. Everything was neat. Perfect. No dust. No clutter. Each room had a single colour. Aunty Maggie liked everything to be perfect. I was only ever allowed into the pink room, where everything was pink. But I had heard tales of the green and the gold rooms. They were special rooms. Aunty Maggie liked to watch me from her window and I knew that she longed to be my mother. I was glad that she was not my mother. But. As Mrs Clark and Mrs Hodgson talked, I thought about Aunty Maggie's baby and the nun. I thought about the cupboard of toys. Whirling. Swirling. Round and round. Hush hush.

Mrs Clark (Number 14) and Mrs Hodgson (Number 2) returned to the topic of Margaret Jones. Apparently. Aunty Maggie and her brother Eddie had *inherited a canny bit of money when their ma and pa had died*. My tummy tightened. Apparently. Aunty Maggie had used the money well and bought a house, but *that waste of space brother of hers* had drank his away. I felt sick. My insides flip flopped. Over and over. Gurgled and churned as they turned. I was going to be sick. I couldn't move. Mrs Clark told Mrs Hodgson that Eddie Jones had been in the paper. *He's a dirty bastard an I hope that thee chop his balls off*. I didn't understand. Inside the flip flapping was at the bottom of my throat. I was trying to stop myself from being sick. I thought about Eddie. Dirty dirty. I didn't want him to visit. He would be coming again soon. *Such a nice man. A real gent and the perfect house guest.* Inside my head, inside my body, it was all too loud. Inside I was making too much noise. Flip flap flip flap **flip flap**. I couldn't hear what Mrs Clark and Mrs Hodgson were saying. The flip flaps yodelled up my throat and bounced off the insides of my head.

*Fancy a cuppa?* They had turned their backs and were wobbling away towards Mrs Hodgson's (Number 2). I wanted to shout and tell them to stop. But I couldn't. I was being invisible.

I sat. Back to the wall. As still as a statue. I wanted to yell. I wanted them to tell me when Eddie was coming back, but instead I let them carry on walking. They kept on walking.

I stood up. Legs against the wall. I began to follow them. A tiny mouse detective. Squeak squeak. Mrs Clark stopped. She turned towards me. She looked straight at me. I stood perfectly still. Mrs Hodgson turned and looked at me too. What's the time Mr Wolf? I stood perfectly still. Rooted. Like a statue. Mrs Clark boomed laughter. Harsh. Throaty. Mrs Hodgson snorted a half hoot. Then they carried on towards Number 2. Wibble wobble. They swished their skirts and shuffled their slippered feet along the grey slabs. They turned back every few steps. Still. Still as a statue. What's the time Mr Wolf? I stayed like a statue. Rooted to the grey paving slabs. Just opposite the lamppost that flamed outside of my mother's house. I didn't move. I wasn't quite sure what to do next.

\* \* \* \* \*

They built a park. Someone built a park. For all the kids from the estate. Somewhere safe for us to hang out. *Keep the local bairns off the street corners.* It was over the Coast Road. At the far side of the other estate. Next to the Scout hut. Apparently. There was a slide. Six swings. A sand pit. And. A wigwam-shaped climbing frame. It was in the local paper. A free paper called *The Guardian*. Apparently. If you stood on the climbing frame. Right at the top. Then. You could see the *sea sea sea*. It said so on the front of the paper. There was a picture next to the writing. It was of Paul Hodgson (Number 2). He was holding on with one arm only. Leaning backwards. Right at the top. He was brave.

I cut out the photograph of Paul Hodgson on the wigwam climbing frame. Cut it out with my scissors that made a wavy edge. I put it in my parka pocket. I walked over to the park. Took myself across the Coast Road. Looked left. Looked right. Looked left again. Walked. Looked into the houses on the other estate. They were like the houses in Disraeli Avenue. But different.

I knew about colours. I knew about the colours of doors. I knew about all of the houses in Disraeli Avenue. I had memorised them. I knew the combination. Thirteen had red front doors. Seven had green front doors. Five had blue front doors. Seven had yellow front

97

doors. The garages matched the front doors. Except for Number 17. Mr Lewis had a yellow front door and a green garage. I didn't know why.

The colours of the doors on the other estate were different. Different order of colours. But. But the houses looked the same. It wasn't right. It was complicated. Too complicated. I couldn't cope. I couldn't cope. My head was twirling. Couldn't make sense of it. The houses looked the same. They had to be the same. It didn't make sense.

I wanted to get to the park. But. But the colours of the doors were stopping me. Solution. I walked along the street with my eyes closed. With my hands in front of me. Counting steps to lampposts. Thirty-seven. Trying to stay in a straight line. One foot in front of the other. A continuous line of steps.

I made it. It took a long time. But. I made it. And without walking into any people or lampposts.

There was a gate into the park. It was open. There were lots of children there. Noisy. Squealing children. I saw Karen and Lucy Johnson (Number 19). Paul Hodgson (Number 2) was there too. With the Pescott twin lads (Number 27) and Sarah Simpson from Number 16 Gladstone Street. They were sitting under the ladder up to the slide. They were sitting on the grass. Close. Talking. Laughing. Paul Hodgson had a stopwatch. His nana had bought it for his last birthday. He took it to school. Timed everything. Had it confiscated twice by Mrs Stouter.

I walked over. Across the grass. Around the daisies. Over daisies. Careful not to squash any. Careful. Careful. Past the swings. Five of the six were being used. Past the wigwam climbing frame. Four boys and two girls were at different heights. Round the sandpit. No one was in it. Rumours of dogs and toilets had already spread across the estate. I stopped next to them. Didn't speak. Karen Johnson looked up at me. She giggled. Then whispered something to Paul Hodgson. She put her two hands around his ear when she spoke. In case the words escaped. I didn't move. I didn't speak.

*We're trying to break the record for the longest snog. You wanna try?*

Paul Hodgson was talking to me. He was asking me to join in. I didn't speak. Just sat on the floor next to them. Slightly out of their circle. Like a pointy nose on the side of a perfectly round face. Cross-legged. Listening. But not really understanding. I was reading the writing that was under the slide. *Sarah woz 'ere*. And a picture of an egg looking over a wall. Karen Johnson told me to pay attention.

It was serious. Record-breaking serious.

The girls were given numbers. Karen Johnson. One. Sarah Simpson. Two. Lucy Johnson. Three. Jude Williams. Four. I was number four. Then. The boys were given numbers. Paul Hodgson. One. Simon Pescott. Two. Graeme Pescott. Three. I didn't understand.

I sat still. Playing a game. Making friends. Trying really really hard not to say anything daft. Had best keep quiet. *Ssh Jude. Ssh.* Paul Hodgson was in charge. He was going to say two numbers. The first two that came into his head. Then. Then those two people would have to kiss. A real kiss. He would time them with his stopwatch. Make it all official.

**First.**

Numbers one and one.

Stand up Paul Hodgson and Karen Johnson. Simon Pescott held the stopwatch in his right hand. And Karen Johnson's Hubba Bubba in his left.

GO.

They went on and on and on. No tongues. I could see no tongues. Graeme Pescott stopped them after 5 minutes 29 seconds. He was bored. I wasn't. I liked watching them.

**Next**.

Numbers two and two.

Stand up Sarah Simpson and Simon Pescott. They didn't wait for the GO. They used tongues. They were boyfriend and girlfriend. Paul Hodgson had his stopwatch. Simon Pescott put his hand up Sarah Simpson's shirt. She started squirming. Tickled. Giggling. They stopped kissing. 4 minutes 17 seconds.

**Next**.

Numbers 4 and 3.

Me.

Stand up Jude Williams and Graeme Pescott. We stood up. Paul Hodgson let out a cheer.

## GO.

I put my lips onto Graeme Pescott's. I held my breath. He pressed his lips against mine. Hard. He put his arms around my waist.

Pulled me to him. He was smaller than me. He was little. I needed to breathe. He tried to push his little spiky tongue into my mouth. Tried to push push push it in. I needed to breathe. *Quick. Quick.* I needed to breathe.

I pulled back.

I gasped for air. Gasp gasp gasp. 1 minute 15 seconds.

Everyone laughed. Rolled around giggling. Paul Hodgson. Lucy Johnson. Karen Johnson. Sarah Simpson. Simon Pescott. Rolling round and round and round the grass. My cheeks were burning. Red. Red. Red. I felt faint. Wanted to sit down. Couldn't.

*You're supposed to breathe. You fuckin virgin.*

Graeme Pescott was angry. We hadn't beaten any records. I had made him look silly. He was angry angry angry. He was going to punch me. Punch punch punch.

I turned. I ran. Out of the park. Through the open gate. Past the garages and doors that were the wrong colours. Back towards my mother's house. *Quick quick.* As fast as I could. Across the Coast Road. No left. No right. Quick quick. I never looked back.

I stopped running when I got to Disraeli Avenue. When I saw the white sign with the black letters. I stopped next to it. Bent down.

Ran my finger over the letters. They were real. They were still there. I was in the right place. I had found the right street. My throat hurt. Really hurt. I thought that I was dying. It hurt that much that I thought that I was dying. It was serious. I had been kissing. I had caught a kissing disease. Caught rabies. Or maybe leprosy. Or maybe cancer. I was going to die. I was going to die. Kissing made you die. No one had ever told me that.

\* \* \* \* \*

In my dreams you're there.
At the top of the slide.
Waving me to join you.
One kiss. One kiss.
A small price to pay.
Number four. Number four.
A kiss. A kiss.
Adam.
A boy.
Adam.
A man.
You wave to me.
In the darkness of night.
You tell me to come and join you.

Her bag of secrets. Her bag of her. Still buried. Untouched. Waiting.

* * * * *

| | |
|---|---|
| DFT 678T | GYS 606S |
| EVS 343V | POK 776T |
| No | NPK 911V |
| GOY 443V | RTS 446T |
| KON 908V | GOT 654V |
| GBT 777S | FVX 404W |
| No | FDT 609X |
| No | PHC 665X |
| No | MYG 553W |
| DEW 664T | No |
| GOP 143W | MTR 320X |
| CWS 694V | LPY 529W |
| No | SRT 744S |
| PLB 533X | KHC 807R |
| No | No |
| FKT 264R | FFH 335V |

* * * * *

My green notebook rested on the windowsill of my bedroom. I wrote
and I wrote and I wrote. I noted what I could see from my window.
I stretched and strained my neck, then my head and then my eyes. I
couldn't see all the houses. Not from Number 9 Disraeli Avenue.

So I would walk. Up and down. Up and down the grey slabs.
Stopping. Crouching. Resting my precious green notebook onto my
knee and noting. Always scribbling and noting. Checking. Double.

Triple. Quadruple. Checking. No room for errors. Precise. True. A notebook full of truth.

\* \* \* \* \*

RED CAR. DFT 678T

        RED CAR. GYS 606S

RED CAR. EVS 343V

        BLACK CAR. POK 776T

NO CAR.

        WHITE CAR. NPK 911V

BLACK CAR. GOY 443V

        GREEN CAR. RTS 446T

YELLOW CAR. KON 908V

        RED CAR. GOT 654V

WHITE CAR. GBT 777S

        MAROON CAR. FVX 404W

NO CAR.

        YELLOW CAR. FDT 609X

NO CAR.

        RED CAR. PHC 665X

NO CAR.

        GREEN CAR. MYG 553W

YELLOW CAR. DEW 664T

        NO CAR.

WHITE CAR. GOP 143W

        BLUE CAR. MTR 320X

WHITE VAN. CWS 694V

BLUE CAR. LPY 529W

NO CAR.

RED CAR. SRT 744S

YELLOW CAR. PLB 533X

BROWN CAR. KHC 807R

NO CAR.

NO CAR.

BLUE CAR. FKT 264R

GREY CAR OR MAYBE SILVER. FFH 335V

\* \* \* \* \*

I came home from collecting. I had been at it all day. Sat on a bright red deckchair. My father had found it outside our house. After the Street Party for the Royal Wedding. I liked the red deckchair. It made me comfy while I worked. While I collected. I had waited on the corner of Disraeli Avenue. With my green notebook. And a pencil. Keeping note. Making notes. Collecting.

Rita was in my mother's house. Her friend Bet was there too. I didn't know Bet. I hadn't seen her before. She wasn't from the estate. She was from Wallsend. Rita used to work with her. Bet was in my mother's front room. Lying back on the flowery sofa. With her blue stilettos up on the sofa. The heel was digging into the arm rest. It would make a hole. I wanted to tell her to take her shoes off. I would get the blame for the hole. I didn't speak. Her long smooth legs stretched out. I couldn't see any hairs. She wasn't hairy like Rita. She was smoking a cigarette and Rita was pouring from a plastic bottle of cider. Into a china mug. My mother's best china.

I stood in the doorway. *That's Bill's fuckin strange bairn.* Bet tilted her head to look up at me. She didn't say anything. Just smiled. A nice smile. Showed her perfectly straight yellow teeth.

Bet had big hair. Piled on the top of her head. A monument of yellow hair. Constructed with nipping hair pins and lacquer. It didn't flop. It was perfect. I wanted to touch it. To see if it was soft. But. I didn't. I didn't dare to. Bet's eyes were painted with bright blue eye shadow and a dark blue mascara. Her eyelashes curled up to the ceiling. They were so long. Looked like spider's legs. Her skin was orange. Like Rita's. Sunbed orange. But. But she wasn't fat. Her legs were long and smooth. No dimples. She wore the most beautifully shiny gold skirt. It shimmered under the light and it stuck to her thighs. I thought that it might have been painted on. Or. She had been bent up and her bottom dipped into a pot of shimmering gold paint. Her top was white. You could see her black lace bra through it. She was pretty.

**But**.

She said something. I had no idea what. When she spoke her words were wrapped in gravel. Sharp edges. Rough. Bumpy in the wrong places. Difficult to understand. Too difficult to follow. Over the water accent. Not Geordie. Different.

*Fuck off Jude.*

I understood Rita. She told me that she didn't want her friend having to look at my ugly face. I went to the bottom red step. Back against the wall. Knees to my chest. Arms wrapped around my shins. I listened. I liked to listen. I tried to decode. To interpret the gravel-filled words. She was exotic. She was different from anyone that I had ever met. She was practically foreign.

Apparently. Mr Lancaster (Number 7). He lived next door with Mrs Lancaster. Our garages joined together. Bet knew him. I think that she said that he was *one of her punters*. I didn't understand. He went to her house. Every Thursday. After work. Told Mrs Lancaster that he was working late. He was. Bet said that he was working late. Working late giving her *a good seeing to*. I didn't understand what she meant. She said that he paid her sixty quid. Apparently. The pleasure *was all hers*. I didn't understand what she was saying. Rita did. Rita was booming. The house was full of the sound of her witch cackle. She was happy. She liked Bet. She liked what Bet told her. I didn't understand. Bet must have been a butcher like Mr Lancaster. She didn't look like a butcher. I knew three butchers. Mr Lancaster. Mr Dewstep and Mr Dewstep's Saturday boy. Bet didn't look like any of them. I was confused. I didn't understand.

Bet went before my father came in from work. She caught the 5.28pm bus to Wallsend. Rita didn't want any *awkward questions*. I was still sitting on the bottom red step when Bet left. Bet said

108

bye to me. Rita said that I wasn't to tell my father about Bet. I had nothing to tell. Hadn't understood what I had heard. Rita didn't tell me off. She didn't hit me for listening. I liked Bet.

Later when I was in my room. I heard Rita talking on the phone. She was talking to Mrs Hodgson (Number 2). Telling her all about Bet working for Mr Lancaster. Saying it was to *go no further*. Hush hush. Whirling. Twirling. Round and round. Apparently. Mrs Lancaster was *tight lipped in more ways than one*. And. Mr Lancaster liked *using his big chopper in his whore's meat*. Rita found her story funny. Really funny. She was a comedian. Ha ha ha. Cackle cackle cackle. An evil laugh. I didn't understand the words. I didn't understand what she was telling Mrs Hodgson. But. But it was to go no further. Another secret. Another hush hush. I didn't understand. Rita had worked with Bet. I wondered if Rita used to work for Mr Lancaster too. I wondered if she used to be a butcher too. I didn't ask her. I dared not ask her.

\* \* \* \* \*

NUMBER 1. MR AND MRS NORTH. RED CAR. DFT 678T. NUMBER 2. MRS HODGSON. RED CAR. GYS 606S. NUMBER 3. MR AND MRS DRAKE. RED CAR. MATCHES FRONT DOOR. EVS 343V. NUMBER 4. MR AND MRS BLACK. BLACK CAR. MATCHES THEIR NAME. POK 776T. NUMBER 5. MRS GRANT. NO CAR. NUMBER 6. MR AND MRS WOOD. WHITE CAR. NPK 911V. NUMBER 7. MR AND MRS LANCASTER. BLACK CAR. GOY 443V. NUMBER 8. MR AND MRS

DOUGLAS. GREEN CAR. RTS 446T. NUMBER 9. BILL AND JUDE WILLIAM. YELLOW CAR. KON 908V. NUMBER 10. MR AND MRS RUSSELL. RED CAR. MATCHES DOOR. GOT 654V. NUMBER 11. MR AND MRS SYMONS. WHITE CAR. GBT 777S. NUMBER 12. MR AND MRS WARD. MAROON CAR. FVX 404W. NUMBER 13. MRS THOMAS. NO CAR. NUMBER 14. MR AND MRS CLARK. YELLOW CAR. SAME AS MRS JOHNSON'S BUT SHINIER. FDT 609X. NUMBER 15. MR AND MRS SHEPHARD. NO CAR. NUMBER 16. MR AND MRS SMITH. RED CAR. PHC 665X. NUMBER 17. MR LEWIS. NO CAR. NUMBER 18. MR AND MRS ANDREWS. GREEN CAR. MYG 553W. NUMBER 19. MR AND MRS JOHNSON. YELLOW CAR. SAME AS MR CLARK'S. DEW 664T. NUMBER 20. MRS CURTIS. NO CAR. NUMBER 21. MR AND MRS ROBERTS. WHITE CAR. GOP 143W. NUMBER 22. MR AND MRS WALLACE. BLUE CAR. MATCHES FRONT DOOR. MTR 320X. NUMBER 23. MR AND MRS SMITH. WHITE VAN. CWS 694V. NUMBER 24. MR AND MRS WALKER. BLUE CAR. LPY 529W. NUMBER 25. MR AND MRS SCOTT. NO CAR. NUMBER 26. MR AND MRS BRUCE. RED CAR. SRT 744S. NUMBER 27. MR AND MRS PESCOTT. YELLOW CAR. PLB 533X. NUMBER 28. MR AND MRS STEVENSON. BROWN CAR. KHC 807R. NUMBER 29. MR AND MRS DORAN. NO CAR. NUMBER 30. AUNTY MAGGIE. NO CAR. NUMBER 31. MR AND MRS GIBBONS. BLUE CAR. MATCHES FRONT DOOR. FKT 264R. NUMBER 32. MR AND MRS ALEXANDER. GREY CAR OR MAYBE SILVER. FFH 335V.

\* \* \* \* \*

Mr and Mrs Johnson went abroad. To another country. Karen and Lucy Johnson went with them too. They left the country. Left England. And not on a day trip to South Shields. They went to Spain. To Estartit in Spain. Real Spain. They travelled for days and days. On a huge coach. A coach with a toilet on it.

My father had to take them to Newcastle bus station. In the middle of the night. He dropped them off so that they could catch a coach and travel all the way around the world. It was going to take them hours and hours and days and days. Then. They were going to stay in a huge tent. One that had a cooker and a fridge in it.

Rita didn't want to hear about it. She said that they were *big-headed bastards*. I wanted to hear about it. Rita called my father *a lazy arse*. She said that she *deserved a fucking holiday*. Rita shouted and stamped her feet. I hoped that she would pack away her smelly things. I hoped that she would leave my mother's house forever. She didn't. I wanted Mr Johnson to talk about his holiday in Spain. I wanted to hear all about it. I thought that they might see my mother when they were away. That they might see her in Spain. Then. They would come back. And bring a letter for me. That they were bound to bump into her.

They were gone for sixteen days.

I counted the days till they came back.

111

One

two

three

four

five

six

seven

eight

nine

ten

eleven

twelve

thirteen

fourteen

fifteen

sixteen.

My father picked them up. From Newcastle bus station. At six o'clock in the morning. They came in for a cup of tea. They woke me up as they came in for a cup of tea. Rita didn't get out of bed. I did.

Karen and Lucy Johnson had red noses. They had burnt their noses and the skin had peeled. Their backs were peeling too. The skin was coming off. They showed me. Their skin was a red-brown colour. They had bracelets made from brightly coloured threads. Their new friends had made them for them. On the campsite. They had had such fun. Swimming. Table tennis. Netball. Talent competitions. Karen Johnson hadn't wanted to come home. She had cried all the way on the coach. She was going to live in Estartit when she was big. It was heaven.

## I wanted to go there.

Mrs Johnson was grumpy. She didn't want a cup of tea. She wanted her bed. She wanted to put some cream on her bites. She had *been eaten alive*. A foreign creature had liked the taste of her. It had come into the tent every night. *It didn't bother with the rest of them.* Just her. I was scared. Scared that it had followed them home. That it thought they lived in my mother's house. It might like the taste of me. It might eat me alive. Mrs Johnson was so brave. She was lucky to be alive. I wondered if she had teeth marks all over her body. Or maybe lumps and chunks where the creature had eaten her. I tried to see. But. But she didn't like me looking at her. She got angry. She told me to *fuck off*.

Mr Johnson didn't like her saying things like that. He shouted at her. Mr Johnson was still holding his huge straw donkey. It was a present for Rita. It was the most beautiful thing that I had ever seen. It was half my height. Wearing a hat. With a big smile. I hoped that Rita would let me have it. Mr Johnson had a medal. He won a prize. Mr Muscles. He showed his bicep muscles when he said it. He was wearing a t-shirt and his arms were very brown. Very very brown. No peeling.

He bought my father a bottle of whisky. For the lifts there and back. Mrs Johnson went back to her house. To Number 19 with the girls. My father and Mr Johnson opened the whisky. I was told to go and get dressed. They had *man stuff* to talk about. No one had mentioned my mother. I didn't ask if they had a letter for me. Best not ask. They were all tired.

After Mrs Johnson went back to her house. Rita got up. She went downstairs in her nightie. No knickers. No bra. I could see her saggy boobs. I could see her hairs. Through her white nightie. I could see them. My father could see them. Mr Johnson could see them. Rita liked her donkey. She liked Mr Johnson. She liked the whisky too. They were drinking and smoking. In the kitchen. At the wooden picnic table. Beside the timber panels that were nailed to two of the three walls. They smoked. And they laughed. In the simple setting. At my mother's table. It was hardly used anymore.

My father phoned in sick..

I stayed in my room all day.

* * * * *

Red cars = 6
Green cars = 2
Yellow cars = 4
White cars = 3 (1 white van)
Brown cars = 1

Grey or maybe silver cars = 1
Maroon cars = 1
Blue cars = 3
Black cars = 2

Number of cars = 23 cars. 1 van
No cars = 8

# 1983

**September 5 1983.** Miss Waters.

Three years, five months and ten days since my mother's death.
Two years and seven months since my walk with Eddie.


New uniforms. Shiny shoes. No creases. No dirt. Clothes slightly
too big. Ready to be grown into. I had a new uniform too. I was
getting big. Rita and my father had no choice. They had to buy me
new things. I liked the feel of the fresh clothes. No wrinkles. Clean.
I had a new grey skirt. Two new blue blouses. A blue and yellow
stripy tie. A new cardigan. I needed new knickers. Mine were grey
coloured and had a rip at the seam. A thread of grey elastic grew
from the cotton. *It grew and it grew and it grew*. I wanted to
pull it. I wanted to. I stopped myself. I stopped myself in case my
knickers fell down. To the floor. In front of everyone.


I wore knee-length socks. They wrinkled and scratched. I longed
for ankle socks. Karen Johnson (Number 19) had pretty white ankle
socks, trimmed with lace and a tiny satin bow. They were dazzling.
They were perfect for Karen Johnson. *A reet pretty bairn.* I liked
my new clothes, but I prayed for a new bag. I wanted a black one
that would go on my back and I could hang keyrings from the zip.
Karen Johnson had one with E.T. on it. I wanted that one. It was a
lot of money. It cost her thousands of pounds. Her dad had bought it
for her from the market in Wallsend. Mr Johnson was rich. I wanted
an E.T. bag. I wanted it more than anything in the world. I prayed

for an E.T. bag. I prayed for an E.T. vinyl pencil case too. It was shiny and black. With E.T.'s head on it. Free stuff came with it. An E.T. biro. An E.T. pencil. An E.T. ruler. An E.T. rubber. And. An E.T. pencil sharpener. Everything matched. I liked it when things matched. I also longed for new sharp pencils. They didn't have to be E.T. ones. Just ones that I could use. Sharp and new. And felt tips. A packet of felt tips. They could be cheap. Just ones that didn't squeak. Ones that came in a plastic wallet, with a pressie stud. I prayed. And I prayed. No one heard me. No one ever heard me.

I walked through the school gates, down the curvy path and round the sharp corner of the E-shaped building. It was quiet. No one else about. Just me in my new uniform. The big grey playground ran along the back of the E. It was a rectangle with two brick-built bike sheds at either end. They doubled up as goal sheds. For the boys who played football. And as dance rooms. For the girls who were practising their Eurovision Song Contest dance routines. I wasn't one of those boys. I wasn't one of those girls. I liked to sit in corners. In nooks and crannies. I liked to sit and watch. And listen.

I saw it.

As I turned the corner. I saw it.

It was bang
                    smack
in the centre of the rectangle playground.

It was bang

        smack
     **wallop**.
      ***Sigh***.

So very beautiful. A new. A brand new. A spick and span shiny new
climbing frame.

## Finders keepers.

I would become the Queen. I would climb to the top of my castle.
I would claim it. Without really thinking. I just climbed. I touched
every bar. I counted every touch. Sixty-two bars. Sixty-two touches.
Each touch made that bar mine. Finders keepers. As I touched. I
climbed. I climbed to the top. I watched all the children and all
of the parents arrive. I watched the late comers rush push into the
school playground. I had to touch each bar before the other children
did. I had to make the bars mine. Quick quick. I did it. I did it.
Just in time as the other children arrived. It didn't matter that they
climbed and that they touched my bars. It didn't matter anymore. I
had touched them first and we all knew that finders keepers ruled. I
had a climbing frame. It was mine.

I wanted to climb down. But. But I couldn't. It had seemed a good
idea. But. But I couldn't go down. Down was too far. I decided
that I would stay at the top for ever. It was too slippy slidey to
go down. I decided to grip. I decided to stay the Queen of my
perfectly square kingdom. Watching. Fingers stiff. Watching.

Always waiting. I sat at the top of the metal climbing frame. Other children scrambled about. Playing tig tag. Off ground. On ground. They were laughing. They were loving the smooth metal bars of the climbing frame.

I felt the cold bars through my grey skirt. I clung to the smooth spotless construction. It was new. It was high. I could practically touch the clouds. I would be able to if I let go. I couldn't let go. I would fall. I didn't want to fall. It was a long long way down. I clung. I gripped. I could see the tops of heads. I could see shoes. I could see hair partings. I could see the roof of the E-shaped building. If I jumped. Like an Olympic long jumper. If I jumped and then kind of flew through the air for quite a bit, perhaps doing four somersaults on the way. Then. Then I would land onto my flat feet on the E-shaped roof of my primary school. Then I would find out if I could fly. I didn't think that I could, but I had never tried it before. I didn't want to. I might fall. There was a chance that I would fall. And it was a long long way down. So I gripped till my knuckles turned white. Like clouds. My knuckles were clouds. Clouds decorating the cold metal bar. The curved silver bars linked together. With nuts and bolts. Joined. Linking together the outlines of the squares. Into a hollow Rubik's cube. It was so pretty. It was a perfect square. A silver present for us to enjoy. Constructed onto the concrete. I was the first to touch it. It was mine. Finders keepers. I stayed at the top and watched. I didn't move. I watched.

The head teacher, Mrs Stouter, came into the playground. She gripped the bell. Held her breath. 10

9

8

7

6

5

4

3

2

1.

Blast off.

Ding ding ding ding **ding ding**.

Run. Run. Run. Time for school. The rushing and pushing of
parents and children. All barging through the yellow double doors.
Packed lunch boxes. Bags. Thick coats. Shoving and ramming.
Rush rush rushing. Turning right into the cloakroom. Grabbing a
coat peg. Bagsying a peg. Parent and child together. Barging in
together. They would be handing over their child into a new class
and a new school year. A new term. Beginning. I didn't want to go
in. Not yet. I didn't have a mother or a parent to rush me in. I didn't
have anyone to hand me over.

The noise went. Suddenly. Instantly. It was silent again. The noise
was inside the E-shaped building. Filling the rooms and the corridors
and the heads of everyone inside my school. I was alone. Again.

Alone in the silence. Normally. I liked to be with the quiet. I liked no noise, so that I could hear my thinking. Usually. I needed to hear the words that were bouncing inside of my head. Not that day. I wanted the noise to come back. I wanted someone to show me how to get down from the climbing frame. Alone. Quiet. Frightened. Trying not to think about the long long way down. Gripping. A solid flag sticking up. The Queen is in residence. Spoiling the perfect square. Stiff. Scared. Waiting to fall.

She saw me.

I saw her too. She was walking towards me. Smiling. A nice smile.

*Jude? I was hoping you'd be here today. I'm Miss Waters. Can I come and join you?*

She knew my name. Miss Waters. My new teacher. She knew my name before I had to find the words to tell her. I liked her already. Then. She climbed to the top of the hollow cube. She climbed like a boy. She wasn't scared. She swung her legs, her trouser-wearing legs in and out of the squares. She touched my bars. I liked that she touched my bars. Miss Waters. A smiling Miss Waters. In black trousers with a delicate white stripe. She clambered and swung and hauled and hooped. Until she reached me. She sat next to me. Her legs flat across the top of the square. She held on. But. But her knuckles were not white. She told me that she liked to climb. She

121

liked to look down. She told me that she had always been small. A tiny child that no one had noticed. She told me that she was fed up with looking up all the time. She liked my climbing frame. She said that it was mine before I even had to tell her. She understood. She told me that she liked to watch people too. But. But that we really must hurry. That we really must climb down. That lessons had to begin and that she had all these ideas and thoughts that were about to burst out of her. She said that we really must hurry. Before she forgot them all. But that the lesson really couldn't begin without me. She needed me to begin her lesson. I was special. It was time to leave my kingdom.

## And I did.

And we did. I didn't say a word. Not a peep or a squeak. I didn't say that my shoes were slip slip slidey or that my fingers were glued to the circular bar. I didn't tell her. I just did as she did. I swung and I hauled and I hooped. I followed her across the grey concrete playground and up the two steps that led into the doorway of the yellow double doors. Miss Waters waited as I found a peg. Quick quick. And together we walked to the classroom. In silence. No need for words.

Parents and children were crowded into the classroom. Squashed. Chatting. Angry. They didn't like waiting. *She's a strange bairn that Jude.* Miss Waters smiled. She spoke to all the parents. Looked them straight in the eyes. Her eyes had lines going all the way around. Like spectacles dug into her skin. The lines crinkled when she smiled. She smiled all the time. She met all of the other parents. Not my parents. Not my mother. Not my father. The parents smiled too. Her smile. Her twinkle. Spread. A rash of grins. All the parents caught it. They couldn't do anything about it. She gave them a smile and stuck it onto their faces. I watched. I waited. Then they went. Waves and kisses to their boys and to their girls. The new year began.

She was little. Tiny. She liked to sit on her desk. Legs dangling over the edge. She had no fat bits and looked a bit like a gingerbread man. A perfectly shaped gingerbread man. Her hair was ruffled and tuffled all over her head. It was short in length. But it tumbled to the bottom of her neck. A brown colour. Full of kinks. Full of life. Her hair moved with her. It was soft. Floppy. With sparkles of grey flashing through every now and then. She'd sit at the front and talk to us. Her arms flew around. Her palms stretched out. Like frying pans. Making us smile. Catching our laughter. Flipping stories up to the ceiling. And then catching them in her large palms. Tossing stories. Up and up and up. She made me laugh.

Sometimes she'd stop talking. She would push her fingers into her floppy hair and ruffle. Ruffle ruffle tuffle ruffle. Then she'd take out her fingers. After she had ruffled a thought. Then. Then her hair would stand to attention. Kindled hair. Sparked into action by her magic fingers. Then she would carry on talking and her arms would fly and her palms would stretch outwards and upwards. After some lessons. After lessons full of ideas. Her hair would have grown. Flamed to the ceiling. Waving. I watched her hair grow. I watched her fingers. Ruffle tuffle ruffle. I watched as her thoughts and her fingers sparked. As the grey sparkles flashed. She had magic fingers. She was alive. She made me alive.

She talked about books. She loved books. Traditions. Stories. Tossing, flipping and flapping stories. Myths. Knights. Fairytales. Heroes. Princesses. Gods. She loved talking about a man called Atlas. I didn't know him. He didn't live in Disraeli Avenue. She said that she felt his strain. I didn't understand.

She told us that we should be turning off the television. She said that the television was *robbing our creativity*. I didn't understand. She said that we should read. We should read everything and anything. I didn't watch television. I sat for hours. I just sat doing nothing before I knew Miss Waters. She talked about books with her arms flying everywhere and her hair getting higher and higher. Excitement. Love. Her arms flip flapped about and her eyes sparkled. I wanted to read. She made me want to read. I told her that I had read the first chapter of *Danny Champion of the World* twenty-seven times. I had read all of *Matilda* and *The Twits*. Thirteen times each. I told Miss Waters. She said that I was very clever. I told her about the New Lymouth Library. I told her that it was a rectangle. Like a shoe box. And that inside the library there were eighty-seven Mills and Boon novels and three Roald Dahl books. I told her that there were signs everywhere. 'Absolute silence at all times.' And

124

that the grumpy librarian liked to read her *Introducing Machine Knitting* magazine. Miss Waters laughed. Miss Waters smiled. A big wide smile. A smile that stretched right up to her twinkling eyes. Miss Waters said that Roald Dahl and C.S. Lewis were her all time favourite writers. I didn't know who C.S. Lewis was. I told her that I didn't know who C.S. Lewis was. Then she went to her own special bookcase. She pulled out a slim paperback. Slowly. The spine was creased and the front right corner was ripped. Gently. She pushed it to my chest. *You must read this Jude.* I clutched the book. I absorbed her words. It was a book by C.S. Lewis. There were more. It was a series. 1, 2, 3, 4, 5, 6, 7. She gave me number 2, because it was her favourite. She wanted to share it with me.

*The Lion, the Witch and the Wardrobe.* She had given me a world where strange was normal. Where animals could talk. Where children were brave. And strong. And clever. Where good conquered evil. Where fur coats hung in a wardrobe. She gave me an escape. I read the book fourteen times in nineteen days. I took it back to her. I told Miss Waters all about Lucy and Peter and Mr Tumnus and Edmund and Susan and Mr Beaver and Giant Rumblebuffin and Aslan and the White Witch. I told her all about it. And she smiled. Big wide smiles. Then. She told me that the book was mine. That I could keep it forever. Her eyes were shiny with water. But she was smiling. Wide across her face. Then she told me that I was the reason why she wanted to teach. She cried. They were happy tears. I didn't understand. She told me that I was special. I wished that I could tell her how special she was. I wished that I could empty my head and tell Miss Waters everything. But I couldn't. I couldn't find the words.

Miss Waters. I didn't know how old she was. I think that she was older than me but younger than Aunty Maggie (Number 30). She might have been as old as my mother. She didn't have a husband. She didn't have any children. She told the class that she didn't have any children. She lived to teach me. We were all her children. But. I was the reason why she was a teacher. She had told me that. Miss Waters taught me that I should read books. And I did. I read all the books that I could find. Miss Waters told me that it was okay to be different.

I loved her. Really I loved her. I wished that I could go to her house. I wished that I could follow her home and see where she lived. But. She drove a brown car and I couldn't keep up running after it. I tried. She saw me and waved. She didn't stop. I loved that she told me of worlds and experiences that my father never would. I loved that she told me of lands that my mother would have known. I loved that she came to my school.

\* \* \* \* \*

**October 7 1983**
Mr and Mrs Symons got a new car.

NUMBER 1. MR AND MRS NORTH. RED CAR. DFT 678T. NUMBER 2. MRS HODGSON. RED CAR. GYS 606S. NUMBER

3. MR AND MRS DRAKE. RED CAR. MATCHES FRONT DOOR. EVS 343V. NUMBER 4. MR AND MRS BLACK. BLACK CAR. MATCHES THEIR NAME. POK 776T. NUMBER 5. MRS GRANT. NO CAR. NUMBER 6. MR AND MRS WOOD. WHITE CAR. NPK 911V. NUMBER 7. MR AND MRS LANCASTER. BLACK CAR. GOY 443V. NUMBER 8. MR AND MRS DOUGLAS. GREEN CAR. RTS 446T. NUMBER 9. BILL AND JUDE WILLIAM. YELLOW CAR. KON 908V. NUMBER 10. MR AND MRS RUSSELL. RED CAR. MATCHES DOOR. GOT 654V. NUMBER 11. **MR AND MRS SYMONS. RED CAR. HYT 664X.** NUMBER 12. MR AND MRS WARD. MAROON CAR. FVX 404W. NUMBER 13. MRS THOMAS. NO CAR. NUMBER 14. MR AND MRS CLARK. YELLOW CAR. SAME AS MRS JOHNSON'S BUT SHINIER. FDT 609X. NUMBER 15. MR AND MRS SHEPHARD. NO CAR. NUMBER 16. MR AND MRS SMITH. RED CAR. PHC 665X. NUMBER 17. MR LEWIS. NO CAR. NUMBER 18. MR AND MRS ANDREWS. GREEN CAR. MYG 553W. NUMBER 19. MR AND MRS JOHNSON. YELLOW CAR. SAME AS MR CLARK'S. DEW 664T. NUMBER 20. MRS CURTIS. NO CAR. NUMBER 21. MR AND MRS ROBERTS. WHITE CAR. GOP 143W. NUMBER 22. MR AND MRS WALLACE. BLUE CAR. MATCHES FRONT DOOR. MTR 320X. NUMBER 23. MR AND MRS SMITH. WHITE VAN. CWS 694V. NUMBER 24. MR AND MRS WALKER. BLUE CAR. LPY 529W. NUMBER 25. MR AND MRS SCOTT. NO CAR. NUMBER 26. MR AND MRS BRUCE. RED CAR. SRT 744S. NUMBER 27. MR AND MRS PESCOTT. YELLOW CAR. PLB

533X. NUMBER 28. MR AND MRS STEVENSON. BROWN CAR. KHC 807R. NUMBER 29. MR AND MRS DORAN. NO CAR. NUMBER 30. AUNTY MAGGIE. NO CAR. NUMBER 31. MR AND MRS GIBBONS. BLUE CAR. MATCHES FRONT DOOR. FKT 264R. NUMBER 32. MR AND MRS ALEXANDER. GREY CAR OR MAYBE SILVER. FFH 335V

I was so angry when I saw their new car. I shouted at them. They were driving past. They must have seen me jumping. Jumping in anger. On the grey slabs.

Angry. **Angry**.

I had so much work to do.
> I had new sums to do.

I had to do them.
> Straight away.

Couldn't wait.

My green notebook. Waiting on my windowsill. I had to tear out the other pages. I had to tear out the pages with the wrong numbers. With the wrong number plates. They were messy. They were wrong. Be gone. Be gone. I ripped them out. My green notebook had to be perfect. They spoiled my green notebook. There were pages ripped out. It wasn't the same anymore. I had to buy a new one. A new green notebook. I found the same one in Brian's Newsagents. It cost 47p. I copied everything out of the old ruined one and into the new perfect one.

**Red cars = 7**

Green cars = 2

Yellow cars = 4

**White cars = 2** (1 white van)

Brown cars = 1

Grey or maybe silver cars = 1

Maroon cars = 1

Blue cars = 3

Black cars = 2

Number of cars = 23 cars. 1 van

No cars = 8

\* \* \* \* \*

Nitty Nora the Dickie explorer was coming. A letter was being sent home to parents. That wasn't her real name. The school nurse was called Suzanne Jones. She was thin. Rectangular. As high as the ceiling. Her shoulders were perfectly flat. She never smiled. She hugged her black clipboard and she made ticks and crosses next to each of our names. She examined our heads. Our ears and our mouths and our eyes. In the staff room. During lessons. Never during playtime.

I had nits again. Every year she found them. Every year she gave me a bright pink slip to give to my father. I walked out of the staffroom. Clutching the pink slip. Everyone knew.

They could see the tiny creatures jumping and bouncing and dancing on my head. Bounce bounce bounce. I never scratched. I wanted to. But. But I was frightened that the nits might crawl under my finger nails. And burrow into my skin. Paul Hodgson (Number 2) told me all about nits. He had a book with a picture of one. It was huge.

The children knew it was best not to get too close. Nits could jump. Really high. Really far. Nits could jump from head to head. Bounce bounce bounce. They laid eggs in hair. Or even into your scalp. They would build houses. Bounce off to collect sticks. Twigs. Leaves. Anything they could find for their shelter. Paul Hodgson (Number 2) told me that once you had nits, you had them forever. Forever and ever and ever. He said that I'd have to tell everyone that I ever met that I had nits. He said that I was *infested*. That I was beyond hope. I didn't understand.

I gave Rita the bright pink slip. No use telling my father. Rita didn't read the slip. I had to tell her that I had nits. Like Paul said. I had to tell everyone. It was my duty. I was *infested*. Rita screamed when I told her. She jumped away from me. But. She did buy some special shampoo. From the late night chemist in North Shields. She washed her own hair. And my fathers. Scraped a metal comb through her hair. And my father's. Found a couple of adult nits. No eggs. I didn't understand. She didn't wash my hair. She wouldn't come near me. Told me to lock myself in the bathroom. Told me to scrub. Scrub. Scrub my hair. *Divvent come oot till all the buggers are gan.* I could use her shampoo. It smelled like the oil that leaked from my father's Mini. I liked the smell.

I scrubbed till my fingertips hurt. I tried to feel for the homes. I was terrified that the nits would bite off my fingers. They didn't. Then I combed my hair. Over a white piece of paper.

Sixty-five drowned creatures. Twenty-four eggs.

I folded them all. Folded the white piece of paper around them. I kept them. In my navy blue cylinder tin. It had a gold trim and $E^{II}R$ in gold lettering.

\* \* \* \* \*

```
Exhibit number four -
my collection of nits.
```

\* \* \* \* \*

November 25 1983. I was ten years one day old.

Miss Waters was teaching us about traditional tales. Little Red Riding Hood. Hansel and Gretel. We were going to write our own stories. I had never written a story before.

My tummy ached and pulled and knotted and dragged. I was sweaty. I was smelly. Under my arms. On my tummy. Under the lumps and bumps that were growing on me. It was sticky. I felt ill. I felt really

really ill. I couldn't tell her. I couldn't tell Miss Waters. She would phone my dad at work. She would phone him to come and get me. Then. Then he would shout at me. Then. Then he would send me to my room. Then. Then he would come in. Then. Then he would shout me into the corner. Then. Then he would scream in my face. Then. Then he would slap me over the head. Around the ears. Over my cheeks. Until the red stings turned into hand prints. Until they decorated my face. Until I curled to the floor. I didn't want Miss Waters to call my father.

I put up my hand. *Please may I go to the toilet Miss Waters?* I went to the toilet. Hardly able to walk. Dragging. Dragging in my tummy and down my legs. I lifted my grey skirt. Tucked it under my chin. Pulled down my grey white knickers.

Blood.
Red.
Brown.
Red.
Blood.

I was dying. I was bleeding to death. I was dying on the inside. It was coming out. Drip drop dripping out. Eddie was coming out. Eddie had killed my insides and now they were coming out. I was dying. I was bleeding to death.

I didn't scream. I wanted to. But I couldn't. I hurt too much.

I wanted to curl into a ball. *Pain pain go away. Pain pain go away.*
I didn't know what to do. I dared not move. If I moved then my
insides would fall out. They'd fall into the toilet. I needed my heart.
I needed my lungs. I needed them. I dared not move. I couldn't
move. I tried to stop the tears. *Big girls don't cry. Do you hear
me? Big girls don't cry.* But. But they trickled down my cheek.
The blood trickled out of me too. My insides were coming out. I
wanted to be back in class. At my desk. Listening to beginnings, to
middles, to ends. Not here. Not dying in the tiny cubicle, with the
tiny white toilet, with the tracing paper toilet tissue and the dirty
concrete floor. I was going to be sucked down into the toilet. First
my insides. My organs. Then my bones. Then my skin. My clothes
would remain. My blood-stained knickers would be the only clue.
Lying on the dirty floor. They would wonder where I had gone.
They would wonder for the rest of the day. Till the bell didn't ring.

I was the bell monitor. I pressed the doorbell button to end the
school day. I spent my school day wishing that I would forget.
That I would forget to ring the bell and we could stay in school.
Forever. The other children wouldn't be happy. They would shout
and scream. They had things to do. They had fish fingers and chips
waiting for them. I had to ring the bell. I never forgot. I spent the
whole day worried that I would forget.

I had thirteen minutes. My digital watch told me. I had thirteen
minutes. Then I would have to press the doorbell button. Then
everyone could hop, skip and jump home. I had to ring the bell. But.

But I couldn't move. I was dying. I was falling into the red water.

I heard her.

*Jude?*
Silence.
*Jude. Are you in there?*
Silence.

I saw her sparkling eyes, peering over the top of the cubicle. She must have climbed onto the toilet. She looked into my eyes. She looked into my tears. Her eyes told me not to worry. Her eyes told me that I didn't have to say any words. She looked to the floor. She saw my knickers. Blood. Red. Brown. Fresh.

*It's ok Jude. It's ok. You've got your first period. You're a woman now. I'll be back in one minute.*

She went away. She came back in three minutes and twenty-seven seconds. My watch told me. It was ok though. She came back. I unlocked the cubicle door. She had a pair of lost property knickers, a plastic bag and a pad. A mattress for a mouse. Huge. It had two hoops on it. One at the top, one at the bottom. She pinned it to the knickers. *It'll do till you get home.* I didn't want to go home. I didn't know what to do.

She talked me out of the toilet. She put my blood red knickers into a plastic bag and she walked me to Mrs Stouter's office. *Sit there Jude.* She pointed to the naughty chair. I didn't understand. Then. She went in and closed the office door. Hush hush tones. Then. She came out. Smiling. I didn't have to ring the bell. Someone else would. I didn't have to worry about anything. They had spoken to my father. He wasn't coming in. Miss Waters would walk me home. She would walk me to the shops. She would buy me some more pads. She would tell me all about what was happening to me.

And she did. She did everything that she promised. She told me about the blood. And my new boobs. And the sweat. And about sanitary pads. I wanted to tell her about Eddie. I wanted to tell her all my secrets. I wanted to skip and to jump and to laugh out loud. I wanted to hold her hand. I wanted. But I didn't. I couldn't find the words. I couldn't find the beginning. I couldn't find all the things that used to be inside. They had fallen out of me. Down the toilet. Flushed away. Gone away.

Rita saw us coming. She was sitting in the front room. She liked to watch the neighbours. She came to the door. Glaring. *What the fuck have you done now?* Miss Waters didn't smile at Rita. Her eyes didn't sparkle at Rita. She handed her a bag. A bag with my sanitary pads in them. Then she turned and walked away. Not a word. Not a goodbye. I wanted a goodbye. I watched her go. She didn't turn back. I looked at Rita. Rita had opened the bag. She cack cack cackled. She looked at me. She smiled. Not a nice smile. *So that's why yee fucking stink.*

# 1984

Rita moved into my mother's house. *It made sense. No need to catch the Number 28 bus from Wallsend to Marsden.* Letters plopped through the box with her name on them. Rita Gustavson. Her clothes, her chocolate and then, on March 19 1984 a photograph of a dead King Charles Spaniel appeared in my mother's house. Loulou had been run over. *A reet tragedy.* Now she was buried in a Pet Cemetery in Jesmond and her photograph enshrined in a gilt frame.

Then Rita got fat. She was huge. She ate all the time. Her plates of food were heaped. Potatoes with everything. Mashed. Chipped. Sliced. Gobble guzzle gobble. Scoff scoff. She was *eating for two.* I didn't understand. She devoured food. I watched her. I felt sick as I inspected her. Shovelled food not quite making it into her mouth. Lingering crumbs clung to her bleached toothbrushy moustache. Sticky droplets trickled down her chin. Guzzle scoff scoff. She talked with her mouth full. She laughed showing her mouthful. Rita lay around my mother's house. My father patted her solid fat belly. *How's me bairn?* I didn't understand. She waddled. She huffed and she puffed. She was an orange monster. Nasty nasty beast.

My father thought it *best that they married.* I thought it best that she went back to her own stinking house and left me alone. I hated her. I hated her cheap perfume that wafted into my bedroom. Invaded my air. A bottle of copied scent, bought for 50p off a stall on Wallsend market. *Hardly tell the difference.* Cat pee and dead flowers mixed together. *Hardly tell the difference.* I hated her squeaks and groans. I hated that she lived in my mother's house. That she slept in my mother's bed. That she hung her fat woman's clothes in my mother's wardrobe. She got fatter and fatter and fatter. I dreamed of rolling her down the stairs and rolling her out of the front door. Away. Be gone. Away. Roly poly woman. Round and round and round.

My mother had not returned for me.

*jude, i have gone in search of adam.*
*i love you baby.*

I was beginning to think that she never would. When the time was right, then I would have to search for my mother. Her bag of secrets. Her bag of her. Still buried. Untouched. Waiting. Waiting for her return. I didn't know how long I should wait. How long before I gave up. Before I threw away the black bin bag. Back out for the bin men. Like my father had wanted.

\* \* \* \* \*

Rita and my father called me into the kitchen. They had three *reet special* things to tell me. They were getting married in seven days. Rumble. And. They had a special bridesmaid dress for me. And. Rita was going to have a baby any day now and my father thought *it best they wed.* Flicker. I thought it best that she left my mother's house and went and had her stinking baby in her own house. I felt sick. I felt panic. Everything was going to change again. Bang.

Those butterflies exploded into a fluttering frenzy inside my stomach. Fright. They needed to escape. I didn't open my mouth. I feared they would flurry out of my throat. They would attack Rita. I would be in trouble. I kept my mouth shut. Tight. Tight. Tight.

\* \* \* \* \*

Six days later. At night. Rita and my father were at The Traveller's Rest. The night before Rita's big day.

I took down the hammer from my father's tool rack. It was very old. A thick dull metal head, with a wooden handle covered in scratches and dents. It spoke of experience. My experience. My pain. It was heavy and cold.

The pain released the butterflies.

Tap

    Tap

        Tap.

Flutter flutter flutter.

\* \* \* \* \*

I sat at the bottom of the stairs. I clutched my red swollen wrist. It was after eleven. I should have been in bed. I heard my father. He was coming along Disraeli Avenue. My father was singing. *I'm getting married in the morning*. He wanted everyone to know. I had been sitting still for hours. Alone in the darkness. I didn't dare to let go of my wrist. It would snap off to the ground. I thought that it would snap off and drop to the ground.

Rita wibble wobbled in. Her purple stilettos strained and groaned under her elephant weight. She stared into my eyes and then slowly moved her gaze down to look at my clutched wrist. She screamed. A piercing witch's cry. She screeched. *Yee fuckin bitch. Yee whore's brat, wantin to ruin me special day.* She would not let me ruin her day. *Me special day.* She wanted me out of her house. I would have to suffer. *You're a fuckin dog. Hoy the brat ootside and let kip in the cald.* She kicked me. Over and over. Pain stabbed into me. Again and again and again. Stab stab stab. Hard kicks with the point of her purple plastic stilettos. Mad. Fierce. Vicious. Evil. She tried to kick my face. I curled over into a protective ball arched on the blood red carpet. She kicked my right shoulder. Stabbing pain rushed down my right arm and peaked at my elbow. Stuck. Throbbing. My father had stopped singing. He was silent. He watched her till she stopped. Then I felt her slump to the floor with a screeching shrill.

Thud. Rita on the floor.

I did not move. *Gan te bed Jude.*

I clutched my wrist and struggled up each of the steps. I wanted my mother. I needed my mother to come home. I lay on my bed. Unable to sleep. I named all the countries that my mother had visited.

Spain ... France ... Scotland ... **America** ... London ... **Libya** ... **Malta** ... **Tibet** ... Victoria ... **Boston** ... **Greenland** ... **Spain** ... France ... Scotland ... **America** ... **London** ... Libya ... **Malta** ... **Tibet** ... **Victoria** ... Boston ... **Greenland** ... **Spain** ... **France** ... Scotland ... America ... **London** ... **Libya** ... Malta ... **Tibet** ... **Victoria** ... **Boston** ... Greenland ... **Spain** ... **France** ... **Scotland** ... America ... **London** ... **Libya** ... **Malta** ... Tibet ... **Victoria** ... **Boston** ... **Greenland.**

It did not help. I wanted to be with my mother.

\* \* \* \* \*

The day of marriage. A stepmother. Wicked. Evil. Fat. I was 10 years, seven months and two days old. Four years and three months from my mother's death. Three years and four months and twenty-one days since my walk with Eddie. June 26 1984.

All the neighbours came. They stood outside the house, clapping as Rita and my father left. They said how *bonny* Rita looked. She didn't. She looked all swollen and red. She looked like a big fat overripe strawberry dipped in clotty cream. Rita wouldn't talk to me. She wouldn't look at me. As far as she was concerned I didn't exist. I was invisible.

I was a bridesmaid. Didn't expect to be. Mr. Johnson (Number 19) had two pretty little daughters. *They were tiny little things.* Karen was in my class at school, the same age as me, but skinny. *A reet pretty bairn.* Her sister Lucy was two years younger than us. *A bonny bairn and reet clever too.* They were bridesmaids too. Rita thought they were cute. They would look *bonny on her photographs.* I was to stand behind one of them. Not at the front of the photograph. Let them cover most of me. I was to do as I was told. It was her special day and I wasn't to ruin it. Mr and Mrs Johnson had room in their car. They could *fit me in.* Lucy and Karen were going with my father and Rita. All together in a Kingcab taxi. *Reet posh.* They were going to arrive in style. It would be nice for them. *Best not show favourites.* It would be special for me to go with Mr and Mrs Johnson. *A nice change.*

I sat through the wedding. In a Registry office in North Shields. They signed their names and smiled for photographs. Click. Click. Flash. I wondered where my mother was. I imagined that she was travelling to me. She was coming to rescue me. She would be standing outside of the door. Watching. Waiting for the ideal moment. I stared at the door, waiting for her to push in. Waiting. I lived my life waiting. She would burst open the door, rush in and light up the room with her ocean eyes. Sparkling. Dazzling. Illuminating.

I watched the door. My wrist ached. My wrist throbbed. I didn't allow tears to fall. *Big girls don't cry. Only whinnying bairns cry.* Swollen wrist. Red. Aching. Hidden beneath a grubby bandage, found in the bathroom cabinet. Found behind the perfect thumb print smeared on the bottom right-hand corner of the mirror. I had wrapped it. I had struggled. Pounding. Throbbing. I had fastened it with a pin. Hush hush. Swirling. Round and round. Mr Johnson had asked what I had done. I said that *I fell out of bed*. Lies. More lies. Pain. More pain.

The wedding finished. The new Mr and Mrs Williams. The doors opened. Happy chatting people spilled out of the room, ready to welcome the newlyweds. Confetti and rice ready to be thrown. I stayed. The neighbours left the room. Rita and my father left the room. I stayed rooted to the wooden seat. Back row. Three in from the left. Alone. Invisible. My mother wasn't coming. I knew. The moment that I knew. I lowered my eyes. Hope gone. Nothing left. No countries to recite. Nothing. My father and Rita were married. I was the only remaining trace of my mother. I didn't know what to do. The bottom of my throat ached. My eyes filled with tears. I could not cry. My father came back into the room and boomed for me. *H'way. Get in the car.* I had to move. I had to get a lift with Mrs Stevenson (Number 28). She was waiting for me. Hurry hurry. I wasn't to spoil Rita's special day. I wasn't to cause any trouble.

\* \* \* \* \*

I was allowed to go to The Traveller's Rest. *A bit of a do.* All the neighbours were excited about the *buff-et*. I followed the trail of happy chatty locals into the building. I stood in the doorway. Alone. Slightly to one side. The guests continued to stream in. I had never been into a pub before. My father's local. My father's special place. It was small. Smoke filled the rectangular room. It was loud. Neighbours shouted over the *Come on Eileen* that boomed from the jukebox. The floor was carpeted. Yellow swirls and green flowers mingled together. The ends of the carpet were frayed. Worn away. I placed my foot onto it. It squelched. I didn't move. I didn't take the step. I looked ahead and tried to read the painted banner, pinned to the yellow wall with four shiny drawing pins.

Rita and Bill. Congradulation's.

It had a hand-painted attempt at a horseshoe after the 's of Congradulation's. It looked like a moon. A blue crescent moon. Smiling. Laughing down at me. *Ho ho ho.* Under the banner were mounds of food. Poised on foiled platters. Covered in cling film. They were arranged onto a lacy white plastic table cloth and stretched over three rectangular tables. Paper plates formed a neat pile, signalling where the queue should begin.

The bar was along the right-hand wall. It was narrow. Stretched. A woman was serving behind it. She had jet black hair. Perfectly straight and from the doorway she looked glamorous. Blood red shiny lipstick. Big dangly earrings. Jingle jangle. Her hair was pulled into a perfect ponytail. It flopped down her back and glistened under the light. She wore a red satin blouse. She had big boobs. Really big boobs. They were trying to climb out of her top. She was very glamorous. Like a movie star. There were five stools in front of the bar. The men were getting drinks. First drink free. *A tab*

143

*at the bar.* Pints all round. Happy men. Laughing men. All talking. The woman behind the bar was laughing. I couldn't hear her over the music. She flicked her head, swished her hair and opened her mouth wide. She looked very happy. She liked her job. She had a nice job.

The women were rushing for the best seats. Push push. The nearer the food, the better the seat. Smoky glass ashtrays decorated the round wooden pub tables. Nineteen tables, each with four chairs. Seventy-six seats. I tried to count the guests. I tried to calculate if there were enough seats. The guests were moving. They wouldn't stay still. I needed paper. I needed a pencil.

Aunty Maggie.

Flutter. I stopped. The neighbours came in couples. Married couples. Aunty Maggie wasn't married. *Never had been.* Hush hush. Whirling. Swirling. Round and round. Twirling secrets round and round. I felt sick. The butterflies were awakened. I searched the room. Scanning. Scanning the room. Eyes flicking for danger. Eyes looking for Eddie. Brown cardigan. Greasy hair. I looked for him. Surely Aunty Maggie would have brought him as a guest. *He was such a nice guest.* I felt sick. I leaned against the door frame, unable to take a step. I wasn't safe. I wanted to be in my bedroom. Sat behind my door. Back against it. Arms wrapped around my shins. Knees pulled up to my chest. Pulling into myself. I wasn't safe. The seats were being snapped up. Push rush. Hurry hurry. The ashtrays were filling. Smoke was being puffed in every direction. I was rooted in the doorway.

A wave of excitement swept across the room. Rita began to take the cling film off the food. *A reet canny spread.* Rita told everyone to *stuff ya gobs.* There was a rush to the pile of paper plates. Mrs Hodgson (Number 2) and Mrs Andrews (Number 18) were first. They had won. They beamed with excitement and giggled to each other as they wibble wobbled along the length of the tables. The queue was formed. I stood in the doorway. Slightly to one side. Searching. Frightened. Alone. Food everywhere. Food food food.

Aunty Maggie came to me. She told me to come and join the queue. She was alone like me. I could sit next to her. I joined the queue. Tiny flip flaps remained, as I stood in between Aunty Maggie and Mr Scott (Number 25). The food was disappearing. Panic. People were piling mountains onto the tiny paper plates. The plates were buckling under the strain. I watched. I counted the chicken drumsticks. Only thirty-seven left. I needed to eat. I needed food.

Sandwiches. Egg, salmon, corned beef. The corned beef still had an edging of white fat. Triangular cut sandwiches. Crusts chopped off *to be posh.* I liked crusts. Vol-au-vents. Ham or chicken in a grey sauce. The sauce looked like grey sick. E.T. sick. Not nice food. I didn't like the look of them. I wouldn't eat them. Aunty Maggie said that they were delicious. I didn't believe her. Chicken drumsticks. Served with a white serviette wrapped around the bone. Twenty-eight left. I had four. Twenty-four left. Cheese and pineapple. United on a cocktail stick. Foil-covered potato hedgehog with the mounted sticks jutting out in different directions. The hedgehog had sultana eyes and half a sultana stuck to the end of a Blu Tack nose. Happy food. I liked the hedgehog. I didn't want anyone to take the sticks. His spikes were going. The hedgehog was sad. Sausages. Out of a tin, drained of brine and placed onto a stick. Foil-covered potato head with cocktail sticks spiking out as hair. *Ho ho ho.* Sultana eyes. No nose. An orange slice for a mouth. A happy head. Soon to be bald. Happy to be bald. Boiled eggs. Smooth and whole. Perfectly glossy and beginning to smell. I ate one whole. Shoved it into my mouth as the queue pushed me along. Sausage rolls. Small morsels with a crisp layer of burn on top. Delicious. Limp lettuce. Grated carrot. Sliced tomato. Tasteless celery. Chocolate fingers displayed like a fan, on a paper doily. Trifle, laced with sherry. Oozing alcohol and sprinkled with hundreds-and-thousands. The colours of the sprinkles all blended together. A smudged rainbow. Chocolate gateau. Right at the back. Still defrosting.

Neighbours laughed. Neighbours drank. Pints all round. Babycham in tall glasses. Clink clink. Presents. Cards. My father and Rita wrapped around each other. Food food food. *They are so in love. Isn't it wonderful about the bairn they're expectin? Bill is so happy.* I sat. I ate. I watched.

A toast. *Speech.* *Speech.*

My father thanked everyone for coming. My father thanked his *bonny missus. The new Mrs Williams.* My father thanked his witnesses. My father thanked his bridesmaids. Everyone was to enjoy themselves. Everyone was to eat. *Eat. Eat.* I sat at the table furthest from the bar. In the left-hand corner. In between Aunty Maggie and Mrs Ward (Number 12). I didn't speak. I ate as much as I could. I ate till I could hardly move. I ate till I would burst. I ate till it began to stick in my throat. I went to the toilet and I was sick. It just happened. I bent over to pull up my knickers. And I was sick. I saw the chicken. I saw the egg. I saw the trifle. I tasted them all again. I tasted the bitterness. I liked the bitterness. I went back to my chair. I sat. I watched. I listened. I ate.

I watched my father. I watched Rita. I watched the neighbours, come and go. Talking about things that I didn't understand. I knew that my father wished that I wasn't around anymore. He had told me enough times. I was too like my mother. *Fuckin mad.* My mother had gone. Off to see someone called Adam. I had no family. Nothing. My father had a new life. A new future. A baby on the way and a new wife. I had nothing. I was surviving in a world of obstacles. I was waiting.

But I had one hope. Hidden. Waiting. One hope that I wouldn't let go of. I still had her bag of secrets. The bag of her. My mother's things. It was still buried. Untouched. Waiting. Waiting for the right time. And. When there was really no hope. Really really. When I gave up. When I really really gave up. Then I still had my mother's bag of secrets.

Caroline Smailes

\* \* \* \* \*

A few days after the wedding, the closest neighbours Mrs Symons (Number 11) and Mrs Lancaster (Number 7) became Rita's bestest friends. They came into my mother's house and would spend afternoons sitting in the lounge. They drank mugs of tea, dunking in chocolate bourbons and custard creams. Biscuits out of packets, placed onto a saucer and carried in on Rita's tray. They were there when I got home from school. Rita was a solid roly poly. Nothing gooey about her. The baby about to burst out of her tummy. Her feet were swollen. She was hot. She was sweaty. She was really red all of the time. A big plump juiceless plum.

I sat half way up the stairs. I listened. Back to the wall. Knees tight to my chest. Arms wrapped around my shins. Head resting on my knees. Listening. Mrs Symons was telling Rita and Mrs Lancaster about Mrs Hodgson (Number 2). She was filling Rita in on everything that she had missed before she moved into Disraeli Avenue.

Apparently. Mrs Hodgson had been married once. I didn't know that. Her son Paul was in my class at school. He was 10 like me. Apparently. When Paul was a toddler, Mr Hodgson had been *called for jury service.* I didn't understand. He had been the *envy of the street having a whole week paid off work.* Two weeks after the end of the service and Mr Hodgson came home and told Mrs Hodgson that he was leaving her. *Poor hinny was cooking his egg and chips at the time.* Apparently. He'd met *some lass* when he *should have*

148

*been focusing on sending some bugger down for grievous.* I didn't understand. Mr Hodgson had finished his egg and chips, packed his bags, then taken a pint of milk from the fridge and left. *Not so much as a blush or bye bye. He just buggered off.*

He had left her for some lass called Sky Thursday. Though her real name was Wendy Jackson and she was from Coastend. She was into crystals and tarot cards. *A bit of a nutter.* Now Mr Hodgson lived in a council flat in Hingleworth, with Sky and their three kids. *He was always a randy bugger.* I didn't understand. Apparently. Mr Hodgson was a changed man. He walked round in sandals, wore hand-knitted jumpers and played the didgeridoo. *Turned into a bit of a nut like his lass.* Rita and Mrs Lancaster cackled and cackled and cackled. Rita said that she'd have to be careful or she was going to *piss her pants.*

Apparently. Mr Hodgson didn't bother much with his *poor bairn Paul. Only a nipper when his father buggered off.* Mrs Symons felt *sorry for the little fella* and she felt he *was crying out for a bloke in his life.* Mrs Hodgson was *on the social* and Mrs Symons said that she was better off without the *didgeridoo-playing weirdo.* Mrs Hodgson hadn't married again. But. Apparently. Mrs Symons did have it *from the horse's mouth* that Mrs Hodgson had *had a bit of Mr Johnson.* I didn't understand. Rita and Mrs Lancaster were booming. Screeching. Cackling. Crowing. Shrieking with laughter. Their amusement bounced against the walls.

Mrs Symons told Rita and Mrs Lancaster that they shouldn't repeat a word of it. Had been told in confidence. A secret. Hush hush. I wouldn't tell anyone either. I had more secrets. Whirling. Swirling. Round and round. Twirling secrets round and round. I would never tell them any of my precious secrets.

I heard Rita saying that she needed a pee before she pissed her pants. I turned and dashed up the stairs. I ran into my room, just as Rita was waddling out of the lounge. She had heard me thunder up the stairs. She knew that I had been listening. She shouted up. *Better not be noseying in on me business.* She huffed and she puffed and she wibble wobbled weebled up the stairs. She didn't come into my bedroom. She went into the bathroom. She was in there ages. Seventeen minutes. I knew, because I was waiting. A quivering sentry. I waited. I waited for her to scream at me. I waited for her to slap my ear. Fuzz buzz.

I heard the door unlock. She wobbled out through the doorway. I sat behind my door. Back against it. Arms wrapped around my shins. Knees pulled up to my chest. Pulling into myself. She shouted to Mrs Symons. *It's time. I've wet meself and me belly is killin.* I didn't understand, but Mrs Symons and Mrs Lancaster did.

\* \* \* \* \*

>Curly.
>My bundle.
>Cry and I come to you.

Arms reaching out from your comfort,
Eyes sparkling
Filled with dreams.
Sleepy bundle.
Close your eyes
Curl into those dreams.
I will protect you.

Crystal Williams was born on July 25 1984. I was nearly 11 years old. I was nearly 11 years older than Crystal. Rita stayed in hospital for a week. I didn't get to see her baby. The neighbours came to visit. In that week I noted that someone from every one of the 31 other houses came to call. Some brought gifts and didn't step into the hallway, some brought gifts and drank coffee at the wooden kitchen table, others sat with my father in my mother's front room and smoked cigarettes and drank from tin beer cans. *They were wetting the baby's head.* My father liked these visitors the best.

I longed to see the baby.

Aunty Maggie had brought rice and two tiny pink knitted cardigans with pearly miniature buttons. The cardigans were buttoned up and ironed so that the sleeves stretched out. Waiting to be hugged. Mrs Clark (Number 14) brought a casserole and a pack of bibs and with each ding dong my father poured drinks, gathered presents and welcomed his guests. My mother's house was full of laughter. I felt excited.

My father described Crystal to me. She was tiny. She had a splattering of jet black hair. Her fingers were curled and her nose was squashed. She had a tiny red birthmark on the left cheek of her bottom. A Cabbage Patch Kid. I longed to see her. My tummy churned and tossed. I needed to know that she was safe.

I wasn't allowed to visit. Rita was tired. Rita needed her rest. I couldn't sleep. Flipping in my stomach. Visions of a tiny plastic-looking baby doll jumped around my head. Hope. Fear. I longed to meet my sister. I had never seen a baby before.

I came home from school. Rita was home. She was sleeping. My father was sitting in the lounge. No cigarettes. No tin cans of cold beer. My father held a tiny swaddled bundle.

Crystal was home.

I stood just outside of the doorway. Spying into the room. My father was staring at his tiny fortune. He was holding her tight. Absorbed. Together. Love. I couldn't move. I sucked up the image. I stayed perfectly still. Trying to be invisible. My father looked at me. His eyes were full of tears. I didn't understand. He asked me to meet my sister. I smiled. Wide smile. A real smile. I moved to my father. I peeped. I saw a tiny squashed face enveloped in a bright white blanket. Compact. Constricted. Safe. She was wrinkled. She was perfect. She was helpless. Catapulted into a world that wasn't safe. Exposed. Fragile. I was overwhelmed. Tears trickled down my cheeks.

My father was watching me and for that brief moment, I felt that he liked me. I wanted to tell him about Eddie. For a split second I needed to tell him about the bad people that came to our street. I wanted him to know. I wanted him to be ready. I wanted him to fight off the bad people. A gallant knight winning his spurs. Like in the hymn at school. I didn't tell him. I didn't talk about Eddie. I couldn't find the words. I couldn't find the beginning. I couldn't trust him to protect Crystal. I had to save her from harm. I decided to guard her. I would be gallant. I would defend my baby sister. She was precious and I wouldn't let anything happen to her. I would be her protector.

Crystal was so tiny. She was the most beautiful thing that I had ever seen. Her eyes were blue. Pale and occupied. She knew me. She grasped my attention. She absorbed me. She wrapped her tiny fingers around my index finger. She told me that she needed me. Her eyes spoke. Rita told me that she was only my half sister. I didn't understand her. Rita was loopy. She was a mad woman. Crystal was my tiny baby sister. I wouldn't let anything bad happen to her. She needed me. For the first time in my life. For the first time I was needed. It was my responsibility to make Crystal safe. I had to protect her from Eddie. I had to.

My father would feed her. My father would change her. Rita was always tired. She would lie in bed watching a black and white portable television. Sometimes my father would let me hold Crystal. Those were my favourite times. Sometimes Crystal would lie on the floor and I would lie next to her. Just watching over her. Just smiling at her. Eyes flickering for signs. I anticipated harm. I watched everything. Rita needed breaks. I longed for these moments when Rita wanted to escape. These times were for me and Crystal. Rita wasn't watching. Rita wasn't glaring at me. Crystal would stare into my eyes. She knew. She knew everything. I told her all of my secrets. I told her all about Eddie. I warned her about Eddie. She understood. She listened.

With Crystal in my mother's house everything changed. I wanted to wake up in the morning. I wanted to hurry home from school. I didn't want to go to school. I didn't want to leave her alone. She shouldn't be alone. I worried about her all day. I didn't concentrate on school work. I thought about Crystal. I worried that Rita would give her to Aunty Maggie to look after. I worried that Eddie would come back. Panic. Fear. A need to protect. I had a sister. Eddie would not harm my sister. Rita would not harm my sister. It was my duty. It was my role. I would protect Crystal. I had to.

It was overwhelming.

My father told me that he had always wanted a daughter. I didn't understand. He had been given a second chance. He was going to be a real dad this time. I felt happy for Crystal. My father would look after her. Two pairs of eyes. We would save her.

I kept a record. I wrote about Crystal. In my green notebook. I described her. Everything. I noted her firsts. Meticulous attention. Never missing a moment.

Stares at me. 3 weeks. 15th August 1984.

Smiles. 3 weeks and 4 days. 19th August 1984.

Moves eyes to watch me. 6 weeks and one day. 6th September 1984.

Smiles just for me. 6 weeks and three days. 8th September 1984.

Drops things on purpose. 8 weeks and 2 days. 21st September 1984.

Stares at hands. 13 weeks. 24th October 1984.

Laughs. 13 weeks and four days. 28th October 1984.

Babbles. 14 weeks and 3 days. 3rd November 1984.

Cries when I leave the room. 15 weeks. 7th November 1984.

Grabs and holds big things. 15 weeks and 3 days. 10th November 1984.

Pulls my hair. 17 weeks. 21st November 1984.

Every little thing was a wonder. She was so very perfect. An angel. Sprouting wings out of the slightly protruding bones on her smooth white back. Innocent. Vulnerable. Fresh. I watched her. I recorded everything. I knew her. I was able to tell if she was hurt. I could distinguish her cries. I knew.

Rita began not to mind. I entertained Crystal. I made it easy for Rita to relax. She could gossip with her friends. Tittle tattle. Crystal was

155

safe with me and I gave Rita the peace and escape that she craved. She was never nice. She was never thankful. She stopped being cruel for a while. It stopped when she needed me. It stopped from time to time. I dragged myself up. I cared for myself. I began to live. Crystal forced me to live. Crystal forced me to grow up. I became responsible. I was responsible for her security. Her sheltering. Her safety. More weight for me to carry. Added. Multiplied. Quadrupled weight. But. But I could manage. I could carry it all.

Rita liked not to see me. She liked me not to speak to her. No need to speak. Hush hush. She let me be with my Crystal. She allowed me to become a gallant knight. Like Joan of Arc. I was special. I didn't hate Rita as much. She had given me Crystal. And. As long as Crystal was safe, then everything would be okay. I was tired. Always tired. But. I needed Rita to let me near to Crystal. It was easier to protect her when I was allowed close to her. I did what Rita asked. Silence. Silence. Hush hush. Never a word.

I watched Rita as a mother. She was a pencil outline. Not quite what a mother should be. She held Crystal. Sometimes. She cuddled her. Sometimes. She soothed her. Sometimes. Everything in small snippets. Boredom threshold allowing. I hated her inadequacies. I hated that she didn't put Crystal first. I had all the responsibility. I had all the weight. I couldn't relax my watch. I was Crystal's protector.

# 1985

February 3 1985. I was eleven years two months and ten days old. My nasty dreams began. Three years, eleven months and twenty-nine days since my walk with Eddie. He entered me as I slept. I could hear his *ho ho ho*. I could taste his dribble. I could smell his cigar.

Wakey wakey.

The smell of his cigar was all over me. All around me. The smell seeped from my skin. Came out of my bed sheets. It enveloped me. It was within me. He is within me. As I closed my eyes. As I floated back into the Land of Nod.

Zip zip.

I was awake. I was wide awake. His dirty smell. Like the dead skin in between my fingers when my plaster cast was removed. Flaked from me. His sound. Zip zip. Bounced around my room. I was afraid that he was there. In the darkness. In the corner. In the doorway. I could not move. Stiff with fear. He was everywhere. Waiting. Waiting. I needed to feel safe. I needed to sleep. I could not sleep. I feared sleep. He came when I slept.

I had a safe place. The boxes remained arranged under my bed. Just enough. Just enough space. I could scramble in. Balls of dust. A tiny metal top hat. Red and yellow counters. Broken bits of plastic. Old knickers. Crumbled sweet wrappers. I could have pushed my way over them. I could have burrowed. I could have been flat on my tummy. I could have been safe under my bed. But. When I woke from my nasty dream. Even though I knew that I needed to be in my safe place. I could not move. I was rooted to my bed.

My nasty dreams paralysed me.

It was real.

He is real.

He is within me.

Always within me.

In the darkness he shouts to me.

\* \* \* \* \*

I can't cope. It's here again. That mind-disturbing feeling. That deep internal rendering.

Again?

It comes again.

And again.

It possesses me. I can't cope. There is no escape.

Again?

Again.

It's here again.

I can't cope. That vision-blurring motion. That head-spinning potion.

Again?

Again.

It won't leave me.

Again?

It's my only friend. I can't ignore it.

Again?
**Again.**

I'd do anything for it.

Again?

Again.

Again.

*Again.*

It's too late. I can no longer escape. It controls me. I am obsessed.

\* \* \* \* \*

I had a friend. I had a best friend. My friend knew my secrets. My friend was a secret.

My body was changing. I would eat whatever I could find. I would eat as much chocolate, cakes and biscuits as my savings would buy. I liked sweet things. I hid the wrappers in a green Fenwick's plastic bag. In the bottom on my wardrobe. Stolen from under

Aunty Maggie's sink. It used to be folded. It used to be perfect. No creases. Now it was full of my dirty secret. My father said I was too fat. They hoped that Crystal wouldn't be fat like me. Rita said my legs were too chubby for trousers. Rita had fat thighs with dimples on them. They slip slapped together when she walked. I didn't tell her that she was fat. *You're a greedy pig, Jude.* I listened to their words. I absorbed their words. I ate more chocolate. Chocolate made me feel happy.

I had no school friends. They thought that I was strange. Teachers thought I was odd. The parents who hung around the school gate thought that I was weird. I had to be at home. Looking after Crystal. No time for anything else. After a while, I realised that I was a fat and ugly freak.

So I ate.

Chocolate became my friend. I ate and I ate. I ate till I hurt. I ate till my sides were going to split. I ate till I throbbed. Till my insides groaned. Then. I went to the toilet. Then. I pushed two fingers into my mouth. Then. I tickled the root of my tongue. I tickled until the chocolate came back and covered my fingers.

I liked being sick.

The first time that I was sick was an accident. It was at Rita and my father's wedding. June 26 1984. I was ten years, seven months and two days old. I ate as much as I could. I ate till I could hardly move. I ate till I would burst. I ate till it began to stick in my throat. Then. I felt sick. I had to go to the toilet. I didn't mean it to happen. I had bent over. To pull up my knickers. I was sick. I didn't need to use my fingers. I tasted the food again. The bitter bitter tasting food. Then. I had returned. Back to my chair. I sat. I watched the celebrations. I listened. I ate again. I felt calm.

I had found a friend. A friend to fill the gap. To make everything better. Eating. Food was my special friend. I invaded the fridge. I collected food. I stored food. Hidden under creased jumpers in the bottom of my wardrobe. I planned. I plotted. I schemed. I gathered. I sneaked. I felt excited. I thought about food all the time. Thinking about food stopped me feeling anything else. I stole. I stored. I hoarded. Ready. Always ready. Throughout the day, the need to eat built and built and built. It took over me. I tried to stay in control. For Crystal. For my little girl. I tried. But something. Something would take away my control. A smell. A sound. A word. A breeze. Something. Then. I began to panic. Panic panic panic. I panicked and I panicked and I panicked. I panicked until I ate. The eating blotted away everything. I didn't have to think. Just for that brief time. The eating made the world silent. I couldn't stop myself.

I ate and I ate and I ate.

Then I was sick. Two fingers into my mouth. I decorated my fingers and I decorated the toilet bowl. Sometimes the gagging sound was loud. It echoed around the bathroom. It shouted down to my father and Rita. They did not notice. They never noticed anything. Then afterwards. After I had cleaned my fingers. After I had wiped away my sick. After I had flushed the toilet and brushed my teeth. After I had brushed away the sour taste that clung to the insides of my mouth. Then I felt sad. Sometimes. I felt numb. Sometimes. I felt. Then. I had nothing again. I felt fat. I was fat. *I am a fat pig.*

\* \* \* \* \*

**4:19pm**
**June 17 1985**
Ring a ding a ring a ding a ring a ding a ring.

*Get the fucking phone, Jude.*
Hello. Who's speaking please?
*Sarah?*
Silence.
*Sarah, is that you?*
Silence.
*Sarah. It's Bill's mam. Is that you Sarah?*

I dropped the phone. It clanged off the little round table. The little wooden table trembled as the receiver bounced onto it. Clang clank clink. I stood back. I stared at it. I glared at it. The squeaky woman had said my mother's name. She had said that she was Bill's mam. She was my father's mother. My father had a mother. I moved backwards over the red carpet. Shuffle shuffle shuffle. Till my heels

162

touched the bottom step. Scared to touch the phone receiver. It was vibrating. Sarah? Sarah? It was wobbling on the small round wooden table. It was alive. I didn't want to speak to her. It didn't make any sense to me. My father had a mother. I didn't understand. I twisted onto the bottom red step. Back against the wall. Arms wrapped around my shins. Knees pulled up to my chest. Pulling into myself.

*Sarah? Sarah?*

I heard her loud twang. She was shouting. Rita came wibble wobbling in. She was carrying Crystal. She shoved her at me. *What the fuck yee doing yee strange bairn?* She picked up the cream phone receiver. She held it to her ear. She was all breathy and puff puffed into the phone.

*Who do yee want?*
Pause. Huff puff.
*She doesn't live here anymore. Who are yee?*
Pause. Huff puff.
*Nah.*
Pause. Puff puff puff.
*His missus.*
Pause. Huff huff.
*I'd best get Bill.*

Rita placed the telephone receiver onto the round wooden table. Carefully. She looked at me. Pulled Crystal back to her. My little girl cried. Not happy. Confused at what was going on. Then Rita smiled. Not a nice smile. Then she wibble wobbled along the red carpet and into the kitchen. I didn't understand what was happening. My father was in his garage. She must have wobbled in through the wooden door from the kitchen. I strained to hear. Hush hush tones. I heard clattering and clanging. Then. My father marched out of the kitchen, huge strides along the carpet and snatched the phone.

*What d' yee want?*
Pause. Pause. His fingers clenched the phone.
*What the fuck d' yee want me to dee bout it?*
Pause. He was angry.
*How d' yee get me number?*
Pause. His angry voice.
*She's deed. It's what yee wanted isn't it?*
Pause. Pause.
*Yee divvent mention his name te me.*

He saw me. His eyes met mine and then he flicked them away. A momentary connection. Momentary. He knew that I was listening. *Fuck off upstairs Jude.* He shouted at me. He glared. Fierce. Red eyes. Angry. I scurried upstairs. Quick quick. I knew to get away. I knew to run as fast as I could. Away away. I stopped at the top of the flight though. I stopped. I made myself invisible. I peered down. My father was standing with his back to the staircase. He was glaring out through the frosted glass front door.

*I divvent want te talk aboot this ower the phone.*

Pause. Steam coming out of his ears.

*Nah. I divvent give a fuck.*

Pause. His head was getting bigger and bigger and bigger.

*Me bairn Jude.*

Pause. Pause.

*Divvent talk aboot Adam.*

My father slammed the phone back onto its base. Rattle rattle rattle. The wooden table quivered and shivered. Rita took a step forward. She must have been standing just out of my view. Crystal wasn't with her. Rita's arms were folded under her boobs. Pushing them up to me. I looked down onto them. My father turned to her.

*Me fucking da's at death's door.*

I didn't understand. My father twisted and looked up the stairs. I breathed in. Gasp gasp. I breathed my head out of his sight. I caught his angry eyes.

*Tha was yee nana.*

Then he marched off, back into the kitchen and left me not daring to exhale. He left me standing as still as a statue at the top of the stairs.

I had a nana. A **nana**. A nana. Adam. **Adam**. Adam.

**Adam**. **Adam**. Adam. **Adam**. Adam. **Adam**. **Adam**. **Adam**. **Adam**. A nana. I had a nana.

I didn't understand. I didn't open my mouth. I didn't ask the questions. I knew to leave my father alone. I knew that he was angry. Really really angry. I just didn't know why.

Panic panic.

\* \* \* \* \*

I went to my wardrobe. A loaf of bread. A jar of jam. Strawberry jam. A packet of digestive biscuits. Two Mars Bars. A chocolate Swiss roll still wrapped. Stolen from the cupboard. Rita was angry. She liked Swiss roll. I didn't like Swiss roll. I hated the feel of the cake on my fingers. I opened the wrapper. Ripped it with my teeth. I pushed the cake into my mouth. I hovered over the Fenwick's plastic bag. Mustn't get crumbs anywhere. *Push push push in*. I didn't chew. I swallowed lumps. *Hurry hurry*. The clock began to tick from the first mouthful. I had to be quick. It was harder to be sick if I left it too long. *Quick quick. Push push push in*. Lumps and crumbs fell onto the plastic bag. I didn't touch them with my fingers. I opened the jam. Took a slice of bread and folded it into the jam. Scooped the jam onto the bread and then shovelled it into my mouth. Blobs of jam trickled down my chin. No time to stop. No time. No time to wipe my chin. *No time. Quick quick*. Biscuits. One two three. No taste. I never tasted. I shoved. I pushed. I swallowed. I saved the Mars Bars for last. They looked the nicest.

They were proper food. *Hurry hurry*. Wrappers off. Into the mouth. My teeth tingled with the texture. The toffee oozed out. It slipped out of my mouth and joined the jam. No time. I wanted to suck. No time to suck. *Swallow swallow*. *Quick **quick***. I had an empty pint glass. Hidden in the wardrobe too. I sneaked to the bathroom. I filled the glass with water. Back to my bedroom. Gulp gulp gulp. I forced myself to drink. *Quick quick*. I folded the wrappers and crumbs into the green plastic bag. I pushed them back into my wardrobe. Covered them with two old creased jumpers. Then. I went to the bathroom.

## I locked the door.

Routine. I turned on the taps. The water covered my noise. I lifted the toilet seat. I knelt in front of the toilet pan. *Ready ready*. I pushed two fingers into my mouth. I tickled the root of my tongue. I tasted the mixed-up food. Sour. Bitter. I tasted the food for the first time. The lumps and strings of sweet food dangled and dribbled from my fingers. Clung to my fingers. My eyes streamed water. Not tears. Not crying. Water gushed from my eyes. I fumbled for the toilet roll. Chocolate fingerprints decorated the green toilet tissue. *Mess mess mess*. I wiped my face. I wiped my lumpy chin. I wiped the sick away. Then. I cleaned the mess inside the toilet bowl. Then. I flushed the toilet. Then. Brushed my teeth. Then. I washed my hands. My fingers smelled. The stench of the dirt in my tummy stuck to my fingers. I washed and I washed and I washed. Until I washed the smell away. Then. I went back into my room.

I went to lie down on my bed. I went to lie down and think about my nana.

* * * * *

Paul Hodgson (Number 2) had a nana. He was eleven like me and he had a nana. I didn't know how long he had had her for. All I knew was that she came on the bus. Every Saturday morning. She came at 9:27am. Paul told me that she brought him a ten-pence mix up and the *Beano*. I used to watch for her coming. She never saw me. I wondered when he got his nana. He was a little bit older than me, but I was sure that he'd had her for ages. I didn't know. I lay in bed. It was dark. The lamppost was flaming. I kept my curtains open. I let the fragments of light shine into my room. I hated the dark.

I lay in bed. Curled on my side. Twisted into a question mark. Looking out into the night. I pictured my nana. She would be small and squidgy. She would wear rouge and full slips with a lace trim. She would use small tight curlers and dye her hair till it was the darkest black. She would never answer the door without her teeth in and her lips would always be painted ruby-red. My nana would wear Golden Tan tights that concertinaed at the ankles. She would have to wear stretchy peep toe sandals because of her huge bunions and they would cause her to hobble slightly as she walked. Her bunions would make her need a wooden walking stick. But it would have silver tassels hanging from the handle and it would shimmer in the light. She would invite me for Sunday lunch. Roast beef swimming in gravy. Gravy made from the meat and not out of a packet. Served with mounds of roast potatoes which were crisp on the outside and fluffy in the middle. Then she would appear with homemade cherry pie for dessert, sprinkled with extra sugar and served with evaporated milk. Then. She would appear with a huge piece of lemon meringue pie. Then. She would appear with home-baked scones, topped with strawberry jam and fluffy cream. I wouldn't be sick.

My nana would make me cups of tea with five sugars and have tins and tins of biscuits. Custard Creams. Chocolate Bourbons. Fig Rolls. Jammie Dodgers. Ginger Snaps. Never Rich Tea. She would have a sideboard brimming with photographs. My photographs. Jude aged 6 weeks. Jude on her first birthday. Jude at the coast with a bucket and spade. Jude's first day at school. She would count the hours. The minutes. The seconds till she saw me again. She would grant me wishes with the wave of her shimmering walking stick. She would spin and twirl and hop and dance and sing. She would tell me stories of long lost cousins, of uncles, of aunts, of my father, of my mother.

My eyes kept flopping closed.

A nana. I had a nana. It was a special gift. My tummy was gurgling. Talking to me. Suggesting. Adding to my imaginings. My nana may even be the Queen of England. That would explain why I had never met her. She was really busy doing very important things.

She loved me. Really loved me. But she was really really busy. Busy chopping off heads and sending naughty people to the Tower of London. My nana was the Queen. I fell asleep with images of my dancing nana bouncing around on the backs of my eyelids.

* * * * *

**3:44am**

**June 18 1985**

The phone rang. It sounded different. It shouted. It shattered the silence.

*Ring a ding a ring a ding a ring a ding a ring.*

My father thundered down the stairs. Thump thumpety. **Thump thump thump**. Not stopping to flick the light switch. I sat up in bed. Back perfectly straight. My bedroom door was open. It was always open. I listened.

*Alreet?*

Pause.

*What d' yee want?*

Pause.

*Alreet.*

Pause.

*I divvent knaa what yee want me te do aboot this. Yee made yer feelings quite clear ower fifteen years ago.*

Pause.

*What difference does it make tha she's deed?*

170

Pause.

*Divvent yee dare mention Adam.*

Pause.

*I'll come te the funeral an I'll bring me bairns, but that's al.*

*Nothin else has changed.*

Pause.

*Alreet.*


I heard my father ding ding the receiver back onto the base. Then I couldn't hear him move. He must have been standing still. I couldn't hear. I wanted to get out of bed. I wanted to creep to the top of the stairs and peer down. The darkness scared me. The darkness kept me rooted to my bed sheet. My father was panicking me. He was not moving. He was not climbing the stairs.


Crystal screamed.


She screamed in protest. Stuck in her cot. Woken in the night. Alone. People were awake. She was awake. She wanted to know what was going on. She spoke for me. She screamed the questions that I could not sound. Rita screeched from my mother's bed. *Yee've woken the fucking bairn. Yee can deal with her.* My father roared up the stairs. *Sort her oot yorsell . Me fucking da's just died.*


Crystal screamed. Continuous. Without breaths. She was ten months and twenty-four days old. She wanted to be free. Rita liked her to be trapped. Controlled. Stuck in her cot.

My father's father had just died. He had died down the telephone. I didn't know what to do. Crystal was screaming. Rita wasn't moving. She must have gone back to sleep. I didn't know what to do. I didn't know what to do. I climbed out of bed. I forced myself into the darkness. I feared the zip zip. I forced myself. I was brave. I was a brave knight. At the doorway. I scrunched my eyes closed and jumped the tiny hurdle to the box room.

Crystal's pink room. Pink walls. Pink carpet. Pink curtains. A Noddy nightlight that terrified me. Blue hat. Red nose. Red cheeks. Brown hair that appeared like a bunch of grapes from beneath his hat. Scary blue eyes that never closed. Stretched open. Stared. Glared. His thin crooked mouth was opened slightly. A tiny hole. The dim light escaped through that tiny hole.

Crystal was standing up in her wooden cot. Gripping onto the rail. Her vest was covered in blobs of dried banana. She needed a bath. She was smelly. Sweet smelling smelly. Her nappy was squelching. Over-spilling past the studded join of the vest. It was heavy. Pulling her down to the bottom of the cot. She needed to be changed. Perfect tears cooled over her bright red cheeks. Clear snot dripped into her wide open mouth. *Ssh. Ssh. Ssh.* I told her not to make my father angry. I tried to make her *ssh*. She wouldn't. She wanted me to pick her up. Rita would explode. Crystal had to go back to sleep. Rita would be angry. She would come in at any minute and see me in Crystal's room. She would scream at me for waking her. She would slap me. She would kick me. I should have stayed in bed. I shouldn't have left my room. The darkness made people grumpy. The darkness was controlling. Crystal was getting more and more upset. My father was still downstairs. Rita was still in her room.

*Quick quick. Decide. Decide.*

I picked up my baby sister. She gripped her arms around my neck. She gripped her legs around my waist. Tight. Her soft cheek stuck to mine. She wanted to be as close as possible. She was not letting go. Her screaming stopped. She sobbed. Softly. Calmly. She felt safe again. I went back into my room. I sat on the edge of my bed and then carefully lifted my legs. Slowly. Smoothly. I lowered my back. I lay flat to the bed. Crystal on my chest. Clinging. Sobbing. Drifting back into the sleep that our dead granddad had interrupted. Hush hush. Hush hush. She drifted away away. Hush hush.

I lay awake. I listened to her breathing. She was safe. Flat on my back. My baby sister forming a shell. Protecting each other. I couldn't fall asleep. I had to stay awake. I couldn't drift off. Awake awake. I had to stay awake. I waited for daylight.

My father stayed downstairs. He did not return to bed. I could hear Rita tossing and turning and the bed groaned under her roly poly roundness. I lay holding my baby sister. Arms wrapped around her. Secure. Stiff. Not daring to sleep. For fear that she would roll to the floor. I forced myself to stay awake in case Crystal rolled and broke her head on the floor. I forced my eyes open. For fear that she may awake without me realising. That she may crawl and fall

fall

fall

down the stairs to her death. I had to stay awake. I had to protect her. My role was to protect my baby sister.

At 6:17am I shuffled myself to the edge of the bed. I gripped Crystal and lowered my feet to the floor. Slowly slowly. Hush hush. I stood. Gripping her close to me. Slowly slowly. I walked into her pink room. I lowered her into her cot. Carefully carefully. She did not stir. I knew that she would wake soon. It was fine for her to wake with the rising sun. I crept out of her room. Creep creep. Slowly slowly. I sneaked downstairs and toward the front room. My father was asleep in his armchair. Slumped to the side. One two three four five six seven eight tin cans lay on the carpet. My father snored and dribbled. Slowly slowly. I tiptoed back to my bedroom.

* * * * *

## June 24 1985

He had the day off work. Because it was his father's funeral. They gave him a whole day off. My father liked having days off. *Full pay for sittin on me arse all day*. He had been sitting. Reading his newspaper. Smoking his cigarettes. Drinking one two three tins of beer. We were going when he was *fuckin ready te gan*. I sat. On the bottom step. I wore my grey school skirt and a black blouse that was Rita's. I had folded the cuffs to make it fit better. The black socks were my father's and had holes in the toes. My toes didn't peep through them though. The socks were very very very big. They didn't fit. But my school shoes covered the holes and the not fitting. I had to be all in black. Not my knickers though. Best no one saw them. They were grey. Used to be white. I dared not move from the bottom step. In case I got dirty. In case my father went without me. I waited. Waited to go. Smiling. Excited. I was going to meet my nana. My twirling swirling nana.

Rita and Crystal were staying at my mother's house. A funeral. *No place for a bairn.* No place for Crystal. I was old enough. I was a big girl. I was brave. I was a knight. Eleven years and seven months old. I was allowed to stay off school. A special occasion. I was excited.

The church was in Fenwick. On the main road into Newcastle. Busy busy main road. My father parked on the road. The church was in sight. He found a little gap for his yellow Mini to squeeze into. Then. My father rushed ahead. He must have known that he was late. He must have known that something was wrong. There were no people around. No black-clothed people. I huff puffed. Trying to make my legs go faster. Trying to run run run after him. He was rush rushing. His black jacket was flapping. He was flying through the wind. Along the road. Then through the gate into the church grounds. I was trying to keep up with him. Trying. Really trying.

He didn't look back.

175

People were spilling out of the church. The funeral had ended. We had missed my granddad's funeral. Late late late. I couldn't cope with being late. My father stopped. In the middle of the path. The path that led up to the church entrance. It made an S-shape. From the gate. To the church. We were at the tip of the snake. He stopped. I stopped too.

There were lots and lots of people there. I counted thirty-seven. Then thirty-eight. A vicar came out. A crowd. The crowd had gathered around two ladies. Two sniffing ladies. Blowing their noses into paper tissues. Cigarettes balancing in their mouths. They were huddling together. Trying to block the wind. Trying to light their cigarettes. Needing to smoke. Trying to smoke. Then more tears. More blowing into tissues. More lighting of cigarettes. Then. Huff puff. Dragging and puffing. Sighing. Crying. They weren't looking at my father. They weren't looking at me. They were absorbed in their cigarettes. In each other. In being sad. A crowd of thirty-five sad-faced people gathered around them. The vicar had gone back into the church.

The two ladies. The two that the crowd circled. The two ladies were both round. One had curled lilac hair. Tight curlers. She was in black. All in black. Like a bowling ball. With high high heels and a very short skirt. She wore black tights that looked like the nets that you could buy on the seafront. If she dipped her legs off Lymouth pier, then she would catch crabs in them. Real crabs. The other lady had long black hair. Streaks of silver flashed as the wind blew. Up up into the air went her hair. A kite of hair. She wasn't as old as the other round lady. But she was as fat. She had a longer skirt on. Flat shoes with silver buckles. Her cigarette stayed in her mouth. Balanced in the corner as she fumbled in her huge black shoulder bag. She pulled out a little dog. A real little dog. He was wearing a black knitted coat. She held him to her chest and hugged him. The dog didn't yap. Didn't yack. He must have been happy to be out of the bag. I wondered what other animals she had in there.

My father turned to me. *That's yer nana and me sister.* Then. He moved. He began to walk. The older round lady saw him. My nana. She saw him. Then. Then she let out a screaming yowl. The worst noise that I have ever heard. Like ten cats fighting. High high. Screaming. It went on and on and on. She fell to her knees. Fell onto the concrete path. Her arms stretched out in front of her. Yowling a constant noise. Not words. A stretched squalling note. On and on and on. Her stumpy arms stretched out to my father. I didn't move. I was too scared to move. The screaming, wailing round lady was terrifying. I didn't know what she would do next. Scary scary lady. My father went to her. He knelt to the floor. He picked her up. My father was a crane. A strong strong man. The round lady dangled in the air. She laughed. I moved forward. I moved into the crowd. Through the crowd that had folded into my father and my nana.

I couldn't get through. I couldn't squeeze in between the black skirts. The black cardigans. The black black wall of people. No

more yowling. Instead. Chitter chatter. Yackety yacking. I was
invisible. All eyes on my father and his mother. My nana.

*Who's he?*
- Bill, her laddie.
*Didn't know sheh had a lad.*
- Aye. Hasn't seen him for years though. Yeh see, his first missus
was a murderer. Killed her bairn. I think his name was Adam. The
murdering cow broke Betty's heart.
*Nah.*
- Aye. Bill isn't with her now though. Sheh's deed and he's got a
new missus.

## Whirling. Twirling. Spinning inside my head.
### **Adam**.
Again.
### **Adam**.

I felt a hand grabbing my coat. Pulling me through the crowd.
My father brought me to her. She was supposed to be my nana. I
think that he made a mistake though. She didn't have a shimmering
walking stick. Her hair wasn't the deepest black. She didn't smell
nice. She didn't twirl and swirl and dance and prance. She didn't
have any cake. Her lips were very thin and they came together in a
point. She wore red lipstick that covered her four front teeth. She
didn't have nice eyes. Not sparkling. Not kind eyes. She didn't hug
me. She didn't touch me. Instead. She looked at me. Up and down.

Up and down. Then she gave out a cackly gulpy giggle. *Funny lookin bairn ain't sheh? Like her fuckin mam ain't sheh?* Then. Then she turned her back to my face. I heard her asking my father about Rita. About Crystal. About when he would bring them to her house. I didn't understand. She wasn't my nana. It must have been a mistake.

I stood. Looking at my pretend nana's back. She was an impostor. A fake. A fraud. Any minute. Any minute. My father would realise. He was being tricked. She wasn't my nana. I knew. I knew my nana. My nana was a special gift. She was the Queen of England. Not her. Not the round woman who had turned her back on me. My nana loved me. Really loved me. My nana was the Queen. Probably at home. Baking. Baking jam tart. Cherry pies. Fairy cakes. She was dancing and bouncing around her royal kitchen. Twirling. Swirling. Sparkling. Round and round and round and round.

My father interrupted my pretty thoughts. Told me that he was going to drop me back in Disraeli Avenue. Then. Then I'd have to get ready for school. He was going to the wake. *No bairns allowed.* I didn't understand. Within six minutes. I was back in the yellow Mini and heading towards my mother's house. The words that I had heard. The yackety yacking in the crowd. *Hasn't seen him for years though. Yeh see his first missus was a murderer. Killed her bairn. I think his name was Adam. The murdering cow broke Betty's heart.* Whirling. Twirling. Round and round.

179

That was it. That was the last time that I saw my nana. That was the only time that I saw my nana.

\* \* \* \* \*

**1:10pm**

I arrived at school. I didn't go through the welcome door. I didn't go through the door that would take me to the secretary's office. Instead. I went to the playground.

I sat at the top of the metal climbing frame. I felt the cold bars through my grey skirt. I clung to the smooth spotless construction.

It was a

long
long
**long**
**way**
**down**.

I clung. I gripped. Gripped till my knuckles turned white. The curved silver bars linked together. With nuts and bolts. Joined. Linked together by the outlines of the squares. Into a hollow Rubik's cube. It was a perfect square. Constructed onto the concrete. It was mine. Finders keepers. Sixty-two bars. Watching. Fingers stiff. Watching.

I was alone. Again. I didn't want to go into school. I was having a day off. I was a big girl. I was having a day off to go to a funeral.

But I didn't. I didn't get to go to the funeral. And. And I didn't get my day off.

It wasn't right.

The whole day was wrong.

It wasn't how it was supposed to be.

*Hasn't seen him for years though. Yeh see his first missus was a murderer. Killed her bairn. I think his name was Adam. The murdering cow broke Betty's heart. Hasn't seen him for years though. Yeh see his first missus was a murderer. Killed her bairn.*

*I think his name was Adam.*

*The murdering cow broke Betty's heart.*

Words whirling. Twirling. Round and round and round.
Whirling
      twirling
           round
               and
           round
      and
round

and

     round

        and

           round

           and

        round

     and

round.

          I had to make them stop.

I turned around. Carefully. Slowly. Moving my legs. From the inside to the outside of the square. Slowly. Slowly.

Then I let go.

     I
     let
     go
     of
     the
     bar
     and
     I
     jumped
     to
     the
     floor.

I put out my right wrist to stop my fall. It buckled under my weight. My body buckled under my weight. Crumpled to the concrete floor. I didn't move. I waited to see if my body would shatter into a thousand pieces. It didn't. A wave of pain swept across my body. It peaked. It stayed. Stayed over me. With me. No longer alone. No tears. No bubbles. *Big girls don't cry. Do you hear me? Big girls don't cry.*

I picked myself up and I walked into the welcome entrance. School. A numbness. A nothing. All over me. A nothing. I smiled to the secretary. She looked confused. I walked past my classroom. Past the cloakroom. Into the toilet. Into a cubicle. I locked the door.

\* \* \* \* \*

Miss Waters came into the toilet. 2:47pm. She came looking for me. I saw her sparkling eyes, peering over the top of the cubicle. She must have climbed onto the toilet. I looked into her eyes. They looked scared. Her eyes told me that she was scared. Her eyes told me that she couldn't find any words. She looked to my arm. I was sitting on the toilet. Clutching my swollen right wrist. On it. In left-handed scribble. In black felt tip pen. I had written.

I had written Adam.

She went away. She came back in four minutes and fifteen seconds later. It was going to be ok. *It's going to be ok Jude. I've told Mrs Stouter. Your dad's going to come and get you.*

I didn't want him to. He would shout. He would scream. He would hit me. Punch punch punch. I didn't know what to do.

She talked me out of the toilet. She walked me to Mrs Stouter's office. *Sit there Jude.* She pointed to the naughty chair. I didn't understand. Then. She went in and closed the office door. Hush hush tones. Then. She came out. Smiling. They had phoned my mother's house. He wasn't there. *At a wake.* Miss Waters would drive me home. Quick quick. Rita was there. She would need to talk to her.

Rita saw us coming. She was sitting in the front room. She was waiting. She came to the door. Glaring. *What the fuck have yee done now?* Miss Waters didn't smile at Rita. She told me to go inside. I went up the stairs. I went to my bedroom. I did what Miss Waters wanted. Hush hush hush. Then Rita closed the door. Slam. I heard her huff puffing up the stairs.

She stood in the doorway to my room. *Yee carn't fucking tell ye da aboot this. He's got enough te deal with. Yer a fucking screwed up kid.*

I didn't say a word.

*Gan in the bathroom an wash tha writing off ye arm.*

Miss Waters had told her. She knew about my words. But. But. Rita didn't ask. She didn't ask me questions. She didn't shout. She

didn't speak his name. She didn't hit me. I didn't understand. I
went into the bathroom. I began to wash my arm. Stabs of pain with
every touch. Rita stood behind me. In the centre of the room. She
was watching. Reading the word. Seeing the black ink drip

drip

drip

drip

**drip**

into the sink. Then. Then she reached over my shoulder. She opened
the cabinet and stretched in. She took out bandage.

*Sit there.*

Rita pointed at the edge of the pea green bath.

*I divvent want ye mentioning this again. We'll tell Miss Waters tha
wer whent te hospital. It'll be oor secret.*

**Hush hush.** Whirling. Twirling. Round and round and round.

Then she wrapped the bandage around my swollen wrist. Tightly.
My wrist liked it. Then she left me. Alone. Sitting on the edge of the
pea green bath. Away away for a year and a day.

* * * * *

The summer came and went. The summer when I left the primary
school. I left the watching eyes. Miss Waters was getting nearer
to the truth. I was leaving her little clues. She was clever. She was

185

picking up the clues. But. I left. I left before she figured it all out. Before she put all of the clues together and discovered the true identity of Jude Williams.

My summer was quiet. I was quiet. No words to be spoken. But. But inside my head. There were words and words and words. Screaming words and words and words.

My head was swelling and swelling. And tightening and tightening. Help help. Inside hundreds and thousands of words spun round and round. They needed to escape. They needed to be free.

Away away.

I dreamed of opening my head. Of cutting round and round. A perfect round. Then. I could open my head. I could open up and scoop out the words. Scoop them out of my pumpkin head. Then I could throw away the pips. Be gone be gone. Then. I would bake the rest. In a cake. With a crust on it. Marked with a J. For Jude. For me.

> Words.
> Hush hushed words.
> The pips of my life.
> Swirling.
> Whirling twirling.

*Hasn't seen him for years though. Yeh see his first missus was a murderer. Killed her bairn.*

*I think his name was Adam. The murdering
cow broke Betty's heart.*

\* \* \* \* \*

Flick flick.
       Lifting lids.
              Searching memories.
                  Delving.
                         Forcing memories.

              Back to the beginning.
              Back to the beginning.

Remember.
Remember.

              Back to the beginning.
              Back to the beginning.

Remember.
Remember.

              Back to the beginning.
              Back to the beginning.

Remember.
Remember.

Remember.
**Remember**.


On March 26 1980, I was six years, four months and two days old. I was dressed and ready for school. It was 8:06am on my digital watch. My mother was still in bed. I went into her room to wake her. I found her lying on top of her duvet cover. She wasn't wearing any clothes. Her ocean eyes were open. She wasn't sleeping. And from the corner of her mouth, a line

of

**lumpy**

**sick**

joined her to the pool that was stuck to her cheek. Next to her, on her duvet I saw an empty bottle. Vodka. And there were eleven tablets. Small round and white. And I saw a scrap of ripped paper. There were words on it.


**Remember**.
**Remember**.


> *jude, i have gone in search of adam.*
> *i love you baby.*


I didn't understand. But I took the note. It was mine. I shoved it into the pocket of my grey school skirt. I crumpled it in. Adam.
Adam.

It was all about Adam.

188

The funeral. It was a Wednesday. My mother's wake at The Traveller's Rest. I didn't go. I went back to school. I walked myself home. I used my key and let myself into my house. Black plastic bags. Remember. Thrown into the garage. Ready for the bin man. Remember. One bag for her clothes. One bag for her secrets. I took her secrets. Remember. That bag full of letters and beads and her sketch book. I took that bag and I hid it in my room. Buried within a basket of teddies and dolls. I wouldn't look. Remember. I couldn't look. Thought that my mother would show me when she came back. Believed we could take it with us. When she took me away. When she had found herself an Adam. When it was time. Remember.

## Reality.

A
bolt
of
lightning
striking
down
onto
my
scraggy
head.

She wasn't coming back.

It was clear.

It was obvious.

Always had been.

* * * * *

**October 24 1985**

Eleven years and eleven months old.

Five years, six months and twenty-eight days since the death of my mother.

The need to know was pressing. Pressing on the insides of my head.

Needing to escape. Needing to find answers.

The time was right.

* * * * *

I had no choice. I needed answers.

I opened my mother's bag.

My mother's secrets. My mother's life with my father. Answers. A bag full of answers.

Photographs.

Cards.

Beads.

Sketches.

A box.

The box would have once contained shoes. My mother loved shoes. It was hardly recognisable. It had been altered. It had been personalised with my mother's artistic flair. Tiny painted footprints. Glittering stars. Shooting stars. Painted. An apple tree in black charcoal. Blond curls. Glued on. A beautiful box. The lid. The roof to her house of secrets. Delicate italics embodied his name.

## *Adam*

I was being invited in. I had found Adam. To remove the lid. To open. To find. Answers. Secrets. My fingers trembled with fear. With anticipation. With desire.

I sat on my bed. Back against the wooden headboard. I placed the beautiful box in front of me. Gently. Onto my blue duvet cover. I sat back. *Adam. Adam.* Arms wrapped around my shins. Knees pulled up to my chest. Pulling into myself. Terrified to go any further. Knowing that I had to carry on. I pulled my arms around my knees. Gripped my hands together. Locked them together.

No choice. A need.

Slowly. I released my hands. Slowly. I removed the fragile lid. Slowly. I took out each tiny item.

Blue booties. Hand knitted. Tiny.
A curl. Blond. In a plastic money bag. Blue letters and

numbers on the plastic.

Hospital wrist band. Black biro.

*Adam Williams. 13-12-1967.*

A black and white photograph. Blue biro on the back.

*Adam. Aged 2 weeks old.*

A knitted hat. Blue. Satin ribbon ties. Straight. Never tied.

A hand-sewn teddy. Brown. A button for a nose. Never cuddled.

A letter. Yet to be read.

A diary. Unspoken words.

A birth certificate.

*Mother Sarah Williams. Father Bill Williams.*

A death certificate.

*Adam Williams. 29-6-1968.*

A tiny coffin of secrets.

*Adam*

I had found Adam.

A diary. I opened the door.

It used to be a sketch pad. Before my mother had spilled out her thoughts. Her secrets. The thick white pages were decorated with her looping scrawl. Personalised with her doodles and scribbles. Always the same. Sad eyes. Sad almond eyes staring back from the pages. Watching over the secrets. Penetrating. Familiar. The words. The blue ink leaped from the pages. Fragments. Episodes. The spilling of thought. Needing to be rescued from my mother's mind. Precious secrets. Words never given sound.

Waiting.

**Waiting for me to discover.**

**Waiting for me to bring them alive.**

\* \* \* \* \*

## 25th august 1968

i can't sleep. i hear your piercing screams.

whenever i close my eyes i hear your crying.

you are still here.


## 26th august 1968

are you hiding from me? are you hiding in our
flat? where are you adam?
i need to see you again. i need to hold you again.
make me smile again. only you can make me smile.
i need to be with you adam.
i have nothing.
where are you? where have you been taken? i need
you to come back to me.

my breasts still leak.

i hear you cry and they tingle.

the milk drips from me and

soaks into my top.

i let it.
i let the round patches spread around my nipples.

i smell you in my wasted milk.

my body needs you. my body leaks for you.
my breasts ache for you.
i know that each leak is taking you further away
from me and further away from my body.
the tingling gives me hope. hope that you are near.

### 27th august 1968

where are you? i can hear you crying?

### 30th august 1968

you were crying. you thought that i didn't love you.
you thought that i had abandoned you.
>i couldn't cope. i was bursting.
>>it was too much, your crying was too
>>much for me.

i killed you.
>i let you die.
>>i made you quiet.

### 1st september 1968

i close my eyes and i hear you crying.
i hear your desperate sobbing in the darkness. you
can't catch your breath - your screams fill the room.
your screams bounce around inside my head.
>>i killed you.
for this i live in hell. i exist in hell.
god has abandoned me.
i long to close my eyes and never wake.
i feel a grey blanket covering me. i am smothered.
i can see only grey.

*everything is smudged and blurred together.*
*my life is a shaded charcoal drawing.*

## 2nd september 1968

people try to help. they say that god needed another
angel. they say that you were too special to be on
earth.
what do they know?
what gives them the right to comment on my grief?
they know nothing.
i see the relief in their eyes as they leave me, as they
leave our flat.
i know that they breathe again when they leave this
hell hole.
they can go back to their lives. they can go back
to their babies. they never bring their babies with
them.
what do they think that i will do?
what would i do?
what am i capable of?
i don't know me anymore.
they don't know me. no one but you, god and your
da know me.
i am evil. i am an evil woman.
i killed my own son.

### 12th september 1968

god rescued you.

### 13th september 1968

god was protecting you. he took you from my
failure.
i'm not worthy of being a mam. i wasn't worthy of
you.
i prayed you away. i prayed for silence. i prayed for
a break.
god and the devil did a deal.
he took the colour, god took you.
i was paid with this fake silence.
i hear him moving. he's watching me. he's laughing
at me.
i'm scared adam.

### 14th september 1968

people utter words.
they do not contain comfort. they're always the
same words. they tell me what they think that i
want to hear. they are empty words.
i hear their speech and as they talk i close my eyes
and wish my grief onto them.
i wish that they could hear my thoughts, hear my

*secrets and then they would be silenced.*
*if they knew they would stop vomiting their empty*
*words.*
*if they knew what i had done.*
*if they knew what i was capable of.*
*then, they'd become angry. they'd shout and*
*scream.*
*i long for them to shout and scream.*

## 19th september 1968

*your da looks at me with such hatred. he loved you*
*and i killed you.*
*your da hates me.*
*he knows the truth. he knows the secret. he carries*
*the burden.*
*after he found me clutching you. i told him. i told*
*him the truth of what i'd done.*
*he didn't protect you. he failed you adam. your da*
*failed you.*
*he knows that i am evil.*
*he knows that i didn't run and get help. i couldn't*
*move. i couldn't shout.*
*he made the decision to protect me.*
*he kept our secret.*
*my marriage died with you.*

## 22nd september 1968

i can't bear your da near to me.

i hate that he knows my evil ways. he knows that i
am a weak woman. i hate that he didn't save you.
i am nothing.

      i hate him. i hate him. i hate him.

          i want him to leave.

i drink and drink.

      it doesn't help, but still i drink. i can't stop. i
want the hell to go away. i swig vodka straight from
the bottle. it makes me cough. it shocks my throat.
he just sits and watches me.

                he sits and stares at me.

i can't read his eyes. they're empty. he looks
through  me.

i hate him.

      i hate him.

          i hate him.

he undresses me when i collapse on the floor. he
clears away my empty bottles. his silence pisses
on me.

i hate him.

i want him to leave, but he won't.

i hit him. i lash out with my nails.

he resists. he refuses to fight. he hates me. he hates
what i've become.

199

he can't connect his eyes to mine. he won't sleep in
our bed. he lies on the sofa.
we both exist in a nothing.
his silence shouts around the room. his silence
enters into my brain and screams out your name.

### 1st october 1968

evil becomes of evil.

### 10th october 1968

i heard you crying again last night.
i couldn't find you.

### 11th october 1968

i don't believe in heaven and hell. not in the red
and white sense. hell is a council flat in newcastle
upon tyne. hell is cold and people piss in the lift.
i see your dead body stiff in your cot.

### 12th october 1968

i heard you crying again. i stumbled out of bed. i
went into your room. your cot was empty. i could
hear you crying. i searched for you.

i screamed for your da to help me. he pulled me to
him. he held me.
i feel that i'm losing my mind.
little things that i do. little things that i don't do.
i'm not here. i'm not living. everything's grey.
i touch things and feel nothing.
i live in a fog.

## 13th october 1968

grey

       grey

          grey.

a double-decker bus will come and knock me down
and for that split second i'll feel alive.

## 14th october 1968

why? why adam?
why did it happen?
why?

     why?

          why did i need to? why adam?
you were crying. i couldn't make you stop. you were
crying all the time.
i needed you to stop.
my head was buzzing.

i needed silence.
i couldn't make you stop crying.
i had to. i had to make you stop. i had to have
silence. i had to.
but not this.
i didn't want this.
i didn't want it to be forever.
i know i prayed for it.
i know i said i did. i know that i told god that i did.
i didn't think that he would believe me. i didn't
think that he'd take me seriously.
i just needed some silence.
you'd have calmed down. i'd have calmed down.
i just needed stillness. i needed peace and quiet. i
just needed to get out.
i still need quiet. i still hear you. now i can't see
you.
i am going mad adam.
i need to find you again.


### 14th november 1968

i shoved two fingers inside me.
    i flicked them around.
        i thrusted them around.
            i'm all dried up.
                i feel nothing.

## 13th december 1968

happy first birthday.

## 23rd december 1968

your room is waiting for you. your cot waits. your
mobile doesn't move.
how can the world go on?
how can people carry on? don't they realise that
you're not here?
i took a pot of crimson blush paint. i wrote your
name across our window and across our door.

adam

my hands are stained with the paint.

## 24th december 1968

how can they forget about you? how dare they!
six months since your death and they won't
mention your name. you never existed.
your da removed the paint. he scrubbed it.
i stood and watched.
i laughed and laughed at him. it came out all evil
and i sounded like a cackling witch. the devil is
inside me. he controls what i do. your da doesn't
know.
your da never said a word. he just kept on
scrubbing.

### 25th december 1968

did you exist adam? were you here?

am i losing my mind?

did i ever know you? were you really inside me? did i imagine it all?

they talk of stuffing turkeys and roasting potatoes.

they live a life that i will never experience.

### 28th december 1968

'but of the tree of the knowledge of good and evil, thou shalt not eat of it: for in the day that thou eatest thereof thou shalt surely die.'

### 3rd january 1969

i push an empty pram.

i bounce the empty pram down the eleven flights of stone stairs.

i know that i look a mess. i don't wash. i don't brush my hair. i don't care what they think.

i go looking for you.

i just push your pram, ready to find you.

where are you?

they fear that i will snatch their child. i don't want their child.

*i want you.*
*where are you adam?*
*i know that your da is disgusted by me.*
*i can't help it. i don't want to help myself.*
*i need to be with you.*

## 5th january 1969

*i am empty.*
*my stretch marks glisten. baby bands, reminding*
*me of you.*
*i did have you.*
*i strip naked to reassure myself that i once knew*
*you. i stand before the mirror. my scars sparkle*
*in the light.*
*i am tattooed by you.*
*you grew inside me.*
*i felt you. i still feel you.*
*you kicked, you somersaulted. you filled me.*
*i didn't imagine it.*

*i have the marks.*

*i did have a baby.*
*i did know you. i still know your name.*
*let me feel a physical pain. let me feel something.*
*i don't know what is real. i'm numb.*
*i still hear you in the night.*

### 6th january 1969

'and the serpent said unto the woman, ye
shall not surely die.'

### 15th january 1969

i can't draw anymore.
i sit down to draw and end up covering pages in
eyes. they're my eyes that i draw.
i need to feel something.
i don't care what it is, i just want to feel.
i'm a silhouette. i wait in the darkness for light.

### 22nd january 1969

'for god doth know that in the day ye eat
thereof, then your eyes shall be opened,
and ye shall be as gods, knowing good
and evil.'

### 2nd february 1969

our marriage is dull. i never talk to your da. i have
nothing but hatred towards him. he looks through
me. his eyes are cold and heavy. he avoids me. he
doesn't want to come home. he hates being in the
flat.
seven months on and i still hear you. i sit in your

room talking to you. do you hear me?

i need to know where you are.

i want to join you.

i wish that you'd give me a sign.

i need to know that you forgive me.

forgive me and i'll come to you.

give me a sign and we'll be united. i'll join you. i'll
be your mam again.

let me know when i can come to you.

give me a sign.


## 15th february 1969

'she took of the fruit thereof, and did eat,
and gave also unto her husband with her,
and he did eat.'


## 6th march 1969

i was told today that i should be celebrating your
life. i should be celebrating the pregnancy and
those short six months.

how can i do that?

i killed you.

i did it.

i must take responsibility for it.

i need punishment.

*i need to feel physical pain.*

*i should be whipped. i need to feel the lashes ripping into my flesh. i need to feel.*

*i need to be punished.*

*why did i do it?*

*why?*

*because i'm evil. i'm evil in my core. i never deserved you.*

*i never deserved happiness. i couldn't cope with the happiness.*

*you were too perfect. you made my life too perfect.*

*i knew. i always knew that i wouldn't know you for ever.*

*i made it happen.*

*i made you go away.*

*it's within me.*

*i have a self-destruct.*

*i destroy everything that i touch.*

*i don't know how to love in the right amounts.*

*i don't know anything anymore.*

*my pain clings to me. you're in that blanket that smothers me.*

*i hear you. you're trapped. i know that you are trapped.*

*they tricked me. they took you away to torture me.*

## 7th march 1969

*i can't celebrate your life.*

*it's cruel.*

*it's wrong.*

*six months old. six short months.*

*you were just starting to live.*

*i did it. i did it. i killed you. i silenced you.*

*i can't celebrate what never was.*

*no one listens to me anymore. they can't hear you.*

*they don't hear you crying in the night.*

*why are you crying? are you still alone? do you*
*need me? are you trapped?*

*am i right adam?*

*i can't find you.*

*i don't know where to look.*

*i need a sign. i need a sign.*

## 23rd march 1969

*it's amazing what you can do with a bottle of*
*vodka. i drink and then i smash the bottle onto the*
*floor. i take a piece of glass and i fold it into my*
*hand.*

*i like the pain adam. i like the blood.*

> *my life is now grey with flashes of red.*

### 1st april 1969

april fool.

### 2nd april 1969

you're not really dead.

   am i alive?

      the red tells me that i am. it tricks my
mind.

            i'm dead really.
welcome to hell.

### 19th april 1969

'and he said, who told thee that thou wast
naked? hast thou eaten of the tree, whereof
i commanded thee that thou shouldest
not eat?'

### 15th may 1969

grey.
i feel nothing.
the flashes of red make me smile.
when i see red i step closer to you.
you are red.

## 22nd may 1969

'the woman whom thou gavest to be with
me, she gave me of the tree, and i did eat.'

## 29th june 1969

one year since i killed you.

## 10th november 1969

i search for you.
i look in prams.
people leave them outside shops.
they leave their crying babies.
i stand next to prams and wait for the mam to
return. i protect them.
i watch over their sleeping babies, but the mams are
never grateful.
they all know me.
they look to the floor and never speak.
no one dare speak to me.
i am friends with the devil after all.
they all think that i'm strange, that i'm mentally
disturbed.
i am. i have the cuts to prove it.
but i would never hurt their babies.
i may drip blood onto them. they can feed on my

211

blood. i can give them life.

but i would never hurt them.

i look for you, but i know that i'll no longer
recognise you.

people say that i should be 'over it' by now.

over it.

my grief is selfish.

i will never be over it.

a sign adam.

it's all i ask.

### 13th december 1969

happy birthday. two today.

### 12th february 1970

'and i will put enmity between thee and
the woman, and between thy seed and her
seed; it shall bruise thy head, and thou
shalt bruise his heel.'

### 20th february 1970

if i bleed to death will i be bleeding you out of me?

each drop of blood pours you out of me.

he's making me do it.

i need a sign adam.
before all the red is lost.

## 27th february 1970

i wouldn't know you.
i've forgotten your smell. i've forgotten what you
look like.
i'm not worthy of you.
what kind of a mother am i?

## 1st march 1970

'unto the woman he said, i will greatly
multiply thy sorrow and thy conception; in
sorrow thou shalt bring forth children; and
thy desire shall be to thy husband, and he
shall rule over thee.'

## 3rd march 1970

your da told his mam about what i did. he told her
that i killed you.
she came around to the flat and slapped me. she
slapped me twice. sharp stings of life. she came
around with your da's sister and the woman who
lives next door to her. she told me that i'd never be

213

welcome in her house and that if it wasn't for your
da she'd have called the police on me. she called me
a murderer.
her words made me smile. i laughed in her face. i
cackled again. he made me do it again.
she spoke the truth. her slap skimmed the surface,
but the sting faded.
i need more physical pain. i need to be slapped till i
come back to life.
she said that my mam would be turning in her
grave. she was right. of course she was right.
i'm friends with the devil. i live with him sticking
his dry tongue into my ear.
your da didn't come home for two days. i sat in the
darkness waiting for him. he didn't come back.
during the day, two days later, he turned up. he
told me that he wouldn't be seeing his mam and
sister again. he wanted to be with me. he wanted to
give our marriage another go.
i don't care. i have no energy to care. nothing
matters anymore. your da is staying with me to
experience the nothing too. for better and for worse.
when will it be better?

## 4th march 1970

your da told me that he shagged the woman who
lives next door to his mam. he did it when he left
me, when he didn't come back.
i don't care.
next time i hope that he'll let me watch. i could do
with a laugh.

## 5th march 1970

'because thou hast hearkened unto the
voice of thy wife, and hast eaten of the tree,
of which i commanded thee, saying, thou
shalt not eat of it: cursed is the ground for
thy sake; in sorrow shalt thou eat of it all
the days of thy life.'

## 7th march 1970

if i kill myself today i will never see you again.
i know that.
he told me that.
i have to keep going till you are ready, till you
forgive me.
a sign. what is the sign? have i missed it?

### 21st march 1970

i think that i've missed your sign.
i don't know what to do.
last night i crunched broken glass into my fist. the
red wasn't as bright as normal. i am losing you.
you are going from my blood.
i can't go on.
i have nothing.

### 23rd march 1970

'whoso sheddeth man's blood, by man shall
his blood be shed: for in the image of god
made he man.'

### 1st april 1970

i can lie in the bath. i can piss and piss.
          drowning drowning in my own pee.
what
a
way
to
spend
my
day.

## 19th april 1970

i took the lift today.
i took it all day.
sat in it with a bottle of vodka.

>             i took off my knickers
>             and pissed in the
>             corner.

## 12th may 1970

i got caught shoplifting again.
the police got involved. i didn't get charged.
i was stealing a packet of frozen peas. i did it
because i could. i tried to shove it down my jumper
and the bag split.
i walked out the shop, cackling with a trail of peas
falling from my belly.
they called the police and they gave me a lift home.
i still have peas stuck to the inside of my jumper. i'm
going to cook them and give them to your da for his
tea.

## 29th may 1970

i still hear you.
you're trapped in my blanket.
i stretch out to try and grab you. i can't touch you.

217

*he is holding you.*
*he is pinching you to make you cry.*
*give me a sign adam.*

## 29th june 1970
*two years since i killed you.*

## 3rd july 1970
*'in the sweat of thy face shalt thou eat*
*bread, till thou return unto the ground; for*
*out of it wast thou taken: for dust thou art,*
*and unto dust shalt thou return.'*

## 15th august 1970
*the cat from next door scratched on the door*
*again. he was hearing you too.*
*i didn't want you to talk to a cat.*
*you're better than that.*
*you can talk to me instead.*
*i dropped the cat over the balcony.*
*i watched it fall*
*eleven floors to the ground.*
*he let me. he laughed as i did it.*

*his hands grip my breasts and squeeze.*
*i don't know if anyone saw me. i don't care.*

## 5th september 1970

*bill refuses to give me money. he says that i'll spend*
*it on vodka. we can't afford for me to be wasting*
*money. he works really hard. he's saving.*
*the bloke three doors down buys me vodka. i suck*
*him off and he gives me the bottle. i don't care. i*
*like the taste. he shoots out quickly and then i spit it*
*onto his shoes.*
*he can clean it up.*
*bill asked me where i got the drink from. i told him*
*that you gave it to me. he didn't laugh.*

## 17th october 1970

*i have no future.*
*i sit alone in the flat.*
*your da says that we need to move. that we should*
*buy a house, put down some roots and start again.*
*my roots flap in the breeze.*
*your da says that i need to get a grip. what should i*
*grip? my own throat would be a good place to start,*
*but i don't have the strength.*
*your da has been working hard at the factory. it's*

all he does. he works long hours to stay away from
me and he thinks that i haven't realised.
he can't cope with being in the flat.
i think that he hears you too.
i think that he sees your stiff body in the corner of
the front room. he wouldn't tell me.
he wants to buy a nice house, near the coast.
he says that the fresh air, the clean start will do
us good.
i know that he's right. i know that we need to escape
the darkness,
but i'm frightened to leave the flat.
it's our home.
what if you come back?
what if you return and i'm not here?
what if we move and i stop hearing you?
your da says that we should give our marriage one
last chance. we should move where no one knows us.
we should move to our own little house.
we're going to leave everything behind.
bill doesn't speak to his mam anymore.
no one will know where we have gone.
no one will miss us.
i get flutters of excitement.
        how dare i get excited!
to feel is to forget.
but adam, no more accusing neighbours, no more

*hushed voices and no more pointing fingers.*
*it's the right thing to do.*
*fresh air.*
*the seaside for you to play on.*
*i know that we must leave.*
*your da has told me that i must not tell anyone*
*of you.*
*i must leave your memory.*
*i mustn't speak your name.*
*i say it over*
        *and over*
            *and over in my head.*
*he can't stop that.*

### 19th november 1970

*'and adam called his wife's name eve;*
*because she was the mother of all living.'*

### 13th december 1970

*happy birthday. three today.*

### 14th december 1970

*we have found a house.*
*a new house.*

it's just being built. disraeli avenue in new lymouth.
there'll be three bedrooms.
you can have the box room. i'll decorate it for you.
blue? or red?
i thought about putting our blood red handprints
all over the wall.
i don't think your da will approve though.

## 17th december 1970

i can't wait for the summer.
in the summer your da'll show his arms.
he has adam on his arm. i see it and i smile.
i want the world to ask him who adam is.
i want to hear them speak your name.
maybe i should get a tattoo. i could have your
name scratched across my forehead and then they'd
have to ask the questions.

## 19th january 1971

a sign.
where is my sign?
i don't want to leave our house.
how am i going to tell your da?

## 2nd february 1971

'so he drove out man; and he placed at the
east of the garden of eden cherubims, and
a flaming sword which turned every way, to
keep the way of the tree of life.'


## 1st march 1971

we met our new next door neighbour today. the
foundations are down and we went to see. i wanted
to write your name in the foundations. bill told me
to get a grip. i was. i thought that i was.
they were called mr and mrs symons. they asked if
we had any bairns. your da said no. i pulled up my
top and showed them my belly. they looked at me
like i was a nutter. i don't think that they saw the
stretch marks.
they're fading away.
your da said something about me having just had
a miscarriage. did i? when did i?
i don't know if i did.
i don't know anything anymore.
it's all changing adam.
everything is changing again.
your da said that you'd never been born.
were you? were you real adam?
a sign. where is my sign?

## 9th march 1971

'and it came to pass, that at midnight the lord smote all the firstborn in the land of egypt, from the firstborn of pharaoh that sat on his throne unto the firstborn of the captive that was in the dungeon; and all the firstborn of cattle. and pharaoh rose up in the night, he, and all his servants, and all the egyptians; and there was a great cry in egypt; for there was not a house where there was not one dead.'

## 2nd may 1971

i sat today.

i had a box that once contained my wedding shoes.

i placed into it everything that reminded me of you.

i will place this diary into it too.

i mustn't write to you anymore.

your da said it makes me look crazy.

i don't care.

i'll keep this with me,

my tiny box of you.

it's our secret.

i must try to be strong. i must try to live.

i know that you'll send a sign when i can meet you again.

we move to our new home tomorrow.

'for in six days the lord made heaven and
earth, the sea, and all that in them is, and
rested the seventh day: wherefore the lord
blessed the sabbath day, and hallowed it.
honour thy father and thy mother: that thy
days may be long upon the land which the
lord thy god giveth thee.
thou shalt not kill.
thou shalt not commit adultery.
thou shalt not steal.
thou shalt not bear false witness against
thy neighbour.
thou shalt not covet thy neighbour's house,
thou shalt not covet thy neighbour's wife,
nor his manservant, nor his maidservant,
nor his ox, nor his ass, nor any thing that is
thy neighbour's.'

### 25th november 1973

i had to tell you.
you've a sister.
she was born yesterday. her name is jude.
maybe one day you'll meet her.

## 7th january 1980

it's been so long since i've written to you.

you've been buried in your box, but i can't pretend anymore.

i need to talk to you.

i look at jude and i feel a deep ache.

she'll never know you. as she has grown, she has become more like you.

sometimes i can't bear to look at her. i feel that you're within her, trying to communicate with me.

she has a lost look, a hollowness that stares into me.

she's searching for answers. she knows that something is not quite right.

i can't tell her about you.

how do i find the words? how many words do i speak before she realises how inadequate my feelings are for her?

how do i tell her that i'm a child killer?

my thoughts keep flicking to you.

you're my habit. you're in my blood, pumping death into my veins.

i wish that i was with you.

i think of jude, i know that she needs me too but without you i can't be the mam that she deserves.

let me know that you hear me adam.

## 11th january 1980

i lay in the pea green bath. it was full. it was hot
and i floated. my ears rested below the surface
and i heard life. i heard the water breathing. i
felt alive. my flesh was warm and the breathing
shrouded me. i wanted to sleep. i wanted to drift
away into a land where i could breathe again. i
needed to be in a land where i was surrounded by
love. i'm so very alone. i don't know what to do. i
need you to tell me what to do.

## 27th january 1980

'and cain said unto the lord, my punishment
is greater than i can bear.'

## 13th february 1980

last night your da asked me why i'm always so
miserable. he hates it if i mention your name. he
gets angry and lashes out with his fists.
i guess that that's how he deals with his emotions.
he should have protected your memory.
we have no marriage. i wish that i'd someone to
talk to. i miss my mam. somehow you've become a
sordid secret.
should i be ashamed of you? how can i be? you

awakened me. i had purpose and a future.

losing you has turned me into a bitter old woman.

i can't give love. what's the point of loving? jude is such a perfect little girl, but she deserves so much more than i can give her.

if i give her all the love that's bursting beneath my skin. if i do this, then i know that god will take her from me. if god sees me loving another, then he will make another deal. i will kill again.

i'm not worthy of her. i'm protecting her. i withhold my love.

i can't cope with what the future might bring; my life is brimming with insecurities.

## 17th february 1980

i told your da that i didn't feel that i was coping. i said that i might go to the doctors and he told me that they'd think i was mad and lock me up.

your da tells me to get on with life, that i should look at all the stuff that we have and not dwell in the past.

all the stuff that we have means nothing.

i like to think about you.

some days i can't get out of bed,

i lie in the quiet thinking about you.

jude comes in and i pretend to still be sleeping.

she climbs into bed and burrows into my space.
she pulls my arms around her and i know that she
is smiling. her love for me has no boundaries.
she isn't like this with your da.
i'm her everything. she's such a good girl;
she dresses herself and is ready for school.
i scrape back my hair, grab some clothes and force
myself to walk her to school.
i look a mess, but she never complains.
she seems so happy to be with me. she grips her hand
in mine and walks with her head held high.
she loves me. she sparkles with affection.
she deserves better.
what kind of a role model am i?
all that i can teach my daughter is how to be a
killer. i am incapable of love.
i can hardly look after myself, never mind a
daughter.

## 19th february 1980

'behold, thou hast driven me out this day
from the face of the earth; and from thy
face shall i be hid; and i shall be a fugitive
and a vagabond in the earth; and it shall
come to pass, that every one that findeth me
shall slay me.'

Caroline Smailes

## 20th february 1980

your da doesn't really bother with jude;
his world revolves around his beer, his mates, his
football and his tv.
i have to make sure that his food is ready for him
when he gets in, that the house is tidy and his
clothes are ironed.
when did i become his slave?
we have sex when it suits him.
he climbs on top and enters me.
i feel nothing. a log of hollow wood.
he fills me and then rolls off to sleep.
i hate his smell.
i hate his weight.
i hate the feel of his breath onto my ear.
i hate the feel of his stubble on my cheek.
he isn't the man that i fell in love with.
thankfully he doesn't want me very often.
my life is full of routine and emptiness.
i can be in a room full of people and i feel lonely. i
hate noise. i hate crowds. i like to be surrounded by
silence, and then i can fill my mind with my own
noise and thoughts.
i busy myself, but nothing excites me. i have a
gaping hole within me. nothingness accompanies
me. i don't think that i can take much more of this.
i need a sign.

## 25th march 1980

jude, i'm going to die.

tomorrow i'm going to die.

tonight i need to find words.

i can't live like this anymore.

yesterday i went to the doctors. he told me that i
was pregnant again.

i can't be a mam again.

adam has sent me this sign.

so i have tablets and i have vodka.

i don't even know why i'm writing this.

there's so much that you don't know and i doubt
that your da will ever let you see adam's box.

but, i wanted to try and explain why i have to die.

i killed adam.

i killed your brother.

i can't be your mam without adam.

there's so much that i need to tell you, so many
things that you need to know about being a lass. i
have no right to tell you them. i'm no good at being
your mam.

i know your da. he'll meet someone else and she'll
look after you. she'll be your new mam.

i can't bear to write anymore.


i'm never far from you –
i can't say goodbye.

231

*one day jude, one day i'll let you know that we're alright.*

*adam sends you a big hug and kiss.*

x

\* \* \* \* \*

Adam was responsible.

Adam was evil.

My mother wasn't wicked.

My mother was wonderful.

My mother was the most beautiful and magical woman to ever live.

Adam had taken my mother from me.

Adam had tricked my mother into leaving me.

Adam was working for the devil.

He was nasty. He was **evil**.

Evil

Evil

**Evil**.

My mother was so very unhappy.

Adam made her unhappy. My father made her unhappy.

I hated them.

I hated my father.　　I hated Adam.

I wanted my mother. I needed my mother.

She should never have left me. She made the wrong decision.

Adam forced her to make the wrong decision.

I hated Adam.

I hated my father.

My mother.

My mother was so very unhappy.

She wasn't evil. She couldn't be evil.

It was my father.

## My father and Adam.
## Not my mother.

My mother was so very beautiful.

I didn't know what to do. I didn't know.

Killer

**Killer**

**Killer**

**Killer**

**Killer**

**Killer**

Killer

**Killer**

**Killer**

**Killer**

**Killer**

My mother was a killer. My mother is a killer.

Murder. Murder.

I had to make a decision. Quick Quick. No time to waste.

Quick.

## Quick.

I had answers. I had more secrets. But. But I could cope. I had to cope. I had to. I had to protect my mother.

I had to keep the words unspoken.
Locked away.
No need to talk about it.

Quick quick. I replaced all of the tiny items. Back into the box. Back into the box that had once contained shoes. A long long time ago. Now it held the weight of the world. It carried the weight of the world.

Onto the floor in my bedroom.
Stomach flat to the blue carpet.
I stretched out my arms.
I dived under the bed.
My fingers brushed against my $E^{II}R$ Silver Jubilee tin.
I dug my toes into the carpet.
Edged myself forward.
Ducked my face to the floor.
Breathed in the cloud of dust.
Scrambled a little further under.
Half a head under.

I placed the box.
Next to the navy blue cylinder tin.
In gold capital letters. $E^{II}R$. 1952–1977.

The Queen of England would look after my secrets. And my mother's secrets.

I wasn't holding the box. I wasn't carrying it around with me.

**But.**

But still. I carried the weight of the world.

# Ever After (1992)

Ward 23
Overdosing on grief.
Alone.
Slipping
Into an already been
State of decay.
Daffodils
Like hospital pills.
Tick, tock.
You're dying.
Sinking in anxiety.
Tears.
Paranoia
Into the welcoming earth
Of splinters puncturing.
White walls
Need sausage rolls.
Ding, dong.
You're dead.
Ask for a razor.
Remember your name?
Hear them screaming
Into the night.
Electric scales
Like bitten nails.

Squeak squeak.

It's a mouse.

**May 24 1992, 11:27am**

I got a taxi to the hospital. GP told me to. *Just follow the signs to the mortuary and you'll arrive at Ward 23.* I followed the signs. *Ward 24. Mortuary. Ward 23.* My father had agreed to meet me at the entrance. I had had to call him at work. He was leaving early. He wasn't happy. He couldn't keep getting time off work. He was waiting for me. I paid the taxi and together we walked past the mortuary. I understood. We arrived at the ward. 11:44am. My father pressed the intercom.

Buzz buzzzzzzzz.

The door opened.

Slam bang bang.

The door slammed behind me. Click clicked. Locked. A code was needed. I didn't know it. I couldn't leave. *Ask permission to leave the ward.* I was eighteen years and six months old.

A lady approached us. She said that she was a nurse. She didn't look like a nurse. She wore jeans and a t-shirt. We were standing in the corridor. A few centimetres away from the door. The locked door. Noises. Loud noises were whirl whirling around. I didn't recognise the noises. I began to shake. In my knees. In my hands. The nurse had her back to me. She was talking to my father. Hush hush. I couldn't hear what she was saying. I couldn't hear anything. The corridor felt busy. There was no one there. The smell was strange. Wee. Bacon. Sick. Coffee. Blood. Beans. Mingled. Strong. All mingled. All wafting.

The nurse turned around. Facing me. She looked at me as she told my father to go. *Best not make a fuss.* He smiled as he left. He'd nip and see Rita, before going back to work. No hug. No kiss. Big smile. *See ya soon pet.* I stood alone. Rooted to the blue strip of carpet. For very important peoples. For very important mad people to walk along. My bag of stuff quivered on the floor. Brushing my feet for reassurance. White walls. Not daring to speak. Waiting to be told what to do next.

The nurse picked up my bag. She didn't smile. She didn't speak. I followed her along the corridor. She was tall. Stretched to the ceiling. She was grey. Smudged together black and white. She was smudgy. But. Tall. Stretched. Straight back. No face. I looked through open doors. To the right. To the left. Quick march. My eyes flicked.

     Left.

          Right.

     Left.

          Right.

Beds. Chairs. Staring eyes. Faces. A smear of images. Blurred into one mixed up mess.

A sick of images.

I had my own cubicle. Iron. Cold beds, separated by a thin flowery plastic curtain, that didn't quite reach the wall. Lines of light escaped between the curtain and the wall. Looked into my private space. Watched. Watched. Always watched. The nurse told me that *was to be* my bed. Pointing at the silver iron block. A white blanket was stretched across. Ward 23 imprinted in blue ink. Just to remind me. Alert alert. The nurse told me that she would have to check my bag before I could have it. My bag was taken. A hurried shoving of my things into a bag. Knickers. A sketch pad. My green notebook. Glue. Scissors. A navy blue cylinder tin. It had a gold trim and $E^{II}R$ in gold lettering. Colouring pencils. A nightie. Toothpaste. Toothbrush. Soap. A razor. Shampoo.

Two hours since I went to the GP. Two hours since I was told to go into hospital and I had rushed to find what I would need. I didn't know what to pack. I was going to be in hospital for a long time. The mortuary was waiting for me. Choices. My bag was taken to be searched. Strangers were rifling through for secrets. They were searching and searching. I sat on my bed and waited for the nurse to return with it.

The padded cell existed. It was real. It was occupied.

People began to introduce themselves. Excited at my arrival. Young blood. A new story to be told. I was frightened. Rooted to the white blanket on my cold bed. I sat on the edge. Not daring to relax. Not daring to move. Alone. Startled by the madness that surrounded me. I could not speak. Heads appeared around the thin flowery curtain. Clouded eyes. The voices were slurred. They weren't well. I had to remember that they weren't well. I couldn't trust them. I had to be silent. I had to keep myself to myself. But. They seemed so happy. They seemed so happy to be on Ward 23. It was a home. It was a safe place.

# Moira

Moira was nice. She rushed in. Shouted at the staring glaring others. One two three four five pairs of eyes.

*Leave the lassie alone. She's terrified. Poor hinny.*

She came in to me and sat on my bed.
*Come on hinny tell is yer name.*
- Jude Williams.
*That's a pretty name hinny. Nice to meet yer.*

She was wearing jeans and a t-shirt. Like the nurse. She had grey hair that was roughly cut. Short and spiky. Her skin was smooth and brown. She was thin. Very thin. Her fingers were stained with an orange band. She put her arms around me and hugged me. She smelled of cigarette smoke. Moira told me that she was a nurse and

241

that she'd look after me. I had to tell her if anyone bothered me. She'd look after me.

*I'll be yer ma while yer in here.*

I didn't tell her about my mother. I wanted to, but I didn't. She sat with her arm around me. Humming *incy wincy spider*. Rocking me gently backwards and forwards. All the time I looked at the hole in her pink slippers.

The nurse returned with my bag. Moira jumped up and scuttled away. *Run run as fast as you can.* I could have my bag back. The razor and the scissors had been taken. I would have to ask to use them. I would have to be watched when I used them. I didn't understand. Someone would watch me while I cut and pasted. And while I shaved. I didn't understand. She left me with my bag. I sat back. Against the iron headrest. I clutched my bag into me. Black. Soft. As big as me. I could hide behind my bag. I would not cry. I could not cry. *Big girls don't cry. Do you hear me? Big girls don't cry.* I wanted my mother. I wanted to be with my mother.

# My neighbour

I heard a hiccup. Loud. Bounced off the walls. Gasping for air. A lady. Sat on her bed. In the next cubicle. She looked like a hunched old lady. Like she was over a hundred years old and about to die at any minute. She wore a pink nightie and a matching velvet dressing gown. No slippers. Bare feet. She stared. Through her eyelashes.

Sat next to the crack in the curtains. Hairy legs dingle dangling over the bed. She didn't have old eyes. Glaring. Staring eyes. She hadn't spoken. Her bed was next to mine. The thin plastic flowery curtain separated our worlds. I felt her eyes watching. Watching watching watching. Not blinking. She was staring in through the crack. Where the curtain didn't meet the wall. The light was blocked. She penetrated. Her eyes telling me stories. Nasty nasty stories. They were screaming out of her eyes. She was watching. Fear. Panic panic panic. Alone. Really really alone. No safe place. I needed my safe place. Out of control. She had no voice. Just staring. Glaring. Burrowing in with her laser eyes. Burning her story into the side of my face. Turning my cheeks red. Ruby red.

In the middle of the night. For the first seventeen nights. My neighbour pushed her bed out of her cubicle and into the corridor. Scraping. Grinding across the floor. Scratching. Scratching. Scrape scrape scrape. I lay awake. Too frightened to close my eyes. On day eighteen she forced plastic into her mouth. Down her throat. And she choked. I heard her choke. She was dead by the time the nurse finally noticed. They found sixteen pieces of a Walkers Salt and Shake crisp packet in her bedside locker. Each cut into a perfect square. The nurse threw them into the bin. I took them out. One two three four five six seven eight nine ten eleven twelve thirteen fourteen fifteen sixteen. I kept them in my blue cylinder tin.

**Exhibit number five –**
**sixteen squares of plastic.**

The noise was constant. It didn't change with the light. They. The patients. They communicated through squeals and high-pitched wails. They sang to each other. Symphonies. Crescendos. Loudening. Maintaining the climax. Always at climax. They reminded each other that they were near. Playing parts in a well-rehearsed show. Locked in together. All of us locked in together. The screams. The wails. The cries. Combined. Rebounded around the white rooms and out along the white corridor. An unhappy tune that told of the pain and the confusion that had led us all to end up on Ward 23.

The sadness penetrated me. By day twenty-one, their sadness had climbed into me and made friends with my own. Added to my madness. I shifted my view of the world. I watched. I learned. I learned so very much on Ward 23. Moira told me too many things. Tips and techniques that no sane person would share. I was eighteen years, seven months old and twenty-one days, when I learned the easiest and most effective ways to commit suicide.

> *Don't slash your wrists. Too many scars and too messy.*
> *Good chance you'll survive or change your mind in*
> *the middle. Hanging is out. Light fittings fall. They're*
> *not strong enough. Moira had fallen sixteen times.*
> *Shooting is no good. Relies too much on bravery.*
> *And strength to pull the trigger. Not a female method.*
> *Tablets. Sleeping tablets. Strong tablets. Lots of them.*
> *With alcohol. Alone. Where you won't be disturbed.*

*That's the easiest way. Though jumping in front of a*
*train is a guarantee.*

# Derek

He used to be a headmaster. Moira told me that. He taught
Geography in the local grammar school. He had had a breakdown
in the middle of a lesson. Hit a pupil. Broke his nose. It had been
in the paper. The local paper. On Ward 23 he walked. He strode
up and down the long corridor. Up and down. Up and down.
Patrolled. Head held high. Eyes straight ahead. He didn't speak. He
didn't alter his gaze.

I sat next to the window in the visitor's room. A big glass window
that looked out onto the corridor. A strip of blue carpet ran down the
middle. I watched Derek. Up. Down. Up and down. I counted.
Twenty-seven seconds down. Thirty-two seconds up. I watched his
determination. His need to reach somewhere. He marched. Up and
down. Up and down. His hair was jet back. He couldn't have
been old. His eyes told me that something was wrong. Something
had frightened him. He was like me. He lived in the same world as
me. A sad world.

Derek's eyes carried secrets that I would never know. Derek didn't
speak. Not a word. He was tall. He was proud. He dressed in a navy
blue suit and a white shirt. No shoes. Just socks. Every day. He
was smart. He was voiceless. I never heard his accent. I imagined
that he was posh. That his accent was swish like Aunty Maggie's.

245

I watched his feet. Huge feet. I sat and I watched him. Up and down. Up and down. Shoeless feet. Dark socks to match his suit. A proud man.

Every Saturday Derek's wife and two boys came to visit. Derek wore shoes for his boys. They sat around the wooden circular table in the visitor's room. Derek connected his palms. Locked his hands ready to pray. He lowered his eyes and he rocked. Gently. Controlled. His feet moved under the table. Tiny steps. Up and down. Up and down. I watched him. Derek never spoke. I strained to hear his voice. But he never spoke. Gentle rocking. Backwards and forwards. Rhythmic. Tip tap tapping. After a strained hour. A nervous hour of his two young boys trying to tell stories. Connecting eyes with their mother for help. For reassurance. They talked to their mother. They talked for their father. For Derek. After an hour they stood to leave. Derek walked to door with them. I saw their relief. Splashed across their faces. I saw his relief. Splashed across his eyes. He smiled. A real smile. His family left him. Derek's hands returned to his sides. His shoes already left under the wooden table in the visitor's room. Another Saturday over. Derek could return to his patrol. Up and down. Up and down. Up and down.

I went to the toilet. I locked the door.

I never saw a doctor. Not once. The nurses watched. They talked in hush hush tones and they built a file. A yellow file of observations. With my name and hospital number on the front. I wasn't allowed to read it. I wanted to. I wanted to know what they were writing about me. The nurses tried to note everything that I ate, that I drank and how many times I went to the toilet. They asked me if I was sick. I lied. They scribbled my lies. It was humiliating.

Then. Once a week they would weigh me. Make me stand on the scales. I was terrified. Terrified that I would put on weight. That I would put on an ounce. An ounce in a week. Then. Then they'd think me cured. Then. Then they'd tell me to leave Ward 23. I couldn't let that happen. Every week they noted my weight. In front of me. I felt sick. Real sick. I made sure that my weight always went down. It wasn't a challenge. It was a need. So. So they recorded. Kept record. They focused on consumption. On food and drink. They focused on the surface. Not really sure what to do with me. Not sure why I had something called Bulimia Nervosa. Not sure how to cure me. Not really sure. They didn't understand. They thought that I should just stop being sick. That I could just stop. If I wanted to. But I couldn't. I really couldn't. I had forgotten how to eat. I had forgotten how to enjoy food. They thought that I wasn't quite normal. They were right. I wasn't normal. *A reet strange bairn.* I'm not normal. But they never asked the questions. They never allowed the words to escape from me. They never realised that I was trying to communicate. Sicking up the words that I couldn't voice. Trying in the only way that I could find. Trying to tell them all the things that were eating away inside of me. Eating their way through me. Being on Ward 23 made me question normal. Being on Ward 23 made me wish that someone would help me to use words.

Sunday was always cream cake day. Sunday was Ward 23's highlight of the week. I had to sit and watch them. I was forced to watch everyone eat. Apparently. Being around food would make me better. Abracadabra. Wave the magic wand. And. Poof. Jude is better. We were all pushed into the visitor's room. A dull metal trolley was clunked in. Clink clank clunk. The cups and saucers rattle rattled as the trolley clunked. On it was afternoon tea. A stainless steel cake display. Smothered in cream cakes. Thirty sticky chocolate éclairs. Oozing with fresh cream. Pots of tea and coffee. China cups and saucers. No knives. A wave of excitement swept around the room. We sat. The patients sat. Waiting. Anticipating. Dribbling. Rocking. Mumbling. Scratching. Screaming. Waiting.

Always the same. Days blurred into one. Not Sundays. Cream cake day was different. Time no longer had meaning. Time tick tocked in the real world. I had escaped. I existed without ticking and tocking and chiming and rushing and worrying. Measure was removed. Schedule was removed. I escaped beyond the cuckoo. We had sold our clocks. We had abandoned our minds. Free. No rules. No boundaries. Free. Except on Sunday.

Every Sunday. I had to sit with them. Around the round wooden tables. I had to watch them grabbing the cakes. Pushing. Shoving each other out of the way. Grab grab grabbing. They fingered the cakes with their dirty fat fingers. I had to watch them. Always fifteen of us. Me and fourteen others. Pushing full éclairs into their mouths. The cream rushed to the end. It oozed. It fell to the table. It fell onto their clothes. It fell onto the floor. Some licked it from the table. Some left it on their clothes. Some licked it from the floor. Tongues. Moving tongues. Food-covered tongues. Others scooped the cream onto their fingers. Eyes twinkling with excitement. Dollops of fluffy cream topped their fingertips.

I watched them. I watched them suck and lick. Slurping. Chomping. Mouths open. Mouths wide. Teeth showing. Chewing like horses. I watched the disgusting blobs of fat-filled cream sticking to their dirty faces. Covering their dirty faces. I watched the food being twirled around their mouths. I wanted to shout. You're all dirty dirty. Close your mouths when you eat. I wanted to scream and throw plates around the room. I wanted to climb onto the table and jump. Jump jump jump. Jumping till the table strained and buckled under my weight. I wanted to scream. Really really scream. The nurses were torturing me. They are driving me to madness. I wasn't getting better. I was learning. I was learning too much. I was blending into my environment.

I was a chameleon. I am a chameleon.

One Sunday. *No date. No date.* I picked up the fattest éclair. Finger prints screamed out from the chocolate. I closed my eyes. I blocked out the dirty dirty finger prints. I shoved the éclair into my mouth. Push push. Chocolate and cream oozed. Escaped. Decorated my face. Two each. I counted them all. Thirty cream cakes. There had been enough for two each. I had four. They wouldn't mind. They

249

couldn't mind. Some of them couldn't even count anymore. No rules. No manners. Eat eat eat. I hated the madness. I hated me.

I went to the toilet. I locked the door. I was sick.

# Simon

He arrived one day. Replaced my dead neighbour. I recognised Simon from the estate. He lived on Gladstone Street. The next street up from Disraeli Avenue. He was nearly two years older than me. He was nearly twenty-one. He had bright ginger hair and pale blue eyes. He looked quite normal. He was tall. He walked around in shorts. He had legs like Barry Venison. Played football three times a week. Supported Sunderland like my father. He acted normal. He seemed quite normal. Made me smile with rhymes and jokes. Made me feel happy. Then. He talked with absolute pride of how he had died for three minutes. He had taken an overdose.

Pip

pop

pip

pop

pip

pop.

Had found his dad in bed with their male lodger. *Sick bastards the two of them.* I didn't understand. He told me that he hadn't meant to kill himself. *Wanted to give the bastard a shock.* But. He told me that the thrill of dying was addictive. I didn't understand. I didn't understand. He was only staying in for a day or two. Simon told me that he wanted to keep in touch after he left hospital. He wanted to be my friend. But. That he wasn't sure if that would be possible. He still wanted to die. He told me not to tell anyone. Hush hush. Swirling secrets. He was tricking the nurses so that he could be discharged. Clever lad. He was my friend. He gave me a big hug when he left. He said he'd be in touch soon.

Two sleeps later he died.

A nurse told me. They had expected him back on the ward. But. But he died on the way to the hospital. A bottle of tablets and a bottle of vodka. It worked every time. I hadn't told. I let my friend die.

# Gordon

Gordon was small and funny looking. He was tiny and had a tummy that must have had a baby in it. He was twenty-eight. He was ten years older than me. Gordon had tattoos covering every inch of his right arm. Words. Mainly words. He did some of them himself. A needle and ink. They were faded. Dirty. Blue. He lived in a Bed and Breakfast in Whitley Bay. Gordon liked to cut himself. Apparently. A bread knife did the trick. Faint lines glistened across his right arms. Over the tattoos. Cuts. Still raw. Spread across the tops of his thighs. He had tried to kill himself too. Seventeen times. He was classed as dangerous. Gordon was on Ward 23 like me. He had a girlfriend who was married. She came to visit with her child. But. She never stayed long and afterwards Gordon was put into the padded cell.

Gordon told me that he fancied me. Fear. I was thin. I was beautiful. My hair was lovely. My eyes were canny. *Let me fuck you.* He was desperate to fuck me. I didn't know what to do. I couldn't escape him. I had to like him too. I had no choice. I had nowhere to hide.

When I went to the toilet he followed me. I couldn't lock the door. He told me to lie on the floor. It was cold. It was dirty. It was covered in drops of pee. Mad people's pee. The coldness seeped into my body. I was frozen. I lay and I watched him. I felt nothing for him. He pushed down his zip and took it out. It was small and stumpy. Snapped within his stumpy fingers. I looked at it. I looked at him. He told me that he loved me. I would have to love him too. He pushed up my nightshirt. He pulled off my knickers. *Let me fuck you. Let me fuck you.*

I opened my legs. I let him. I didn't scream. I didn't make a sound. He was quick. I felt him graze into me. I didn't care. I was frozen. An ice queen. Short. Sharp. Thrusts. Hard. Hard. Quick. Quick quick. He groaned. He tried to pull it out. Thick yellow lumps. Inside me. Onto my stomach. Onto my nightshirt. He stood. He pushed it back into his pants. Zip zip zip.

He left me. I lay still.

Coldness tingled me. I stood. Thick dribbles. Lumpy. Tumbled down my inner thigh. Rolled down my naked leg and landed on the floor. I left it there. Next to the mad people's pee. I wiped myself with the crunchy sharp toilet tissue. I felt tender. Grazed down there. In there. I pushed my crumbled pink cotton knickers into my clenched hand and I returned to the visitor's room.

The next morning he phoned his girlfriend. He told her that I liked him and that I wanted him to fuck me. She told him that she was going to kill me. He told me that she called me *a skinny bitch*. I liked that I was a skinny bitch. I didn't like Gordon. I had nowhere to hide. Gordon was going to keep on doing things to me in the toilet. No one cared. No one stopped him. I didn't care. I was frozen.

We were told that our ward was to have a party. An Easter disco. Shock. Confusion. Amusement. A chance for us all to wear silly hats and dance around to Agadoo and the Birdie Song. After all. We were mad. Music played. No one heard it. We all had our own noises swirling around inside our heads. Soundtracks played into our worlds. I hated music. Music was too loud. Music interfered with my sounds. My in-head sounds. I sat and I watched. Fourteen of us. I wondered who would be next to visit the mortuary.

# Chris

Chris arrived. He was in a wheelchair. He had broken both of his legs. He had driven into a wall. Had wanted to die. He was twenty. Drove into a wall to die. He was quiet and I liked him. I sat and I talked to him. He was nice. He was sad like me. I didn't want to kiss him. I didn't want to touch him. I just wanted to talk to him. His face was covered in spots. Big-headed spots. Oozing. Yellow heads. Picked. Pocked. I didn't want to touch him. I didn't want his face near to mine. I wanted to talk. I wanted to tell him about Eddie. I wanted to tell him about Gordon. He was good at listening. He was soft. Gentle. Kind. Chris didn't understand. He thought that if I talked to him. Then. Then I must have wanted to be his girlfriend. I thought that he was the same as me. His mother was dead like mine. She had taken tablets to die. I thought that he understood. He wanted me to be his girlfriend. I didn't want to be. I didn't want his face next to mine. I didn't want to be anyone's girlfriend. I didn't know what to do. I didn't know how to say no. I didn't know what to say.

## No no no no no no no no no no.

I stayed in my cubicle. I sat on the bed. Nowhere to hide. The nurse came in. I was a tease. Tease tease tease. I should not talk to Chris again. He was depressed. He was suicidal. I didn't understand. I had not helped. I had teased him. I had talked to him. I didn't understand. I just wanted a friend. I knew his sadness. He was like me. He was alone like me.

Rita, my father and Crystal went to Spain. On a plane. They made the most of my time locked up. They were able to fit in their first-ever trip abroad. They'd taken Crystal out of school. For a quick week in the sun. I was in the best place. No harm would come to me. I would be safe. They needed a break. They'd had a stressful few months. They'd had a stressful few years. Looking after me. Dealing with my problems. It'd be nice for them to get away as a family. To be able to have fun. Without me. Without my problems. I was a problem. I am a problem.

I was allowed out. While Rita, my father and Crystal were in the sunshine. I was allowed out. The nurses thought it best that I start leaving the hospital. Ready for when I was discharged. I wasn't getting any better. I wasn't getting any worse. Best I go out a bit. I needed to try and breathe in the normal air. Couldn't stay in hospital forever. I was allowed to walk around the hospital grounds. It was a sunny day. I was told to stay in the hospital grounds though. Not far from the Mortuary.

I caught a bus instead.

* * * * *

I decided to go back to Disraeli Avenue. I wanted to collect something. Something to help me.

My mother's house was empty. My father, Rita and Crystal were still in Spain. The spare key. Under the large rock. Next to the rose bush. Was obvious. Predictable. I let myself in. I took off my shoes and I felt the soft red carpet on my bare soles. The house was full of a stale smoke smell. A familiar smell. A secure smell. My mother's house was cold. Silent and cold. I needed the silence. I needed the calm.

I walked up the stairs. Memories of those red stairs jumped around inside my head. Images flicked. Then hid. Away away.

I looked in Crystal's room. It was once my mother and father's. Now it was pink. Posters of Care Bears. Of princesses. In beautiful dresses. It wasn't tidy. It wasn't perfect. Lived in. Allowed to be lived in. The box room. Now my room. A single bed. A wardrobe. A bookshelf. A stool in the corner. No posters. My room. My lonely space. Secrets under my bed. And in my head.

I lived in a family home. Their family home. I was hardly ever there. My room was where I slept. Close to work. My room was where I stayed out of their way. But still close. Close to Crystal.

I went into the bathroom. Stood on the linoleum floor. In the centre of the room. Looked into the pea green bath. I faced the bathroom cabinet. I looked into the mirror. So pale. No makeup. Pale. Sad. Sad staring eyes. I opened the cabinet. Looking for that thing to help me. I took a bottle of paracetemol. One hundred tablets. I walked into the box room. Lay on my stomach. On the green carpet. Feet sticking out of the doorway. I stretched under my bed. Pulled out my mother's box. Adam's coffin.

I walked back down the red stairs. Picked up the telephone. Off its round table. Phoned for a taxi. Five minutes to wait. I sat on the bottom red step. Waiting. Counting. Eight minutes and ten seconds later. The Kingcab picked me up from outside the house. Mrs Russell (Number 10) saw me. Mrs Symons (Number 11) saw me. Mrs Lancaster (Number 7) saw me too. I smiled at her. I had given Mr Lancaster a blow job once. In the toilet at The Traveller's

Rest. Five pounds eighty-nine pence. I waved at Mrs Lancaster. She would tell her husband that she had seen me. The Kingcab left Disraeli Avenue. I went back to hospital.

I was away for seventy-two minutes. *Must get back. Must get back. Quick quick.* I needed to be on time. I followed the signs. *Ward 24. Mortuary. Ward 23.* I walked past the mortuary. I understood. I pressed the intercom.

Buzz buzzzzzzzz.

The door opened.

Slam bang bang.

I carried a white plastic bag. Containing Adam's box and my tablets. I wasn't searched. No one said hello. No questions. So. I carried on along the blue carpet. Avoided Derek's route. Alert alert. Very important mad person approaching. Alert alert. Derek patrolled. Walked past me. I walked back to my cubicle.

I sat on the iron bed. Carefully. Carefully. I removed Adam's box from the creased plastic bag. The box. It had once contained shoes. My mother loved shoes. I loved shoes. The box had been altered. It had been personalised. My mother had such an artistic flair. I didn't. There were tiny painted footprints. Not prints of a foot. They were perfectly painted feet. A memory of Adam's foot that my

257

mother had captured. There were glittering stars. Shooting stars. Shining. Sprinkled with a shimmer. An apple tree was drawn in black charcoal. A snake wrapped around the trunk. All down one side of the box. It was so beautiful. I had never noticed the snake before. His tongue was long. Curled. Pointed. A blond curl was glued onto the box. Such a beautiful box. The lid. The roof to her house of secrets. Delicate italics embodied his name.

*Adam.*

Perched on the edge of the iron bed. I placed the beautiful box in front of me. Gently. It was so delicate. So perfect. I placed it onto the white stretched blanket. Covering the 23. Blocking out the imprinted blue ink.

Straight-backed. Stiff. I opened the box and took out each tiny item. Laid them in a straight line.

Blue booties. Hand knitted. Tiny.
A curl. Blond. In a plastic money bag. Blue letters and numbers on the plastic.
Hospital wrist band. Black biro.
*Adam Williams. 13-12-1967.*
A black and white photograph. Blue biro on the back.
*Adam. Aged 2 weeks old.*
A knitted hat. Blue. Satin ribbon ties. Straight. Never tied.
A hand-sewn teddy. Brown. A button for a nose. Never cuddled.

A letter. Already read.

A diary. Spoken words.

A birth certificate.

*Mother Sarah Williams. Father Bill Williams.*

A death certificate.

*Adam Williams. 29-6-1968.*

I opened my mother's diaries. I read her words. I skimmed. I read. I knew them. I knew them by heart. By shape. By page. The words danced around in my head. Rehearsed words in a well-performed play. I knew those words. They pulled my life together. They tied me with a big pink bow.

Adam. It was all about Adam.

I lifted the bottle of paracetamol out of the plastic bag. I took out eighty tablets. Counted them into piles of five. One two three four five. One two three four five. Left the other twenty in the bottle. Spilling from the bottle. I poured cloudy water. From my bedside jug. Into a plastic beaker.

pip
pop
pip pop
pip.

Gulp gulp gulp.

pop
pip
pop
pip
pop.


Gulp gulp gulp.

pip
pop
       pip
           pop
               pip.

                   Gag gag gag.
                   pop

pip pop
       pip
           pop.
Stop stop stop.

               pip
pop
       pip
           pop
               pip.

                   Keep going. Must keep going.
                   pop
                   pip

                pop
           pip
     pop.

                   Gulp gulp gulp.

pip
pop
pip
     pop
           pip
           pop
                pip pop
                   pip pop.

Quick quick quick.

pip     pop     pip     pop     pip.

                           Gag gag gag.

pop pip pop pip pop pip pop pip pop pip.

Keep going. Must keep going.

pip
     pop
           pip
                pop
                   pip
                       pop.

pip

pop

pip

pop

pip

pop

pip

pop

pip

pop

pip

pop

pip

pop.

The powdery bitterness makes me gag.

Gag gag gag.

I fought myself.

*Keep going. Must keep going.*

I forced myself to swallow.

pip
pop
pip
pop
pip.

* * * * *

There was a lighthouse.
There is a lighthouse.

Sits proud on a mountain of rocks. Safe. Tall. Swollen with pride. Scans and shines. Scans and shines. Scans and shines. Flashing out words of warning. Telling passers-by that the eye is watching. Watching. Watching. Always watching. There is a lighthouse. White. Erect. Tall. Proud. Shouting out. Stop. Stop. Stop. Telling passers-by to behave. Restraining. Controlling. Protecting. Yellow eye watching. Always watching.

Below the cliff. Standing tall. Emerging from the rocks. The throne of rocks. There is a lighthouse. The sea laps and licks and gushes and slurps. The sea bows at the feet of the lighthouse. Admiration. Love. Fear. Fear of the all knowing, all watching, all controlling. Fear of the slender white lighthouse.

Inside thousands and millions of tiny people hustle and bustle and scurry and scamper. Moved by a need. Controlled by that need. A need to protect. A duty to serve. Watching. Turning. Scanning. Round and round and round and round and round. Protecting. Preventing. Watching. Always watching. Knights of

the Royal Lighthouse. Serving. Life saving. Watching
watching watching.

I was there.


I was on the tiny curve of land.
The banana-shaped bay.
Two piers.
One at each end.
One lighthouse, beyond the left pier, standing tall on the jagged
rocks.

                                                        Waiting.
I was there.


Being tricked into the cave. Being promised
treasure.
Being lured to my knees. Being promised a map.
Being filled with sand.

I was there.


The light was off.
Must have been a royal event.
A national holiday. A day of rest. They failed. Those
thousands and millions and billions of tiny men with
green skin and orange hair.

They failed to protect.
To prevent.

To watch.
To warn.
To save.

>They failed to shine their light.
>They failed to give me light.

No shining.
No saviour.
Nothing unto me.

>Nothing apart from Eddie.

They failed.

>There is a lighthouse. In Lymouth Bay.

\* \* \* \* \*

A nurse found me. Someone had told her. Someone had seen. It hadn't been long. I was conscious. Lying on my bed. My mother's box. My mother's secrets. Curling into me. I was walked to the emergency department. I heard her talking to the other nurses. *Another overdose. Put my pie and chips in the microwave.* She wasn't impressed. I wasn't impressed.

*Drink this.*

Cups and cups of a salty liquid. I didn't speak. I didn't say a word. Gulp gulp gulp.

Sick.

      Sick.

            Sick.

                  Sick.

Not nice sick. Not my controlled sick.

Sick.

      Sick.

            Sick.

Escaped from me. Carried the tablets out of me. Carried the words shooting. A waterfall of tablets, of water, of salt, of words. Carried the eighty tablets from me and into the cardboard bedpan. Over the cardboard bedpan and onto the floor.

I had no control.

I had to let them escape. I had to let them. The nurses. The patients. I had to let them rescue me. Saved from death. I had no choice.

* * * * *

Three days later the nurse asked the question.
*Why Jude? Why do it?*
Silence.
*Did you realise the dangers?*
Silence.

*You wouldn't die instantly, you know? It'd take days. They'd eat*
*away at your internal organs and you'd die ... slowly ... painfully.*

She liked the words *slowly* and *painfully*. She left a pause. A
pregnant silence. Before uttering the words. They made her smile.
I watched her smile.

She was sitting at the end of my bed. The spare tablets had been
removed and no one was asking where I had managed to get them
from. The box of my mother's things had been taken for *safe keeping*.
No one asked any questions. They didn't ask the right questions.
They didn't ask. They should have asked the right questions. They
should have wanted to clear out my mind. They should have wanted
to make me better. But. They didn't. They didn't care. They didn't
want to care. No room for humanity on Ward 23. The place was
overcrowded already.

*Jude?*
Silence.
*What now Jude?*
- I want to discharge myself.

I had broken my silence.

I wanted to go back to my mother's house. Back to work. Back
to my money. They couldn't stop me. I wasn't sectioned. They
couldn't section me. They wouldn't. They were happy to let me go.

Happy to have one less patient. Happy. No visit to the mortuary. A success story for Ward 23.

I agreed to have counselling. I agreed to go on the six-month waiting list and attend the block of six sessions. I agreed. That would make me better. Counselling was the solution. The only solution. I told them that I hadn't wanted to die. I was attention seeking. I wouldn't do it again. I lied.

I escaped the hell hole.

\* \* \* \* \*

Ward 23. One hundred and nineteen days.
Weight on entry.
Eight stone four.
Weight on exit.
Seven stone two.
Time: 3:26pm.

\* \* \* \* \*

Exhibit number six –
my hospital wrist band.

\* \* \* \* \*

- I'm coming out.
I spoke into the receiver. Silence. Silence.
- Dad?
*Ah heard ye.* He spoke in his usual dull monotone.

- I need to talk about Adam.

Silence.

*Are ye gettin a taxi home?*

He broke the silence. Home. Home. Home. I had no home. I have no home. Home is what other people have. The Johnsons (Number 19). Mrs Hodgson and Paul (formerly Number 2). My father, Rita and Crystal (Number 9). I didn't have a home. My roots flip flapped in the breeze. I travelled in a taxi to my mother's house. Forcing Rita and my father out of their holiday glow.

I got in the taxi. A pilgrimage to my mother's house. The diary entries flip flopped. Refreshed memories. Eddie was spinning in there too. My mother stood awfully still. And Adam. His tiny body. His murder. The images filled my head. They climbed the inside of my mind. My mother killed Adam. My mother killed my brother. My life would have been so very different. Adam made my mother kill herself. Adam made my mother drink. Adam made my mother leave me. He let Eddie enter me. Adam had helped Eddie.

Adam.
Adam.
Adam.

It was all about Adam. I needed to find a way to stop the whirling inside of my head.

The taxi pulled into Disraeli Avenue. Sweat dripped down my back. Panic. Panic. Panic. Disraeli Avenue was different now. I saw the houses, the people and the number plates with the eyes of an adult. With the eyes of someone who could see and could understand.

The semi-detached houses were small. Very small. They were too close to each other. Resembled terraces. Dirty. Old. Decaying and out of fashion. Graffiti decorated the street sign. A local tagger had made his mark. In green spray paint.

The estate had gone downhill. It had aged.

Aunty Maggie (Number 30) had died. Four years ago. She'd had cancer for years. Refused treatment. No one had known. I didn't go to her funeral. I didn't want to see Eddie. I didn't mourn her death. She left me fifty pounds in her will. I spent it on Crystal. Bought her a brown Care Bear with a red heart on its tummy. Bought her an atlas and the complete works of Roald Dahl. I slipped them into her pink room. She noticed only the Care Bear. Big smiles. Big hugs. Aunty Maggie's house had a young couple in it now. Kept themselves to themselves. Had a brand new silver car. They were rich. Didn't really fit in. Rita reckoned that they wouldn't stay in the street very long. *Too far up their own arses. Think they're better than us.* They put in new windows. A month after they moved in. Double glazed. And they knocked down the dwarf wall. Put up a shiny metal fence instead. It made Aunty Maggie's house look nicer. Different.

Mrs Roberts (Number 21) had gone around and filled the young couple in on all that had happened over the last 20 years. Told them all about the community and how close the neighbours were. Too close. Watching each other's every move. Waiting for a mistake. Waiting for something to gossip about.

Rita liked to gossip. Rita had always liked to gossip. I knew secrets about every one of the neighbours. I knew too many secrets. Rita had told me that Mr Johnson (Number 19) was now a proud grandfather. Lucy. One of his pretty daughters had had a baby at 15. Nearly 16. They kept it a secret. She had been sent to live with Mrs Johnson's sister in Wallsend. She didn't get to complete her GCSEs, but she was doing well. Still living in Wallsend with her little girl. It was supposed to be a secret. Everyone knew. Mr Johnson's other daughter. Karen. She was rumoured to be making erotic films. Apparently. One of the neighbours knew someone who had watched *Suzie Sucks*. Rita had delighted in that gem of tattle. Karen Johnson was always destined for big things. Rita quite fancied the thought of being a film star.

Rita told me that Mrs Roberts (Number 21) had had an affair with Mr Johnson. That was old news. It had gone on for years. Apparently. They had had Timothy's blood tested and found out that they had had a little boy together. Timothy Roberts. Mrs Johnson had never found out. Mr Roberts had never found out. But. But the whole street knew about it. *Such a close community*. The neighbours watched Mrs Roberts. They were worried that

271

she would set her sights on another one of their husbands. *Such a close community.*

Rita told me that Mrs Hodgson (Number 2) had moved onto the new estate. She had moved into a new house. Detached. Three double bedrooms. No one spoke to her anymore. Apparently. She thought herself better than them. She'd met a nice new man. No kids of his own and loads of money. Paul Hodgson was going to university. He was studying law. He had escaped. Mrs Hodgson had escaped. They had hope.

My mother's house was nestled in among the incest. In among the lack of morality and the judgmental glares. Rita and my father enjoyed their home and although they could afford to move on, they preferred not to. They liked the community feel. They believed in the community feel. They liked their neighbours. They thought they liked the neighbours. They were all so close. Too close. In and out of each others' lives. Waiting for downfalls. Waiting for pain. Waiting for a chance to gossip. To yack. To yackety yack yack yack. Rita didn't know what I did in the toilets of The Traveller's Rest. The other neighbours will have known. But. Rita didn't realise that Number 9 Disraeli Avenue was brimming with dirty scandal too.

Crystal would be coming home from school. New Lymouth Primary School. I hadn't seen her all the time that I was in hospital. Rita didn't want her to go to the nuthouse. I longed to see my baby sister again. Pangs of excitement and guilt. She'd be home soon.

I needed to talk to my father before Crystal came home. Crystal shouldn't know.

The taxi pulled in front of the house. Close to the lamppost. The one that used to flame. Pulled the wheel onto the pavement, so as not to block the whole road. Nearly hitting the dwarf wall. Everything was so small. Miniature-sized living. My father and Rita rose to the window. Strained expressions. Hands held. I climbed out of the taxi, grabbed my black bag of secrets and closed the taxi door. Rita and my father moved together, out of the front room and into the hall. The front door opened before I reached it.

*Come on in Jude dear. God you're aal skin an bones.* Rita dared to speak.

I glared at her. She was a roly poly. She was baking a cake. A welcome home cake. She smiled at me. She had wanted to hug me. Put her fat stumpy hands onto my back and pitter pat pat me. I wouldn't let her. I would never forget. I glowered. I hated her. I went into my mother's front room.

Rita coughed. Clearing her throat. I turned and glared at her. She was squidgy. Chubby. Squashy. Not in a nice way. She was wearing a black ra-ra skirt. With a pink lycra body on underneath. The type with poppers at the crotch. It held in her lumps and bumps. I tried not to laugh. Her eye shadow was bright pink. To match her outfit. It made her eyes look all puffy and infected. And she wore chunky black plastic beads. To finish off the look. Rita scurried off to make a cup of tea. I stood very still. Very straight. Just in front of Rita's sofa.

*Now, Jude pet. It's aal in the past. Best buried with yer mam, don't yee think?*
I gave out a cackle.
*Now Jude pet. Divvent be fuckin daft.*

He was holding out. Didn't want to chitter chatter. Didn't want the past dragging up. Hauling up. Yanking up. I needed to drag and pull. I needed to open two coffins. The past was my present. I couldn't live. The past was smothering me. Covering my thoughts. Draining my happiness. I didn't know how to feel. No feelings. No emotion. Nothing. I didn't know how to smile. I didn't know how to laugh. Couldn't let myself go. Couldn't relax. Not for a moment. My guard. My eyes. Watching. Always watching. I didn't know how to live. My father broke my thoughts.

*Adam died a long time ago. A wee lad who died. Ah'm sorry that yee found oot about him, but there really is nothin te be gained by dragging this up now.*

He sat down into his chair.

- My mam left me a note.
*What d' yee mean she left yee a note?*

274

He spoke with an aggressive twinge. He was scared. I knew that he was scared.

- She left me two notes.

I bent to the floor. Delved into my bag. My big black hospital bag. Took out my tin. It used to be my father's. A navy blue cylinder tin. It had a gold trim and E$^{\text{II}}$R in gold lettering. I pulled off the lid. It was tight. Still tight. I placed the six exhibits onto the coffee table.

```
        Exhibit number one -
          my mother's note.

        Exhibit number two -
      sticker from nice nurse.

       Exhibit number three -
           Eddie's cigar.

        Exhibit number four -
        my collection of nits.

        Exhibit number five -
      sixteen squares of plastic.

        Exhibit number six -
       my hospital wrist band.
```

My father didn't speak. My father didn't ask. Not one question. He looked. He absorbed. He didn't speak. He didn't ask the question. I shoved the crumpled note to him **(Exhibit 1)**. His cheeks burned. Red red red. Steam rose from them.

*Where'd yee get this from?*

Demanding. Demanding. My father was always a demanding man.

- The morning she died. I took a bin bag too. One that you decided to throw away. Put in the garage. You know, after the funeral.

## *Of course Ah fuckin remember me missus' funeral.*

Too many sssssssssssSSSSSSSSSSSS. Too many sssssssssssSSSSSSSSSSSS. He was angry. Really angry. I had to calm him. I had to calm him. I needed answers. I needed to stay in control. Calm calm calm.

- Didn't you notice her things gone?
Silence
- I hid the bag. I took it and hid it in my room. Buried it in my basket of teddies.
*Yee had nah reet te take hor things?*
- It was my note. It was mine. You had no right to get rid of my mam's stuff.

I was calm. I stared at him. No longer scared. He couldn't hurt me anymore. There was nothing more that he could do to me. I had nothing. I was nothing. I am nothing. But. But I wasn't weak. Not anymore. I watched him squirm. Rita stood by the doorway to my mother's front room. A tray shaking in her hands. She was listening. She knew what was coming.

- I know *all* about Adam.

Silence.

- My mam kept a diary.

Silence. His eyes glued to his locked palms.

- Why didn't you tell me about Adam? Why didn't you tell me about my brother?

*Ah was protecting yee.*

- Well you did a crap job. I knew there was an Adam. I heard all about him at your da's funeral. Until then Adam was my hope. I thought that my mam had gone on a journey and that she'd bring Adam back with her. I thought that Adam would be someone special.

Tears streamed down my face. Rita moved into the room.

**- NO.**

I shouted at the nasty nasty woman. My words forced her to stay where she was. Rooted to her spot. Quivering in the doorway. She was frightened. She wasn't sure what I would do next.

- This is nothing to do with you.

Silence. My father slumped back further into his chair.

- I needed you. I needed your love. I needed you to protect me from her.

I pointed my index finger toward Rita. She quiver quiver quivered a little bit more. I was in control. Not inside. But they didn't realise that.

- You failed me and you failed my mam.

I screamed. My words jumped around the room. Jumped and danced and bounced and leaped. Twirling round and round. My words danced.

- Is this making you uncomfortable? Well, I'm sorry if you don't like it, but I need to hear it. I need to hear the truth.

I shoved my hands into my jeans' pocket. They were shaking. I shivered. I trembled. He was not to see my weakness. Rita had not moved. She was deep-rooted to the spot. She was not defiant. She was scared. She didn't know me. She feared what I was capable of. I had power. I had sweat. I was dripping.

Drip.

Drip.

# Dripping

under my hair. Down my neck.

Down my back.

## Down my front.

Collecting under my breasts. I needed to carry on. I needed to know. I needed to calm down before my baby sister came home from school. She must not know.

I bent to my bag. Again. Stooped. Knees quivering. Hands sweaty. Delved into my bag. My big black hospital bag. I took Adam's box.

I placed it onto the coffee table. I stayed near to the table. Near to my treasures. Rita still shook holding the tray of tea. Adam's box. On the coffee table. In my mother's front room. My father stared at it. Memories. A tiny coffin of memories. His and my mother's memories. He had seen the box before.

## Slowly.

Slowly I removed the fragile lid. They were not to touch my box.
Slowly.
Slowly I removed each tiny object. Item by item. I placed them around the box. Framing. Edging.


Blue booties. Hand knitted. Tiny.

A curl. Blond. In a plastic money bag. Blue letters and numbers on the plastic.

Hospital wrist band. Black biro. *Adam Williams. 13-12-1967.*

A black and white photograph. Blue biro on the back. *Adam. Aged 2 weeks old.*

A knitted hat. Blue. Satin ribbon ties. Straight. Never tied.

A hand-sewn teddy. Brown. A button for a nose. Not cuddled.

A letter. Read.

A diary. Unspoken words. Read.

A birth certificate. *Mother Sarah Williams. Father Bill Williams.*

A death certificate. *Adam Williams. 29-6-1968.*

A tiny coffin of secrets.

My father's eyes filled with tears.

- No. Don't you dare. Don't you dare. I need you to be strong. I need you to be a father.

*Adam.*

My father spoke. His eyes were glazed. Sad. Really really sad. He stared at the items. His eyes fixed. Sadness. Deep. Real. True sadness. His eyes willed the items to be alive. His eyes willed them to spring into action. To become something.

- Tell me. I need to know.

My father coughed. To clear the lump from his throat. The lump of Adam from his throat. Then he spoke. Just like that. No need to ask twice.

*Wi didn't have a phone an lived in a flat. Wi were on the sixth floor an the fuckin lift niwor worked.*

My father paused and nodded to Rita. I heard her scurrying with the tray. I heard her place her best china on the kitchen side. I heard her scurrying back. An obese mouse. Unable to sneak. She came in and hovered on the arm of my father's chair. She didn't touch him. She nodded for him to continue. I was still standing. I felt my knees weakening. I needed to sit. I needed support. I moved to the sofa. Rita's sofa.

*Adam was born on the thirteenth Decemba, twelve days before*
*Christmas. He was reet handsome ... yer mam was only 19.*
*Sheh'd bin an art student, a canny good one at that. Sheh wez*
*funny, canny clever.*

He looked at Rita, she nodded for him to continue. Permission
granted.

*Wi met at a party and that first nite sheh got pregnant. Wi didn't*
*even knaa each other, but wi tried te build a family. Wi were*
*excited about wor bairn and ower the nine months wi married an*
*moved in together. Wi were happy, but it was all tee fast. Adam*
*came alang and yer mam was overwhelmed. Sheh couldn't cope wi*
*it, wi the responsibility. Sheh worried that sheh was deein things*
*wrong. It was tee cold, sheh couldn't tyek him oot so sheh began te*
*miss hor student friends. Sheh'd had te drop oot – yee knaa?*

- Yes she told me.

I watched him fumbling for the right words. He was crumbling.
Breaking. But he continued.

*Sheh changed. Sheh lost hor sparkle. Nothin ah could dee could*
*cheer hor. Sheh loved Adam, but sheh couldn't cope. Sheh just*
*couldn't cope. One day ah came home frem work later than usual.*
*As ah came up the stairs ah could hear hor wailing. Ah'll niwor*
*forget them high-pitched cries. They whent on and on. Ah knew*

*even before ah turned the key an saw hor. Sheh was holding Adam*
*tee close tee hor chest. Tee close. He wasn't moving … Ah knew.*

My father stopped talking. He cleared his throat. His eyes were red.
He was trying to maintain composure. He was trying to be brave.
He was breaking. Breaking. Crumpling crumbling.

- He was dead.

*Had been fe hours. Yer mam told me how sheh'd left him. Adam*
*wouldn't stop bubbling. Sheh couldn't cope. Sheh'd run oot hopin*
*fera bit o peace. Sheh'd needed te clear hor mind. Adam was*
*baad. He had a cold an it'd gone onto his chest. He was cryin in*
*pain an sheh couldn't comfort him. He died when sheh was ooot.*
*Ah divent knaa how long sheh left him for. The postmortem said*
*tha he choked on his own vomit. He died on his own … Yer mam*
*told me that sheh had left him and ah didn't tell the doctor. Ah*
*said that sheh had foond him like tha. Sheh was in ne fit state te*
*talk te anyone to tell them different. Wi had a secret. Ah protected*
*her an in deein so ah betrayed me bairn laddie.*

Rita started to sob. I glared at her. She stifled her cries.

*Sheh got through the funeral. Sheh was in shock. Wi were numb an*
*went in te automatic pilot. The coffin was tiny.*

He paused. Regaining control of his memories. He wasn't dwelling

on details. Quick quick. Getting it out as quick as he could.
Throwing it out.

*Yer mam wez calm ... tee calm. Sheh didn't bubble an sheh held
hor heed up high. Fowk must have thought hor cruel. Sheh seemed
te lack any feelin. Ah nearly told the whole place. Ah stood up
in the middle o the service ... Ah was gonna tell the truth ...
but ah couldn't. Not by then, ah'd shown where me loyalty lay.
Ah couldn't gan back. Affta the funeral, ah realised tha sheh'd
been carried alang wi the momentum. Sheh'd been focusing on
the funeral. Sheh was ne longer numb. Instead sheh wailed and
wailed. Piercing noises without warning, triggered by tiny stuff.
There was ne consoling hor. Sheh would bubble uncontrollably.
Ah couldn't help. Ah couldn't help hor. It was aboot then tha sheh
talked aboot hearing Adam. Sheh thowt tha he was hiding. Sheh
would talk te him ... sheh would hear him crying in the neet. All
neet. Ah'd wake te see hor rocking backwards and forwards a the
bottom of me bed.*

He stopped talking.

- Don't stop. I need to know.
*What else can ah tell yee? Ah stopped luvin hor. What does tha tell
yee aboot me? Ah hated hor for letting me laddie die. Ah hated
what sheh became.*

- What'd she become?

283

*Sheh drank. Yer mam was a drunk. Sheh was an alcoholic who preferred the company o the bottom of a bottle of vodka. Sorry Jude – but yee came here for answers and ah divvent really knaa what yee expected te gain.*

He left the room. I sat in silence. I watched the swirls on the carpet. Around and around. Rita had not moved. She watched me. She did not talk. My father returned with his cigarettes. He placed one, balancing in the corner of his lips and flicked his lighter. I watched him.

*Ah carried the burden. Ah felt such guilt. He was me son an ah'd not protected him. Wi didn't talk an instead ah was left wi 'what ifs?' an 'whys?' Ah tried te forget, ah tried te move on, but every time ah came home te the flat sheh ... sheh wasn't reet. Sheh turned te spending time in his room. Sheh would walk wi an empty pram an kept saying tha sheh was waitin, waitin for a sign.*

- But she wrote that you were trying again.

I clung to hope.

*Wi did. Wi moved to this hoose, but the marriage was deed. Wi lived together, but there was ne love ... nothing.*
He was almost too nervous to say the words.

- There must have been. You had me.

284

*Yee were a mistake. A drunken mistake. After the Semi-Final.*
*Ah'm sorry pet, but yer mam should nivvor had another bairn.*

The truth. Did I need such truth?

## - She loved me.

My voice was raised again. He would not lie about my mother.

*Sheh loved yee tee much. Sheh nivvor enjoyed yee. Sheh clung te*
*yee an spent nights awake listening te yee breathing. Sheh was*
*convinced tha yee'd be taken frem hor tee. Sheh'd something te*
*prove te horself. Sheh needed te be perfect. Sheh needed yee te be*
*perfect. Sheh tried te hide hor cracks from yee. It exhausted hor.*
*Sheh wouldn't let me near te yee ...*

- I needed your love.

*Sheh needed yee te give hor all yee love. There was ne room for*
*me. Ah wasn't allowed te love yee. Ah couldn't love yee ...*

- And now the truth da.

*Ye should nivvor have bin born Jude. Yer mam an ah should nivvor*
*had another bairn. Wi didn't deserve yee ... Ah felt tha te love yee*
*waad be te forget Adam. Ah couldn't.*

- You've never loved me. I needed you. I needed my da to look after me. I needed your love. I needed someone to make everything alright. What did I do to you? I needed you. I had found my mam. My world fell apart. I needed you. I just needed you to show me some love. Anything. What did I do?

*Ye weren't Adam ...*

> The truth.
> It pierced.
> The truth echoed.
> It bounced.
> I heard the truth.
> It warmed me.
> It made me whole.
> I knew.

*Ah was scared of hor. Sheh'd hide empty bottles. Sheh'd spend hundreds o pounds on booze. Ah was scared tha sheh would leave yee somewhere. Wi didn't deserve a second chance.*

- You used to leave me. You and **her**.

Again I pointed at Rita.

*When yee mam died, ah realised that wi'd destroyed another life. Ah gave up on yee ... Ah should nivvor have been yer da.*

286

- But you were and you should've just got on with it.

*Ah'm sorry.*
Sorry.
    Sorry.
        Sorry.
            Sorry.
                **Sorry.**
                    **Sorry.**
                        **Sorry.**
                            **Sorry.**
                                **Sorry.**

He did mean it. I looked at his red cheeks. I looked at his puffy
eyes. His cigarette ash was fully formed, clinging to his cigarette.
*Ashes to ashes*. Absolution.

It didn't matter anymore.
The truth.
The lies.
The gossip.
The evil.
God.
Murder.
Decisions.
Decisions.
Decisions.

# Realisation.

It didn't matter.

None of it.

Nothing.

My mother made a mistake.

She made the wrong decision.

My father had tried to do the right thing.

My mother. My poor mother.

Nothing could be said.

Nothing could be done to change the past.


- And Crystal?

*What aboot Crystal?*

- Do you deserve to be her da?

*Sheh's me chance.*

- Don't you dare fuck her up.


She was precious. She is precious. My baby sister. She was due home soon. I needed to see her. I needed to hug her. I needed to check that she was alright.


No more questions. Nothing else to say. Silence.


Silence.


Nothing else mattered.

Rita left the room. She scurried off. Tea. A cup of tea. There was a need for tea.

Silence. My father didn't say another word.

I cleared away my secrets. I cleared away the `exhibits`. Back into the blue cylinder tin. I put Adam's tiny items. Back into his coffin.

I sat. In silence. Watching. Watching out of the window for Crystal. She would be home any minute.

# Happy Ever After

Suddenly
The handsome prince opened the door
And invited his princess to step onto his special
path.
Their eyes were wide open
Sparkling in excitement
As they advanced out into the unknown.
Not once did the blissful duo withdraw
Advancing over hills
Through rampant rivers
Even fighting off all kinds of peculiar beasts.
They walked for the rest of their lives
Discussing
Exploring
And always knowing
That their union permitted true and natural
happiness.

* * * * *

I worked in The Traveller's Rest. I worked full time. The wages
weren't bad. When the tips were added on. My special tips. I liked
working there. I was a princess when I worked there. Standing
behind the bar. Knowing that if my top was low. Very low. Then my
glass of tips would be full by the end of the night.

**Clink**
     clink
          clink.


I liked the sound of my glass being filled with money. I would change notes to coins. So that I could hear the rattle. And the clink.


I had had sex in the toilets.
Twenty-three times.


During my break.
During my shift.
That boosted my tips too.

**Clink**
     clink
          clink.


Word had spread around the male customers. A few quid and I was ready. *Up for it.*


Blow jobs. I didn't swallow. Calorie control at all times.
Hand jobs. I wasn't very good. Never been shown how.
Sex. Up against the cistern. Legs spread wide. Quick. Always quick.
I monitored it all. Took the money for the drink. No fixed price. It was up to me. I controlled.

Clink
        clink
            clink.

They offered me a drink. That was the code. I would say yes. They
would tell me how much to take. Simple. I took the money. Put it in
my tip glass. Clink clink clink. Then I would tease. I would play.
I would seduce. I would decide what treat they would receive.

I was a lucky dip.

Mr Johnson (Number 19) had been my first customer. He still smiled
a lot. His yellowed mouth with a little gap in between his two front
teeth. He still laughed a lot. Sounded like a horse hiccupping. It
still made me smile. Mr Johnson was a nice man. Not a very good
husband. But a nice man. He always wore jeans and trainers. He
didn't do any sport and he was getting fatter and fatter. He still
wore the blue, soft leather jacket which had huge pockets. It was
fashionable once. A long time ago. He must have been hoping that
it would become fashionable again.

Mr Johnson had given me six pounds and twenty-three pence in
tips. I gave him a blow job. Teased the end with my tongue. Like he
wanted. Like he told me to. It didn't take long. He tasted funny. We
had sex sixteen days later. Seventeen pounds forty. He was quick.
He kissed me on the lips and I liked it. Pushed his tongue into
my mouth. In the men's toilets. Up against the dirty cistern. Hard.

Hard. Hard. My father didn't know. My father could never know. **Hush hush.** Mr Johnson was my favourite customer.

**But**.
It meant nothing. Sex meant nothing.

It was about money.

It was about wages.

It was a job.

An easy job.

There was no need for love and affection. Sex wasn't ever like that. I provided a service. An extra to have with a pint of bitter and a packet of pork scratchings.

I needed the money. I wanted the money. I was saving. Had a box. Used to contain shoes. Clip clop pointy red shoes. I wore them with a red skirt that was too short. *Fit where it touched*. It edged up up up when I bent over. Rita liked that skirt. Now my shoe box held money. Jingle jangling with coins. Ready. Waiting. Building. Saving to travel the world. When the time was right. When the time was right I would leave Disraeli Avenue. I would say bye to New Lymouth. Forever.

I had started working in The Traveller's Rest. Before hospital. Before my father had told them that I was ill. Having tests. Having tests for three months. They knew. Everyone knew. Rita told Mrs Symons (Number 11). Told her it was to go no further. But. But it always did. Mrs Symons had arrived on Ward 23 with a plant for me. She didn't stay. She looked around. Stored a few images. Picked up a few details. Then she went back to Disraeli Avenue. My secret went back to Disraeli Avenue. I imagined her yacking down the phone or spilling details in Brian's Newsagents. I knew that she would. I had heard them. The women in Disraeli Avenue loved to gossip. They loved to yackety yack yack yack. I would have been the talk of the Estate. Reputation. Reputation.

**But**.

My customers didn't mind. They already knew me as a *reet strange bairn*. It didn't change their view. They still wanted to fuck me. They still wanted me to put my mouth around their things. They still wanted to scrape together their loose coins. To hear them accepted into my clink clink clanking glass.

I returned to work. The day after I discharged myself from hospital. I had sex in the toilets within the first fifteen minutes of my shift. Mr Johnson (Number 19).

Eighteen pounds, sixty-seven pence.

* * * * *

Dirty

      Dirty

           Dirty.

I was dirty.

My life was dirty. Eddie had made me dirty. Dirty in places that I could not reach. I could not turn my insides out. I could not scrub. Scrub. Scrub away the scabs that he had left there. Out of reach. Out of reach. My insides were out of reach. I was full. Full with sperm. Full with the dirt of all the men who had entered me.

Dirty.
　　　Dirty.
Dirty.

I began to lose count of all the men who entered me. The faces blurred. The names ran into one. Eddie.

They were all Eddie.

\* \* \* \* \*

## Session one

**November 14 1992**

- I've an appointment with Susie Evens.
*Go through to the waiting room and I'll tell her that you're here.*
She didn't ask my name. She knew my secret.

Susie Evens was everything that her name promised. She was probably in her late twenties. Her clothes were London trendy, petite and with contrasting fabrics and patterns. She wore knee-length brown leather boots and a tailored short brown tweed skirt, which rested about an inch above her knee. She was slim and the smile that she greeted me with stretched to allow her perfectly aligned, white teeth to dazzle. I thought that she was too slight and too faultless to understand eating. I thought that she was too perfectly pretty to understand my inadequacies.

*Come in Jude.*

I followed her into a tiny room. It smelled stale. It was in desperate need of airing. Words of woe had bounced off the white walls, each leaving a decaying lingering stench. She sat down. Perched on the edge of the chair. Opposite me. The chairs were near to the floor and our knees almost touched. I could see her knees. They were bony. She was slender, tall and blond. She was everything that I wished I could be. Instantly awkward in her presence.

*Hi Jude. It's great to see you. As you know, I am Susie … **pause** … and today I want to introduce you to the … **pause** … education … **pause** … surrounding the therapy that you are getting over the next few weeks.*

I wanted to talk about Eddie.

*Here are some diagrams illustrating the Cognitive Behavioural Therapy Formulation, which shows a typical pattern for a sufferer like you … **pause** … for someone who has Bulimia Nervosa.*

She handed the sheets of printed paper to me. Her finger nails were perfectly manicured. Painted with a crimson gloss. I stared at the nails. She pushed the papers closer to me. Push pushed to gain a response. I glanced down at the diagrams. Bulimia Nervosa in an enlarged font. Underlined. Glaring at me.

A label.
Another label.

I had another label to add to the many that were pinned to my torso. Pin the tail on the donkey. Bray. Bray. Bray.

*As an adult you have adapted strict rules which govern your Bulimia Nervosa.*

She pointed a crimson-tipped nail. Onto the diagram.

I wanted to talk about Eddie. And Adam. And my mother. And my father. And Rita. And. And. And.

*You have low self-esteem and this ... **pause** ... has led to extreme concerns about your weight and shape. You have tried strict dieting ... **pause** ... but the precise and rigid boundaries that you have placed upon yourself have led you to binge eat ... **pause** ... This is then accompanied by guilt and has led to self-induced vomiting ... **pause** ... which ultimately leads to low self-esteem. Can you see the cycle?*

She pointed from the black arrows to words. Crimson glow on the white paper.

She didn't know me. I'd never met her before. I feared that I had missed questions, that the softening introduction had occurred without my realising. Her speech was odd. It was performed. Precise. Faultless. Rehearsed.

- I like to vomit.

I spoke quietly.

*Nothing that you can say can shock me. You're no different from any other woman who comes into my room.*

- I'm **very** different from other women. I'm not normal.

My voice was firm. But quiet. Directed down to my fat knees.

*I need to tell you now Jude … **pause** … I won't cure you and I'll probably not even meet your expectations.*

- I've no expectations of you.

*What do you want?*

- I want to be normal.

*And what is normal?*

- I don't know.

Silence.

- I know that there's something wrong with me.

Silence.

- I can't seem to cope with life.

*How did you feel coming here today?*

- I didn't feel anything. I tried not to think about it … went into automatic pilot. I used my usual distraction techniques until I got here.

*You can't use distraction anymore.*

- This is how I survive. I've been doing it since I was six.

I wanted her to ask me why at six. She didn't.

*Therapy is about facing up to things that you try to hide from.*

- I don't know how to do that.

*We'll work together.*

She handed me another piece of paper.

*This is a model of a person. You have thoughts and these are identified as cognitive processes. These thoughts relate directly to our feelings and our behaviour.*
Nod nod. Blah blah blah.
*You have feelings that trigger certain actions and behaviour. We need to work together to identify which feelings are linked to your binge eating. However. We cannot change these feelings until we understand the thought processes behind your feelings. This is to do with interpretation and cognitive processes.*
Nod nod. Blah blah blah.
*Over the next few weeks we're going to try and identify your thought processes, which will lead to a change in your emotions and moods. This will then have a direct effect on your behaviour.*
Nod nod. Blah blah blah.
*We often blame people for making us feel a certain way, when in fact it is our thoughts that have triggered the feelings ... Have you followed that?*

I nodded again.

I hadn't. I had heard her saying blah blah blah.
I was waiting to talk about Eddie. And Adam. And my mother. And my father. And Rita. And. And. And.

*Each session we will base our discussions around this model and
also around the monitoring of your eating habits.*

- Sorry?

*Have you ever kept a diary?*

- No.

*Why's that?*

- Because I can't trust anyone.

*Well you can keep one now. I want you to write down everything
that you eat in a day. All the fluids and foods that you consume,
the place where you ate it, whether you considered it to be a
binge, if you took laxatives or vomited and finally you need to
record the thoughts and feelings which contributed to the event.*

I couldn't think of anything to say. Rehearsed. Rehearsed. Her
speech. Her kingdom. Ruling. Dictating. I didn't trust her. I didn't
like her. She was sterile. She was too clean in her stale-smelling
room. She wanted me to spill my secrets onto paper.

Never.
Never.
Never.

I wanted to bounce words off her wall.

- But won't this mean that food's always in my mind?

*You're talking distraction methods again Jude. You need to face up to your problem and address it.*

- My life is shit already, if I have to record everything and constantly delve into reasons behind my behaviour, then how'll this make my life any better?

*There are no short-term fixes. Things will get harder before they get easier and as I said ...* **pause** *... I can't cure you.*

- Well who can then?

*You can Jude. It is all about making the decision to commit.*

It's all about decisions. It's always about decisions.
I walked from the square room. I clutched the details of my next appointment. I knew she saw my fat.

\* \* \* \* \*

I have a recurring dream. I appear. Walking into a
white room. I look normal. I am wearing clothes that
fit. My body has shape. The curves allow the clothes
to touch and to cling. I move with my clothes. I enter

the room and the door closes behind me. Calm. Silent.
I remove my clothes. I want to remove my clothes. I
stand naked and my torso displays a gaping hole. You
can see right through. You could place a fist straight
through me. In removing my clothes, all that I do
not have speaks through the hole. In my dream my
removed clothes disappear. They vanish and leave
me exposed. Alone. Naked in a room with a round
wooden table, a roll of tape and a photograph. In
my dream I tape a Polaroid photograph of my father
over the hole. I tape only the top of the photograph.
It flaps up with a breeze. The breeze is like a giant's
breath. It comes in small gusts. Like the blowing
out of candles. I tell myself to move. To leave. In
my dream I try to tell myself that it will not work.
That the Polaroid is not enough. That the tape is not
enough. In my dream I do not hear. I never hear.
The wind blows through me. My nakedness exposes
my loss.

\* \* \* \* \*

My period was late. My period was never late. At 29 days I bought
a test. I peed onto the absorbent stick. I laid it on the side of the
sink and watched. I sat on the edge of the pea green bath. I waited.
I watched. A pink sea swam over the two white windows. The test
was working. I had to wait for five minutes. Then I would know. The
control line appeared. A straight pink line. In the window next to

it a fainter line emerged. It didn't get stronger. It wavered between negative and positive. It was trying to decide what to tell me. At five minutes. Exacty five minutes. I read the result. Two lines. Both pink. One much stronger than the other. But. But still two lines.

I was pregnant.

I picked up the result. Held it up to the ceiling light. Illuminating the line. It was faint. But it was there.

I was pregnant.

I had something real. A physical. Something to think about. I had focus. I was unsure if the news was good or bad. But. But I could cope with the chaos. There was an excitement oozing from that stick in my hand. It wasn't a celebration of the life inside me. It was a carnival of chaos. Confusion and disorder. I was filled with excitement. I had a new focus. I had a new distraction. A baby. A baby inside me.

I had no idea who the father was. It could have been any of the customers that I had slept with that month. I played sex like a game of Russian roulette. I tried to recall who and when. Too many to guess. Too many to name. I could divide my tips. My gains. I could subtract. I could remember. But. But I didn't care who the father was. I was the mother. I was going to be a mother. Sex meant nothing to me. I played at sex. It never reached a climax. My pleasure came from the emotion that rejection brought. I was an easy lay. A cheap shag. Men hopped in and out of me. They all knew that I was a sure bet. I was left with pain. Money and pain. I expected their rejection. I lived off their rejection. Money and rejection.

\* \* \* \* \*

# Session two

**November 21 1992**

*How are you today?*

Susie asked in the direction she was walking.

- Fine.

She gestured to the seat opposite her. Our knees nearly touched. She was still blonde. She was still skinny.

*OK Jude. Have you brought your homework with you?*

I looked blank.

*We're going to talk about your food diary and the food cycle that I mentioned last time. Do I need to recap?*

Nod nod.

*Jude, you have low self-esteem and this has led to extreme concerns about your weight and shape. You have tried strict dieting, but the precise and rigid boundaries that you have placed upon yourself have led you to binge eat. This is then accompanied*

305

*by guilt and has led to self-induced vomiting, which ultimately leads to low self-esteem. Can you see the cycle?*

She recited her words. Again.
Fluent.
Rehearsed.
Precise.
Emotionless.
Cold.

How many times had she uttered the speech? The meaning. The weight of the message was lost. Lost within the coldness. Lost within the script. The books read. The books learned. Susie was a puppet. A very skinny puppet who had no chance of ever understanding the secrets that I carried inside.

She did not see me as an individual. I was another one. I was the same as everyone else. No need to alter her mere talk. Preparation wasn't necessary. No need to change anything. Just slot in my name. That's it. Simple.

- Can we talk about something else?
I found my voice.

*I understand that this may be uncomfortable for you. However … **pause** … I have a strict formula that I must stick to. I have a weekly plan.*

- I have questions.

*About the cycle?*

- I'm pregnant.

*Oh.*

She was stunned. I watched as her eyes jumped. She was exploring inside her tiny brain. Opening boxes. Flicking through files. She needed to slot me into another group. I could not become an individual. She would not allow that to happen. Quick. Quick. Define define. Quick quick.

- I need to know if my ... if my **Bulimia** will harm my child.

*Perhaps this will give you a new incentive, a new drive to conquer your eating disorder.*

- I don't want to hide behind things. I want to talk.

*All in good time Jude. I will have to consult with my boss and see if we can arrange for you to see a dietician. This is usually around about week 11, but in these circumstances, I think that it'll be ...*
**pause** *... beneficial to see our community dietician as soon as possible.*

307

- But am I harming the baby?

*You're harming yourself. The baby will always take what it needs. Time is ticking* – she tap tapped her watch – *we really need to address this cycle.*

She began to talk.
Blah blah ... *feelings that trigger certain actions and behaviour ... blah ... work together ... identify feelings ... blah ... your binge eating ... behind your feelings ... blah blah ... interpretation and cognitive processes. Jude?*

I looked at her. Tears filled my eyes.

- Will my baby die?

*You'll be fine. You may even find that being pregnant drives you.*

She looked at her watch. She tap tapped her watch again. Tick tock. Tick tock. My time was up.

*Please maintain your food diary for next time. I expect at least three days this time.*

I stood. I walked to the door. She watched my fat.

\* \* \* \* \*

I bought a new notebook. Pink. With a huge purple heart on the front. I wrote down everything that I would need for my baby.

Breast pads. Nursing bras. Muslin cloths. Breast pump. Breast milk containers. Teats. Bottle brush. Bottle steriliser. Baby sling. Pram. Car seat. A Moses basket. A baby monitor. A mobile. Baby bath. Baby soap or wash liquid. Two soft towels. Two soft flannels. A soft hairbrush. Baby nail clippers. Vests. Babygrows. Cardigans. Socks. Shawl. Scratch mitts. Changing mat. Changing bag. White cotton wool. Baby lotion. Baby wipes. Newborn disposable nappies. Nappy sacks.

I needed to save. No escaping New Lymouth and travelling the world. I had to put down roots. Save my money for my baby. I stopped earning special tips. I stopped letting men deposit their dirt into me. I didn't want my baby to swallow any dirt. I wanted to protect my child. I wanted to make something of myself. For my child. So. I worked. I saved. I didn't tell anyone about the baby growing inside of me.

I planned to take classes. Parenting classes. And to go and see a GP. My GP. Then a midwife. Then visit the hospital. So much to do. So much to do. The weeks were flying past. I planned to tell my father soon. Eventually.

The first things that I bought for my baby. Two things at the same time. A packet of scratch mittens. Tiny. White. Forty-nine pence. A white teddy bear. Hands together. Praying. Four pounds ninety-nine pence. I bought them six weeks and three days after my last period. I needed to do something. I needed to make my baby real. For me. I needed to spend some money on my child. I caught a Number 37 bus to Whitley Bay. I walked around the shops. Looking at racks and racks of tiny things. Blues and pinks. There were so many to choose from. I liked the looking. The knowing. Just me and the baby knowing that one day soon I would have to buy little socks. And little shoes. And little trousers. And little jumpers. I walked around for hours. And hours. And hours. Just looking. Apart from my two tiny items.

I kept my two buys. In a white plastic box. Under my bed. I bought the box too. It was new. Fresh. Clean. It was white. Neutral. For my baby.

I thought about names.

**Boys**
Michael. Christopher. Tyler. Nicholas. Thomas. Dylan. Corey. Jonathan. Ryan. Cameron.

**Girls**
Molly. Jessica. Emily. Megan. Nicola. Danielle. Courtney. Kelsey. Whitney. Alicia. Grace.

I liked to think of names. I looked for names. I asked for names. I remembered names. I wrote them all in my pink notebook.

I was waiting to tell the world.

Waiting as long as possible.

Waiting so that my father.

So that Rita.

So that no one could take away my happiness.

Hush hush. My secret. My special secret.

I was waiting to tell the world.

## My baby.

\* \* \* \* \*

I remembered overhearing someone saying that when they were pregnant, they **just knew** that everything was going to be alright. I **just knew** that it wouldn't be. I was cursed. If I felt love for anyone, then they would be taken from me. I was never going to have a happy ever after.

I was still being sick.

I couldn't stop myself.

**But**.

I began to love the baby that was growing in me.

I began talking to my child.

I could lay my hand over my stomach.

I began trying to smile.
I couldn't help myself.

I was keeping a diary. In my pink notebook. Talking to the baby.
Writing things. Not important. Just about work. And my day. And
what we would do. The baby and me. In the future. About getting
a flat. Just me and the baby. Crystal could help me decorate the
baby's room. It would have to be a yellow room. Unless I found out
the sex of the baby. I would have a scan. A picture.

I couldn't stop myself.

\* \* \* \* \*

Eight weeks and two days after my last period.

I sat on the toilet. Legs separated to see if anything fell. Blood
dripped into the bowl.
**Drip.**
      Drip.
**Drip.**
      Drip.
Drip.
      Drip.
**Drip**.

Red water. Legs open. Watching between my thighs. My wee was
tinged with red. I tried to stop its flow. I had no control. It fell.

Softly. Softly. Sinking down to the bottom of the bowl. Away away. No noise. Softly softly sinking. I watched it fall. One large red clot. A large red clot sank away from me. My hope left me.

I had no control.

My baby was gone.

I reached my hand into the water. Into my pee. Trying to grab the large clot. It came away in my fingers. I desperately scooped it. Blood oozed from it. Drip drip dripping through my fingers. Staining my finger nails. Getting under my finger nails. I was touching my baby. I wrapped it in toilet roll. The clot. I placed it back into the toilet. I flushed away my hope.

My baby.

My throat ached. I strained. Trying to stop the tears. *Big girls don't cry. Do you hear me? Big girls don't cry.* Tears were weakness. They came. They fell. They were beyond my control.

I cried for everything that I had ever lost.
I cried till I could cry no more.
Sitting on the toilet.
Baby falling from me.
Blood drip drip dripping from me.
My stomach cramped.

Clot.

     After clot.

## After clot.

Fell to the bottom of the toilet bowl. Fresh crimson blood drip drop dripped. I sat on the toilet. Terrified to move. My insides were falling out. My fingertips stained with my baby's blood. That single clot. Promised so much. I flushed my child away, into the sewer. Unknown. Alone. Abandoned. Away. Away.

* * * * *

My bleeding seemed endless. It went on for weeks. I never told anyone. I never went to the GP. I was dying. I knew that I was dying.

I was alone in my grief.

My baby was gone. With that faint pink line I had thought of a new beginning. Names kept popping into my head. They wouldn't stop. I couldn't stop them.

## Molly.

I would have called her Molly. She would have been a girl. I knew that she was a girl.

My mind had wandered. Into a future. I had allowed myself to hope. I had had dreams. I had seen a future. I should have known better.

As the clots passed from me. As the blood turned brown. I realised that I had been weak. I had given in to temptation. That enticement of something that I should never have had. I was weak.

I cried for my baby. I stopped work. Just didn't go in. Instead. I spent hours. Days. Curled into a question mark. On my blue duvet. In the box room. I ached. All of me ached. Inside and out. I didn't want to speak. Not even to Crystal. I shouted at her if she came into my room. She didn't understand. I didn't want to feel anything. I didn't want to speak. Silence. I needed silence.

I was angry at me. At my weakness. How dare I hope. I had forgotten the cruel game that was being played around me. It had played all of my life. I had forgotten that my Lord hated me. I should never have hoped. I knew not to hope. My Lord had given me a taste of honey. Sweet sweet honey. I had wanted more. I had needed more. My Lord knew that. My Lord was laugh laugh laughing at my weakness. At my greed. My Lord had watched as I began to change. I let down my guard. Just for a moment. I began to hope.

Then.

Then he fired his fatal shot.

Bang.

Into my stomach. Into my baby. Cruel.

The Lord that governed me was cruel. Evil evil man.

I had died.

Somehow I had missed out the living and instead I was existing in Hell. Hell on earth. Hell was a semi-detached house. Number 9 Disraeli Avenue. My Lord hated me. I was evil. My father used to tell me that I was the child of a whore. I knew all about Adam. I knew all about my mother. I knew that I was being punished. That I should never have been born. I was paying for my mother's sins. I was the consequence of a sin. Destined for sorrow.

I had no right to live.

I should not live. I had to make a decision. I had to be brave. I had to go before Crystal was touched. Before my sorrow invaded her innocence. Before she became like me.

I had to make a decision.

**I have to make a decision**

\* \* \* \* \*

**My palm is crowded.**

Line upon line.

A spider's web.

Intrigue. Complicated. Destined.

I need to find my mother.

The time is right. You know that the time is right.

Blood brought me my sign.

The red washed out all that is inside.

I am pure now.

I am ready now.

I understand.

I understand my mother.

I must go and tell her.

**I forgive her.**

\* \* \* \* \*

I am ready.

Caroline Smailes

I have made my decision.

Off in search of Adam.

A bottle of vodka.

And a jar of paracetamols.

A note.

My note reads:

Gone in search of Adam.

# Thoughts

Caroline Smailes

*Unto the woman he said, I will greatly multiply thy sorrow and thy conception; in sorrow thou shalt bring forth children; and thy desire shall be to thy husband, and he shall rule over thee.*

Epigraph to *In Search of Adam*

## Why is your epigraph taken from Genesis?

That's where *In Search of Adam* begins. We all know that God created Adam from the dust of the ground and placed him in the Garden of Eden. He couldn't live alone, so a woman, Eve, was created from Adam's rib. God forbade this man and this woman to eat from the tree of knowledge of good and evil. But, the woman was tempted by a serpent and she ate.

But.

And this is the significant but.

Eve shared the pleasure with Adam and he ate too. The serpent tempted Eve and she tempted Adam. They were all punished. The epigraph tells of Eve's punishment and *In Search of Adam* stems from a modern-day working-class Eve. Sarah Williams is Eve.

## And where do you begin?

I begin at the very beginning. Where else? I begin with a need to find purity and perfection, to go in search of Adam. In search of the man who is untainted and innocent.

## Are you taking us further than a simple story?

I am taking you as far as you want me to. *In Search of Adam* was born of a religious seed and developed into a reflection on the

321

society that we live in, one where we seek to blame, to point a finger and to gain pleasure from tales of downfall. There is a lack of acceptance of responsibility, a lack of consideration for the consequences of actions and a lack of humanity. It is this that has led to a spiralling down and to the maltreatment of the innocent. It is our children who suffer at our hands. I can rant on, but this is where I started. I started to write with Adam in mind.

**And what came next?**

The story unfolded. The novel begins with a six-year-old child, Jude, finding her dead mother lying next to an empty bottle of vodka, an empty jar of tablets and a suicide note reading 'Gone in search of Adam.' That was the image that wouldn't budge. That's where I had to start. I then tried to examine and understand firstly why the mother would kill herself and then to allow the consequences of this action to unfold. Then. Came the idea for the after-school care of Jude being divided among her neighbours. Then. One of the neighbours had a brother who raped Jude. Then. As another consequence, Jude stepped into a life of self-harm, eating disorders and continued abuse patterns. The novel ends with Jude about to commit suicide with vodka and tablets. A full circle. In the middle of Jude's story, Sarah – Jude's mother – interrupted and told her story through diary entries. Within these diary entries, Sarah tackled the idea of heaven and hell and the awareness that she had sinned. She believed that she had killed her son. Later in the story, through Bill, Jude's father, we learn that Sarah had had a baby, Adam, and that she had suffered from postnatal depression

which was heightened by Adam's incessant crying. When Adam
was six months old, she had left him alone in their flat and
returned to find him dead. She had gone against rules; she had
been tempted by silence. Her husband, Bill, had found Sarah and
the dead baby and had chosen to protect Sarah.

And here lies the connection to Genesis. For their sins, their
eyes were opened and they knew that they had done wrong.
Sarah then lived a life in the shadow of an abusive husband and
her sorrow and longing prevented her from loving Jude. Bill
worked all hours in a desperate need to achieve something and in
doing so rejected his family. So *In search of Adam* was born out
of Genesis.

I must stop you there. I can't believe the rubbish that
you're spouting. You're claiming that my story is a
creative take on the Bible. You're trying to be clever
when clearly you're not and I'm not at all impressed.

### I'm sorry – and you are?

My name is Jude Williams and I'm the bairn whose story
she's telling. I met her when I was in hospital. When
we were in hospital. I was eighteen at the time. What?
She hasn't told you that? I didn't think she would. I
didn't think that she'd like you to know which bits
are mine and which bits are hers. She's perfected this
cover story of her being an all-creative being and
clearly she's not. I told her my story, she mixed it

323

with hers and then she typed the words into what she
attempts to call a novel. Slowly, mind you, she types
really slowly. She's really crap at typing.

**But she's just said that you die at the end. How can you be here if you're dead?**

I've no intention of killing myself. Life's been pretty
shitty, but I'm no coward. Perhaps it's her that's
heading that way.

**So you're telling me that *In Search of Adam* is a true story?**

Yes.

**And it is all true. Every detail is true?**

Yes.

**So all of those horrific things happened to you?**

Some of them and the others happened to her. You don't
believe me? Why would I make that up? How can she
imagine such horrific things? They're too horrific and
too real not to be true. And, if you do believe me,
then surely you must be thinking that she's twisted and
clearly in need of help?

And here lies the problem with *In Search of Adam*. My biggest
problem has been reader/workshop reaction to the content. This
novel did not exist until I started my MA and it has developed

rapidly. I have pushed boundaries and addressed issues, such as paedophilia, rape, bulimia and violence, without shying away from the visual. This has led people to question my motives and to feel sympathy for me. I refuse to answer their direct questions. I refuse to say what is fact and what is fiction. Why should I? It's a story and I believe that it should be read as a story.

**So – you admit that some of your content is fact?**
No. I don't admit anything.

Yes all of it is.

**Why did you write *In Search of Adam*?**
Because it was within me. I wasn't in control of it. I sat and it poured out. My story poured out. I wrote because I love to write. The story spun and turned and sometimes I lost control of it.

That's because it's my story.

No. It's mine. *In Search of Adam* is my own search. My own need to find answers and to explore purity. I feel that a fog has lifted and I've written about subjects that need to be voiced. I played with language. I broke grammatical rules, paid attention to consistencies and stretched language to bring life to the senses. I've played with one-word sentences, one-word paragraphs and refused to use speech marks. I made pretty patterns with typography. I played a truly enjoyable game. The writing

experience made me feel alive, yet it's absorbed my thoughts. It was puzzling, cryptic, problem-solving and exhilarating.
I am alive.

So am I.

**What has influenced your writing?**
Grammatical rules and fairy tales.

What about me?

You don't exist.

But I do. I'm here. You've just spoken to me.

**What influences your writing style?**
I write with one thing in mind, acquired on the MA course. I write with it typed and stuck to my wall:

'Show don't tell or tell in a way that shows.'

**That's a bit cryptic don't you think?**
Not to me. It wakes me up.

She hides behind it and pretends to be a writer.

**And what problems have you encountered?**

*In Search of Adam* is written in the first person narrative, but not only this, the voice of a child. I can describe only what Jude can see and what I believe that Jude would understand. I have found it difficult to describe setting and to give a sense of place, but I overcame this by using dialect and by simplifying descriptions to a small area around Jude's street. Her world is stretched from a housing estate to the coast of Lymouth. The story is Jude looking back on her childhood, but she is still a young adult and her memories are locked within the language available to her at that time. She remembers only key moments, stuck visuals and so only those moments are expressed. I describe fragments of a life.

```
I'm still here you know. I hate it when you talk about
me as if I'm not here.
```

You're not here. I killed you off. I've had to locate my narrator and to make her a believable character.

```
What, don't you believe my story anymore?
```

I think that Jude's innocence and all that she can't communicate allow the reader to trust and want to protect her. She exists within an impressionist painting, The feeling of an understanding, of a memory. I have established a community for her. I have a detailed drawing of her street, with names and histories for every one of her thirty-one neighbours. I know details about door colours, names, ages. I have planned and I have been meticulous.

But you haven't been creative. I've told you
everything. Why aren't you acknowledging me?

## So what next?

I have the outlines for my next two novels. Something a little
more cheery next. I think either postnatal depression madness or
reincarnation. Something to make me smile. Something to give
me a break from Jude whingeing in my ear every five minutes.

I don't have another story to tell you. Does that mean
that you're going to abandon me? Like everyone else...

Please be quiet.

So you can hear me?

# Afterthoughts

# Prompts to discuss or consider

• Jude the collector. Why does Jude collect?

• Consider the significance of the exhibits and the tin in which they were stored (p.82, p.275).

• Think about triggers and reactions. What is the trigger that causes Jude to hide her mother's bag of secrets and what is the trigger that forces Jude to open that bag (pp.187–190)?

• Before the rape, Jude is saving to buy a globe that lights at the flick of a switch. She never buys it. Globes and atlases are symbols that appear within the novel. Consider the significance of these items (p.34).

• A lamppost flares outside of Jude's bedroom window and the lighthouse fails to shine. Consider the symbols of light within *In Search of Adam*.

• A book of decisions and consequences of actions. Is Jude's analysis of her palm accurate (p.34)? Was it greed that led her onto a path of self-destruction?

• Is Jude a consequence of her mother's tragedy or does Jude create her own tragedy?

• Are Jude's actions the result of choice or destiny?

• Consider Jude's relationship with food. What does Jude gain from this relationship (p.159)?

• Why did Jude think the snowman was evil (p.89)?

Caroline Smailes

• Return to Jude's miscarriage in 1992 (pp.312–315). Is it a blessing or tragedy?

• If Eddie had not raped Jude, how would the story have altered? Would a *happy ever after* have been possible?

• Do you think that Aunty Maggie was aware of Eddie's behaviour (p.95)?

• What is your opinion of Sarah Williams? Was she a good mother?

• Are Sarah's actions the result of choice or destiny?

• Who is to blame for Jude's tragic life story? Her mother, her father, Eddie or Jude? Can blame be placed? Should blame be placed?

• Bonds exist. Can you identify and comment on the different bonds within *In Search of Adam*?

• Do you agree with Bill's decision to protect his wife after Adam dies (p.282)?

• Did your opinion of Bill Williams alter/evolve as the novel progressed? Is he a good man? Is he a good father? Is he a good husband?

• Consider February 1981 again. A self-harming Jude chooses her father's hammer. Why (pp.54–57)?

• Consider the peripheral characters within the novel. What influences do these characters have on the choices available to Jude?

• Disraeli Avenue is a close community. Discuss.

• What is the relevance of the road names (p.20)?

• p.95 makes reference to Eddie's past. Does the community have a duty of care towards Jude? If so, do they fail in this?

• Grammatical and typographical choices have been made within the novel. What is gained by altering font style and sizing? What is gained through altering grammatical rules?

• The section from p.17 onwards describes New Lymouth. How does the author indicate class boundaries? How is Jude's class represented? What is the author stating about class?

• This is a novel about family ties. How does Jude's relationship with her immediate family change as the novel progresses? How does Jude's attitude towards her mother change?

• Does Jude die at the end of *In Search of Adam*? Could the ending have been *happy ever after*? Would that have been plausible?

• Twisted fairytale imagery emerges throughout the novel. Jude Williams is a modern day Cinderella. Can you cast the other roles?

• Can you identify the significance of the religious imagery within the novel? The epigraph is taken from Genesis. How religious a novel is this?

• In what way do the events in Jude's life reveal evidence of the author's attitudes? What social comment is being made?

• Why do you think that the novel was written? What is the message behind the words?

# Acknowledgements

For being there at the very very beginning – Jude Williams, Brian Moss and Suzanne Moss. My talented early readers – Karl McIntyre, Emma Darlington, Oli Mell, Paul Maloney, David Simcock, Diana Bradley, Roz Clarke and Ruchita Bakre. The lovely professionals at MMU – Andrew Biswell, Nicholas Royle and Paul Magrs. For waving their magic wands – Clare Christian, Clare Weber and Heather Smith at The Friday Project. For making it all fit together – Julie Pickard, Joanna Chisholm and Lorna Read. For listening to my exclamations when Richard & Judy talked of the 'nearly woman' and for insisting that I didn't press the delete – the stunning Jude Hughes. For their constant support and sparkling encouragement – Johnathan Dennan, Maria McBride, Karen and Patrick Clark, Richard Wells, Sarah Hilton, Ryan Groves, Margaret Coombs, Christopher Kelly, Val and Les Smailes. For the heartening comments and twinkling advice – my initial blogroll of blogger friends. For reading it all, for helping to make it better, for understanding and for being a true friend – Karl McIntyre. For being the person I admire the most in the world and for unquestionable support in everything that I do – the beautiful Paula Groves.

To my Jacob, my Ben and my Poppy – for making me smile when Jude was making me sad. And finally to my Gary – without you, there would be nothing.

# About the Author

Caroline Smailes was born in Newcastle in 1973. She moved to the North West to study English Literature at Liverpool University, before going on to specialise in Linguistics. A chance remark on a daytime chat show caused Caroline to reconsider her life. She enrolled on an MA in Creative Writing in September 2005 and began to write *In Search of Adam*.

Caroline is currently an Associate Lecturer for the Open University and lives in the North West with her husband and three children.

www.carolinesmailes.co.uk

# Coming Soon

**Accomplished and affecting, Caroline Smailes weaves together a catastrophic tale of mismatched lives.**

Ana Lewis is a woman trapped in a black box of her own creation; the black box of her mind. Afraid to blink for fear of puncturing holes in her memory she remains in her room, woefully neglecting her two children Pip and Davie, leaving them to fend for themselves and find any kind of love, anywhere they can. Davie retreats into his own world, permanently soiled and communicating only by sign language, while Pip, fat and desperate, sneaks out of the house at night to have sex with a boy who hates her. Pip and Davie exist in parallel, with only Ana's bedroom door separating her from them. She does not want to see them. They are the present and Ana chooses to live in the past, continually raking over the ashes of a relationship that was never really hers.

£7.99 PB July 2008
ISBN 978-1-906321-70-3